A Gathering Storm

A Dora Ellison Mystery

Book 2

A Gathering Storm

A Dora Ellison Mystery

Book 2

First Edition

By David E. Feldman

Copyright © 2022 David E. Feldman

All Rights Reserved

No part of this publication may be reproduced, distributed, or transmitted in any form or by any means, including photocopying, recording, or other electronic or mechanical methods, without the prior written permission of the publisher, except in the case of brief quotations embodied in reviews and certain other non-commercial uses permitted by copyright law.

This is a work of fiction. Unless otherwise indicated, all the names, characters, businesses, places, events and incidents in this book are either the product of the author's imagination or used in a fictitious manner. Any resemblance to actual persons, living or dead, or actual events is purely coincidental.

For my family

CONTENTS

Chapter 1
Chapter 2
Chapter 3
Chapter 4
Chapter 5
Chapter 6
Chapter 7
Chapter 8
Chapter 9
Chapter 10
Chapter 11
Chapter 12
Chapter 13
Chapter 14
Chapter 15
Chapter 16
Chapter 17
Epilogue

Chapter 1

"We're here!" The front door opened, and Vanessa and Jesse's family spilled into Agatha and Rudy's home.

Agatha squealed with joy and threw her arms around her brother. "My baby brother's here! My baby brother's here!"

Jesse pried his sister away from him, and pretended to look hurt. "You can call me your twin brother, but go easy on that baby shit!"

"Jesse, language," Vanessa chimed in. She was pretty and petite, and wore her hair in shoulder length golden dreads, and was wearing a gold blouse and black slacks. Her makeup was perfect. She pretended to glare at her husband, then grinned at her sister-in-law. She carried a toddler in her arms, while an older boy clutched at her pants pocket with one hand while sucking his other thumb. Vanessa and Agatha embraced, then Vanessa stepped back and looked around. "Where's the little prophet? I want to see our little prophet!"

Agatha stepped to one side, revealing the carrier she had set down to answer the door, and little Samuel, who had been examining the chubby fingers on his left hand and seemed to have discovered his right hand for the first time. He gazed at first one, then the other hand with astonishment.

Jesse laughed. "Ooh, our little prophet! Isn't he perfection?"

"Where are my nephews?" Agatha set Samuel's carrier rocking and, while her brother continued to marvel at the one-year-old, squatted on her heels.

Vanessa put the toddler down. He stood for a moment on unsteady legs, saw that everyone was watching, and stumbled back toward his mother, his arms outstretched, his mouth twisting, as he began to cry and tried to bury his face in her leg.

"Ooh, Buster's walking! Look at you, little man!"

"*I'm* little man," the older boy insisted.

His aunt turned to him and held out her arms. "No, you're the big man. Come to Aunt Ags, Andrew."

"No kissing," the boy warned. "Not Andrew—Drew."

"Excuse me, Drew. And how old are you now, Drew? Seven?"

Drew grinned toward his parents, clearly proud to be mistaken for such an advanced age. "Five. Five!"

"Almost a grown man!" Vanessa watched her husband and boys bask in the love of their family. She was so proud of them all, and so grateful to have a kind, thoughtful husband who would do absolutely anything for her or their children. She leaned toward Jesse and kissed him, something they did frequently and spontaneously. Jesse took his wife's hand, and he and Vanessa beamed with the shared joy of their family.

The house had been decorated with colorful crepe paper, balloons, streamers, signs reading *Happy Birthday!* and *One Year Old!* and a table festooned with framed, propped-up pictures of Agatha, Rudy, and Samuel taken since Samuel's adoption. The Raines's home, which had been gutted and rebuilt after Superstorm Sandy, as had so many Beach City dwellings, was newly raised, so everyone had to climb a set of stairs to get inside.

"Jesse—" came a deep voice from the back door.

Jesse turned, saw Rudy, and threw his arms around his brother-in-law in a bearhug. "Man, Rudy. You're putting on weight!"

Rudy shrugged, glancing down at his six-foot-four frame, all 265 pounds of him. A blue and orange Knicks shirt was draped over his belly. "Guess you won't be having any of my barbecue."

Jesse frowned. "What're you doing in here? I thought you'd be out back, tending the food."

"Came in to see my nephews." Rudy took each of the boys by a hand. "Excuse us. The men need to talk." He led the boys to one side, knelt beside them, and complimented them on their looks and style.

Agatha and Jesse stood side by side, watching their family. The twins looked alike, except Jesse's afro was shorter, and he was five foot ten and a muscular 195, whereas Agatha was bony, smaller, and thinner, wearing jeans and a purple cotton t-shirt, and had her hair tied back in a bun. Jesse's red collared shirt was open at the neck, revealing two gold chains glinting against his bronze chest.

He inclined his head toward his sister's. "You call him Samuel, not Sam or Sammy? Was that his name before?"

"It was, and we do."

Rudy looked at Jesse. "They're sayin' on sports talk to bet big on the Rams."

Jesse shook his head. "Problem with that is, they're sponsored by the betting app, so who do you think their advice is gonna benefit—you?"

Agatha put a hand on her hip and frowned at her husband. "You best not be betting again!"

Rudy held up his hands. "I'm just talking to Jess. Not betting. Talking. See? No money. And I'm thinking about our customers at the bar. Jesse's right, and I got to tell them that. Always thinkin' 'bout the customers, baby."

Jesse stepped closer to his brother-in-law. "Say, we going to do a little hmm hmm hmm before dinner?"

Rudy nodded. "C'mon out back." He held out his nephews' hands to Vanessa, who led them to their baby cousin. "Jesse'll be out back with me, talking Yankees, Giants, and Knicks."

Vanessa smiled. "Mmhmm." She watched the men head for the back door. "Boys," she said, "this is your cousin, Samuel. Isn't he handsome? Can you give Samuel a kiss?" The brothers each somberly and dutifully gave their cousin a kiss. First Drew leaned over the carrier and planted a kiss on the baby's cheek, and then Buster, who had been paying attention, did his best to do the same. "Look at them!" Vanessa marveled. Agatha laughed.

Samuel was clutching one of Vanessa's fingers. "Ooh, this child is strong!" Vanessa exclaimed to her sister-in-law. Her boys remained on either side of Samuel's carrier, soberly standing guard.

Agatha knelt beside Samuel. "This is your Aunt Vanessa, Samuel. We call her Nessa."

"Gggh," said Samuel.

"Hello? Children?" a voice called from the other side of the front door.

"Mama!" Agatha opened the door, saw her mother's arms were full of gifts and cake boxes, and propped open the door. Mother and daughter pressed their cheeks together and kissed. "You look beautiful, Mama."

Miz Liz, as she was called by just about everyone but her children, wore a scarlet shrug over a black dress. She was a diminutive woman with a big personality that could be charming or intimidating, depending on her mood.

"Mom!" Vanessa exclaimed. "You look gorgeous."

"If you're going to lie, Nessa, at least make it believable—though I suppose there's an element of truth in that, when you take my age into account."

Miz Liz held a smooth, cool palm against her daughter-in-law's cheek and looked deep into her eyes. "You *do* look gorgeous."

"Oh, stop!"

"But enough of you. Where's my little men?"

Drew was dancing around his grandmother's feet, and for a moment, she danced with him. "How is my Andrew?"

"Drew! Drew!"

"He insists we call him Drew," Vanessa explained.

Buster stumbled around in circles, in as close an approximation of his brother's dancing as he could manage.

"Oh, and William's walking!" Miz Liz swept her younger grandson into her arms and twirled him around.

"That's Buster!" Drew corrected.

"Well, hiya Buster!" She set her grandson down and leaned toward Agatha. "You tell your men if they're going to smoke, to do it in the basement, so you don't get in trouble."

"Haven't you heard?" Vanessa said. "It's pretty much legal now."

"Not in my family, it isn't."

The doorbell chimed. Agatha looked beyond her mother, then shook her head. "Too late. Cops're here!"

Liz looked alarmed and turned as Agatha opened the door, revealing two women—one five foot eight, white, and heavily muscled, the other smaller and rounder and of South Asian heritage.

Miz Liz turned back and shook a finger at her daughter. "Don't you play!"

"Mama, you remember Dora?"

"'Course I do. I will always admire this girl for what she did for our family and this city."

Agatha held the door and Dora stepped into the room, moving lightly on her feet, despite her size. She wore jeans and a dark blue t-shirt with the logo of Shay's Mixed Martial Arts Gym. She and Agatha kissed, then Miz Liz touched cheeks with Dora, who stepped to one side.

"And this is my friend, Missy."

Miz Liz looked at Missy, who wore a crisp white shirt and navy-blue slacks. She looked back at Dora. "Mmhmm." She raised an eyebrow.

"Mama," Agatha warned, and Miz Liz held both her hands up in front of her, palms outward.

"What do I know? I'm just an old lady."

"And Dora and Missy," Agatha said, "this is my sister-in-law, Vanessa. She's married to my twin brother Jesse."

Vanessa took both of Dora's hands in hers and looked at her, the love shining from her eyes, which had begun to tear. "I've heard so much. It's truly an honor." She turned to Missy. "And we're so glad you're here!"

Miz Liz bent toward her grandsons. "I don't think we're going to need to eat."

"What? Why?" Vanessa asked.

"Oh, no! Not when we have three delicious boys! I could…eat 'em all up!" She poked each boy lightly in the belly, making them giggle. "Eat 'em all up! Eat 'em all up!" The two boys laughed and ran from the room. They peeked in from the doorway to the kitchen and, when their grandmother pointed at their bellies, laughed and ran away again, then snuck back to peek once more. Samuel couldn't take his eyes off his grandmother.

"Now I know those boys in the yard aren't just smoking; they're drinking too," Miz Liz said to Vanessa.

"It's okay, Mom. We're staying over."

"Mm hmm." She turned to Dora. "So, you're a policewoman now, like your..." Her voice trailed off.

"Not yet," Dora said. "I'm just starting at the academy. But yes, like Franny was. I'm sort of doing this in her honor—her memory."

"Have I told you how sorry I am for your loss?"

"I believe you did, but thank you again, Miz Liz." Thinking about Franny was excruciatingly painful for Dora. Franny had been a balm to the pain and trauma caused by Dora's childhood—Franny had understood without judgment, supported without expectations.

Miz Liz turned to Missy. "And are you with the police as well?"

Missy giggled and shook her head. "I work at the library."

Miz Liz turned to her daughter. "With my Agatha!"

Missy nodded. "I'm more reference, while Agatha is more children's, but we all share responsibilities."

"Well, it's a pleasure," Miz Liz said. "Maybe you can help Agatha influence these children to read, instead of..." She turned toward the kitchen. "Do you think if I went out the back door I could catch those boys smoking?" She looked briefly concerned. "I guess I shouldn't say that in front of the police, though they do tell me it's legal now."

Dora laughed. "I promise to look the other way, Miz Liz."

"Okay, then!" The elderly woman headed through the kitchen, toward the back door. "'Cause I got to go see my favorite son!"

Agatha watched her mother disappear out the door and start down the stairs, and pressed her lips together. She continued watching, as her mother clutched the bannister while descending slowly, one step at a time, down the short stairway to the deck. Something about her mother's body language bothered her, but Agatha forgot about it a moment later when she heard

Rudy and Jesse launch into their usual argument over which beer was better, Blue Moon or Samuel Adams.

While she and Agatha prepared the side dishes, Vanessa smiled to herself, grateful for the love of their close family without the roadblocks of misunderstanding and jealousy that burdened so many families she knew, or the pain of relatives caught up in addiction or criminality.

During dinner, she and Jesse held hands under the table whenever their hands were free, and kissed and nuzzled every few minutes. She was so grateful to be so much in love.

Chapter 2

Vanessa awoke and sat up in bed. Later she would try to remember why she had sat up or what had awakened her, but she could answer neither question; she knew only that she was suddenly awake and sitting up, and that Jesse was not beside her.

"Jess?" She spoke softly, remembering that she was at Agatha and Rudy's house. Save for her, the bed was indeed empty. She pulled back the covers and swiveled her feet to the floor and into Agatha's fuzzy gray slippers. Opening the bedroom door, she peered into the hallway. "Jess?" The light from the bathroom cast reflective streaks across the length of the shiny wood hallway floor. She could still smell yesterday's barbecue, wafting up from downstairs. She put an ear to the bathroom door. "Jess?"

No response. So Vanessa pushed and the door creaked open. She stood still, listening, but heard only the faint barking of a dog from somewhere outside.

"Nessa!" came a loud whisper.

Vanessa spun to see Agatha's silhouette framed in her bedroom doorway against the white light spilling in from the street lamp outside the window.

Behind Agatha, a dark shape appeared. "What's going on?" Rudy stepped into the light. "What are you girls doing up at 3:00 a.m.?"

"Jesse's not in bed," Vanessa explained.

"Shhh. Don't wake the boys," Agatha cautioned.

Rudy nodded. "Go back to your rooms. I'll check downstairs and outside." He looked to Vanessa. "He was in bed when you went to sleep?"

She nodded, then stopped. "He...no, he went out. At about eleven. He said he needed—you needed more beer, but I thought he was with you. I assumed you went to the store together."

No one spoke for a moment, then Rudy shook his head. "We were on the couch, watching hoops. When I came up to Ags, he was on the last bottle of Sam Adams. Prob'ly went out for beer and passed out in front of the

TV. Go on in your rooms 'til I come back, but I 'spect he's downstairs on the couch. Hang on a minute." He ducked back into the guest room and came back with a shotgun open over his left forearm, its stock held against his body under his right arm. He was not a big fan of guns, but he kept an unloaded shotgun hidden away in a closet and insisted his brother-in-law's family safely do the same. He slowly descended the stairs.

Five minutes later, he returned, shaking his head. "He's not downstairs." He looked at Vanessa. "And your car's gone."

Vanessa shook her head. "Why would he take the car? He could've walked to the store for beer. He knows not to drive."

Rudy thought for a moment. "Maybe the store didn't have Sam Adams and he went looking…"

"No, he still wouldn't drive. For sure he wouldn't with me and the boys here. Something's not right."

"We should call the police," Agatha said.

"And say what?" asked Rudy. "That Jesse said he wanted more beer and now he's gone with the car?"

"Maybe that's *just* what we say," Vanessa replied.

Now Rudy was shaking his head. "You think the cops are gonna bother with a missing black dude who's been drinking at a party and has only been gone a few hours?"

Agatha looked at him. "We don't know what they'll do unless we try, but it should come from Nessa."

"Agreed," said Vanessa.

• • •

Twenty minutes later, the doorbell rang. Vanessa, now in a blue silk robe over her pajamas, answered the door with Rudy a few feet behind her, minus the shotgun. She looked through the glass peephole to see two uniformed police officers, a man and a woman. The woman was holding up a shield. Vanessa opened the door and stood aside, allowing the officers to enter.

"Vanessa Burrell?" the female officer asked, and Vanessa nodded. "I'm Lieutenant Catherine Trask and this is my partner, Lieutenant Mitchell Weiss. You reported your husband missing?"

"I did. Would you like to come in and sit down? I can make us all a pot of coffee."

"I can do that," Rudy offered.

"And you are…"

"He's my brother-in-law, Rudy Raines."

"Sure, I've been to your place," Lieutenant Weiss said. "Many times."

Rudy nodded.

"Thanks, but we'll pass on the coffee," Trask said.

"Well, come in and sit down." Vanessa retreated into the living room, with Rudy by her side. The officers followed. A few paper plates, napkins, and plastic cups lay on the coffee table, several side tables, and one, large folding table in the otherwise neat, carpeted room; both the carpeting and the painted walls were forest green. "We had family and friends over yesterday. My sons and nephew are upstairs asleep. My sister-in-law Agatha is with them."

"Agatha Raines, the councilwoman," Trask observed, as she and Weiss sat down.

"That's right," Rudy said.

Lieutenant Weiss took out a small, rectangular device. "Is it okay if we record our conversation?"

Vanessa nodded.

"Could you please respond verbally?"

"Yes, recording is okay."

"Wonderful." Weiss was in his mid-twenties, with blond hair, the remnants of a pockmarked complexion, and full lips that tended to purse when he was concentrating, as he was now. He spoke a few introductory words into the recorder and then looked at Vanessa. "Please tell me your brother's—"

"Husband," she corrected.

"…husband's name."

"I did that over the phone."

"Could you please do so again, for the recording?"

"Of course. My husband is Jesse Elgin Burrell. He is thirty-two years old."

"Height? Weight?"

"Umm. Five ten. 195." She gave a grim smile. "He would say 190."

"Race?"

"African American."

"Do you have a photo of your husband?"

Vanessa stood up and went to an end table at the far end of the couch, picked out a matted print from several family photos, and returned with it. "This is a picture from this past summer, with myself and our two boys, William and Andrew."

Rudy gave a wan smile. "Buster and Drew."

Officer Trask leaned forward, and looked at the photo. "Where was your husband last seen?" She was a fit woman in her early thirties, with the chiseled, fat-free features of a body builder, short, curly red-brown hair and a habit of clearing her throat before speaking.

"Here," Vanessa answered.

"As in this room?"

"Well, no." She stopped, thought a moment. "Last I saw him, I was going to bed. We tucked the boys in upstairs—we try to do that together whenever possible. Then I went to bed, and he kissed me and came downstairs to watch sports with Rudy."

Rudy nodded. "Switching back and forth between the Knicks and Sunday night football. But I went upstairs at the half. I have things to do tomorrow and I'm sure our little one will be up during the night. He always is, and I watch him in the morning, when Ags is at the library."

"That would be Agatha," Weiss confirmed. "She's a librarian here in town?"

Rudy nodded.

"Anyway," Vanessa continued, "I was going to bed after tucking the boys in, and Jess came in, kissed me, and said he was going back down to hang out with Rudy."

"That's right," Rudy said. "He mentioned that we were out of Samuel Adams—that's the beer he drinks. We still had some Blue Moon, which is my beer, but he would have wanted Sam Adams."

Vanessa gave a faint smile. "The boys have a running joke about which beer is better."

"And if he was out of Sam Adams, he would likely go out for more, if it could be had on a Sunday night."

"Well," Vanessa said, "Seven Eleven…"

"They'd be open late," Trask observed.

Rudy frowned. "I wish I'd've thought of it then, but we have Sam Adams bottles at the bar." He shrugged. "Hindsight."

Vanessa put a hand to her throat. "Does a person have to be missing for twenty-four hours to be considered a missing person?"

"Not necessarily," Trask answered. "Did your husband suffer from any medical conditions?"

Rudy snorted a laugh. "Cavities. The man had serious teeth problems." Returning to the moment, he stopped laughing.

"No, Officer. He did not," Vanessa answered.

"Just a few more questions, Ms. Burrell," Weiss said. "We'd like to know what he was wearing when last seen, whether he specifically said he was going out for beer, as opposed to going out to *have* a beer, and whether he might have contacted anyone before going."

Trask nodded. "A simple misunderstanding could explain this."

Rudy was shaking his head. "He just noticed we were out of beer."

"He wouldn't have gone to a bar—not with the kids and me here, and not without telling me." Vanessa lightly stroked her throat with the tips of her fingers. "That's just not something he would do. And there's no one else who would have known he was going out, unless he called someone, and why would he have done that?"

"Okay," Weiss said. "We still need hair and eye color, birthday, whether there's anyplace you can think of he might have gone on the spur of the moment. Friends or other relatives who live in the area?"

"Especially given that he may have had a beer or two," added Trask. "Anyone in the area he hadn't seen in a while?"

Vanessa bit her lower lip. "His hair is dark brown. Eyes are green, but sometimes brown." She paused, collecting herself. "Birthday is September 7th, 1989. And none of his friends live around here, and even if he had a lot to drink, he wouldn't do that without talking to me. In fact, he wouldn't do that at all—especially if he had been drinking. He never drives after drinking. Never."

"I take it you've called his cell."

"Called and texted. Several times." Vanessa pressed her lips together and looked into her lap, then up again at the officers. "You said it's not necessarily true that a person has to be missing for twenty-four hours to be considered a so-called missing person, but I've also heard that if you don't find them in the first twenty-four hours, there's a good chance it's too late." Her voice broke. "How can both be true?"

Lieutenant Trask shook her head. "Neither is true. We know this is a difficult time, but please believe that we are and will be doing everything we can to find your husband. In the meantime, if you think of any place he might be or anyone he might have called, don't hesitate to let us know. It's only been a few hours." She handed Vanessa a business card. "This card has my name, rank, command, and shield number, along with a number to call for any updates or if you learn anything that might be helpful."

Vanessa took the card in a trembling hand and nodded.

"Is your husband active on social media?" Weiss asked.

"He has a Facebook page, but doesn't really use it. Teachers are discouraged from using social media. Nothing else."

"Where does he teach?" Trask asked.

"Beach City High. English."

"Okay, we'll have a look," said Weiss.

"Can you think of any reason anyone might want to harm your husband?" asked Trask.

Vanessa didn't hesitate before answering. "None."

"Well, if anything else occurs to you," Trask pointed to the card, "please don't hesitate to call. As soon as we have any information, we'll be in touch."

"What will you do in the meantime?" Vanessa asked.

The officers looked at one another, then Lieutenant Trask answered. "We'll reach out to local hospitals, put out a BOLO to our people—"

"BOLO?"

"Be on the lookout. And if he doesn't turn up in the next few hours, we'll send a press release to local papers with his photo, name, and last known whereabouts."

•••

Rudy closed the door behind the two police officers and turned to see his wife and his sister-in-law hugging and swaying as Vanessa sobbed.

"Maybe I'll stay with the boys so you girls can be together."

Agatha nodded, while Vanessa folded her arms across her chest and shook her head. "I'm not going to sleep until my Jesse's back." She pulled away from Agatha and began to pace the width of the living room as Rudy went upstairs. "We can't let Liz know anything."

Agatha started to say something, but Vanessa cut her off. "Or the boys." She stopped pacing and looked around, then went to the kitchen table and opened a laptop lying on a short pile of newspapers and magazines. "Yours?"

"Yes," said Agatha. "Password's Samuel. Cap S."

Vanessa opened the computer. "Maybe we go to Facebook now and post that he's missing. We can go to the Beach City groups and moms' groups…"

Agatha sat next to her and covered Vanessa's hand with her own. "Why don't we give it a little time? He'll come back, or maybe the police—"

"Fuck time! And I'm not waiting for no police!"

Agatha held her palms up. "Okay. Okay. I understand."

"No, you don't. I love you, but you do not understand. Your man is upstairs with my boys and your little one, and my man is nowhere to be found."

"Do you have any ideas about where—?"

"No!"

"Friends from work? Women from work?"

Vanessa's features went slack. "I'll pretend I didn't hear that."

Agatha shrugged. "I'll pretend I didn't say it."

Vanessa clasped Agatha's hand and looked her in the eyes. "He didn't have friends, especially women friends, because I was his best friend." She caught herself. "*Am* his best friend. Am. Am!"

"Listen to me, Nessa." Agatha continued to hold Vanessa's hand. "Let's make us a plan. We'll brainstorm now, and we'll execute—we'll do it in the morning. Rudy will see to the boys at least until the early afternoon, and I can take the day off. Maybe by then, he'll be back, apologizing for wherever he's been."

"And what he's put me through!" Vanessa swallowed and nodded. "Okay, then. So, what's the plan?"

Agatha spoke softly, but with a strength that comforted Vanessa, whose desperate mind was casting about for anything positive. "We'll make a list of Facebook groups—moms' groups, town groups, PTA and PTO groups, anything local or related to his interests—what were his interests?"

"Hooo." Vanessa sat back and ran her hand through her hair. "He liked to eat, that's for sure."

"But he had plenty to eat here, right?"

Vanessa smiled, but only for a moment. "Seriously. The way Rudy barbecues!"

"What music does he like?"

"Different things. He likes T-Pain, Busta Rhymes, and Bone Thugs-N-Harmony. But he also loves old doo-wop and soul, like he sang with your mom at the party last night."

Agatha smiled. "When he sings with Mama, they sound professional. So, can you get into his Facebook account and see what groups he's in?"

Vanessa thought a moment then nodded. "I think so. I'd have to figure out his password, but knowing him, it's probably Buster and Drew."

"Or Giants, Yankees, Knicks."

"Nah, he doesn't care enough about sports. He likes those teams, but not for passwords."

Agatha slid the computer so that it was in front of her and began typing notes.

Vanessa held up a finger. "You know what he liked? Cards."

Agatha's brows lifted in surprise. "Really?"

"Played poker twice a month in Rudy's back room. Betcha didn't know that."

"I knew he had a game but not where it was or who was in it. I try not to think too much about it." Agatha thought for a moment. "Something else we can do. While I don't know who plays in Rude's game, I can make some pretty good guesses, and these guys—if they don't play in the game, I can guarantee they know who does. Maybe one or more of them will have something useful for us."

Vanessa gave a quick nod. "Great. Let's do it."

Agatha sighed. "We can't do it at 4:00 a.m. We made a good start with this list, and in the morning, we'll do like we said and start executing."

"That boy comes home without a good excuse, he's gonna *get* some executin'!" Vanessa got up, went over to the couch, and sat down heavily with a long exhale. "Hoooh." She snapped her fingers. "You know what else he loved? Astronomy!"

"Really? Jesse?"

"Mmhmm. He had an app you could point at the sky and it would overlay the names of the constellations. He looked at the sky with the boys all the time, and he talked to them about space and planets and stars, and then he'd talk about dreams and the things they could do if they really wanted to." Her eyes welled up and her voice got very small. "Oh, Ags. Oh, Ags. I'm so scared."

...

At 6:17 the following morning, Vanessa's cell phone rang. She and Agatha were still in the living room, where she had drifted off for about an hour and was dreaming about a fishing trip she had taken with Jesse and the boys to a small lake in upstate New York just over a year ago. Buster had been barely a year old and too young to fish, but Andrew—he was still Andrew then—had caught two largemouth bass on worms with his father's help, a fact that was never mentioned in the telling.

She fumbled with her phone. "Jess? Um, yes, it is. Oh my God. Oh my God! When? Where am I going?"

Agatha, who had been asleep in an easy chair, sat up. "Who is it? What'd they say?"

"Ags?" Rudy had descended to the second-from-the-bottom step on the stairs, and was rubbing his face between the thumb and fingers of his right hand, while his left tugged up the waist of his dark blue sweatpants.

From above came a child's voice. "Daddy?"

The three grownups looked at one another.

"I'll go back," Rudy offered. "I'll think of something to say." Agatha gave a quick nod, and Rudy turned and headed back upstairs.

Vanessa let her cell phone slip to the floor. Tears slid down her cheeks, and her mouth opened in a silent scream. It was a long moment before she could speak. "Someone called the police about an unidentified male found in an alley who…who fits Jesse's description. I have to go…go to the medical examiner's office downtown to identify...shit, I forgot to get the address." She bent forward, looking for her phone.

"I know where it is," Agatha said. "I'm going with you."

• • •

Thirty-five minutes later, Vanessa and Agatha entered a spare, tan lobby that might have been a doctor's office waiting room, except for the lack of an office manager and the temperature, which was in the low sixties. The two women stood together, shifting uncertainly from one foot to the other, until a young woman in a gray skirt, sensible shoes, and a blue wool sweater peeked in.

"Who are you here to see?"

"The medical examiner?" Vanessa ventured. When the woman hesitated and frowned, Vanessa looked at Agatha, then back at the woman. "This is... the medical examiner's office?"

"Just a minute." The woman disappeared. A few moments later, the same door opened and the same woman stepped back into the room. "I'm so sorry. I'm Margaret Blufeld, one of three forensic pathologists who work with Dr. Anderson. I'm afraid there's been a miscommunication. You need to go to the police station and ask for Detective Paul Ganderson."

"But I'm here to...try to identify my husband."

"Mm hmm." Ms. Blufeld was brusk and businesslike. "You can talk to Detective Ganderson about that."

"But...you're the medical examiner's office..." Vanessa felt as though she were swimming in molasses. She couldn't seem to hear, think, or speak correctly.

Blufeld gave three quick, emphatic nods. "Detective *Ganderson*. Beach City Police Station. I can give you directions..."

"No. We'll be okay," Agatha said, taking Vanessa's arm to pull her out of the office.

Vanessa allowed herself to be led back out the front door and into the parking lot, where Agatha delivered her to the passenger's side of Rudy and Agatha's grey Hyundai Tucson. Ten minutes later, they were inside the police station. Agatha ran interference and quickly found Detective Ganderson at one of two desks whose fronts were pushed together. He stood and stepped to one side as Vanessa approached.

Detective Paul Ganderson was tall, had probably been bony in his youth, but now, in his late forties, he was gangly and loose-jointed. His dyed black hair had been slicked back with gel, still showing white in spots. He wore a cheap brown suit. He didn't quite smile.

"Please have a seat. I won't keep you, Ms. Burrell."

"Mrs.—Mrs. Burrell."

"Yes, of course." He looked at Agatha and finally seemed to see her. He looked surprised. "Councilwoman Raines."

"Detective."

"Can I find you a chair?"

Agatha shook her head. "I'm fine standing."

As Vanessa spoke, she was looking around the large, open room, which contained twelve desks that were pushed together in six pairs. "We were at the medical examiner's office. I thought that was where you…"

Ganderson pulled an envelope from a file drawer at the base of his desk, opened it, and prepared to remove its contents. "I'm going to show you a few photos, Mrs. Burrell." He emphasized the word *Mrs.*, and Vanessa could feel rather than see Agatha stiffen beside her. "They may be difficult to look at, but it is important, so would you please tell me if you recognize this person."

He laid three photos next to one another on the table, snapping each one down as if he were dealing cards.

Vanessa let out a little cry, like a small, bereft animal, and grabbed Agatha's upper arm with both her hands for support. A sob escaped her lips.

"Mrs. Burrell?"

"Ohhhh—that's, that's, that's Jesse. That's my husband."

Ganderson picked up a digital recorder that had apparently been running, though he had not mentioned that fact, and spoke into it. "Let the record show that at"—he looked at his watch—"8:41 a.m., Monday, August 18th, 2021, Mrs.... Victoria?"

"Vanessa."

"Vanessa Burrell. Mrs.," he emphasized again. "Mrs. Vanessa Burrell identified the deceased in ME photos 81621A, B and C as being her husband, Jesse Elbert—"

"Elgin," Vanessa murmured.

"Jesse Elvin—"

"Elgin!" Agatha said, more forcefully.

"Elgin. Yes. Jesse Elvin—Elgin Burrell." He continued speaking into the recorder, but had turned away, so that Vanessa and Agatha couldn't hear him.

When the detective turned away, a fire had lit in Vanessa's eyes. Her husband was dead and she was being ignored! She stood up and walked around the detective, where he could see her.

"Detective? I need to know what happened to my husband. Detective!"

But Ganderson held up a hand and turned away again. Vanessa followed him.

"Where was my husband found, detective? Would you please answer me?"

Ganderson turned and looked at them both. Vanessa waved, catching his attention.

He held up a finger and, after finishing his recording, placed the recorder on the desk between them. "I know this is a difficult time, Mrs. Burrell, and I'm sure you will have things to take care of, but I'd like to ask you a few questions that may be helpful to our investigation."

Vanessa took a shaky breath. "So, Jesse was murdered?"

"At this time, our job is to find out everything about your husband, so we'll have as much information as possible going forward."

Vanessa huffed out a breath. "Seems to me we need to be finding out everything about the guy who did this!"

Agatha lay a hand on her sister-in-law's shoulder.

Vanessa swallowed, nodded and proceeded to answer detailed questions about Jesse's whereabouts throughout the day prior to his death, his teaching job, his relationships with everyone in the family including Vanessa, his friends, car, hobbies, places he frequented, how much he drank and whether he used drugs.

When he was finished, Ganderson stood up. "We'll let you know as soon as we know anything more, Mrs. Burrell." He nodded to Agatha. "Councilwoman."

The sisters-in-law headed for the door. When they were outside and walking toward the car, Agatha looked pointedly at Vanessa.

"I do not like that man," she said.

Chapter 3

Dora Ellison stopped at home to shower and change out of her sanitation clothes before going to the funeral home. Being around garbage all day tended to leave one in need of a shower, though Dora had the unique attribute of rarely if ever sweating, whatever her level of exercise or exertion.

The wake and viewing were from 2:00 to 4:00 p.m., and again from 7:00 to 9:00 p.m., for two days only.

Dora went with the intent to convey her condolences, but she felt she might be in a position to do more, and wanted to express as much to Vanessa, and perhaps to Agatha and Rudy as well.

She found the family in the back of the larger of two rooms at Trabor's Funeral Home, which was midway between Beach City and Rockland Township, where the Burrell family lived. The room was tastefully decorated in restrained elegance—gray walls and carpet, paintings of peaceful landscapes, glossy polished wood tables featuring the occasional vase. Vanessa was seated next to Miz Liz in the center of a group of people that included Rudy but not Agatha, along with several couples she knew to be both friends of Agatha and Rudy's and customers at Rudy's bar. Agatha was off to one side with Samuel, who was in his carrier, and Vanessa and Jesse's sons, both of whom wore perfect little suits. She was prepared to take all three boys outside, should their chatter get to be too loud for the wake.

The casket was at the front and closed at Vanessa's request. About a third of those present wore N95 or cloth masks that had been in use since the COVID-19 virus had become widespread early in 2020. Virus protection was still prevalent a year and a half later, but with infection levels and deaths on Long Island dropping, many, particularly those who were vaccinated, now eschewed masks. Many refrained from shaking hands or kissing; others did not.

Vanessa and Miz Liz were gripping one another's hands. Vanessa looked exhausted, but Dora was surprised to see that Miz Liz, despite being well into her seventies and having lost her only son just two days before, was a commanding presence.

"What are you saying?" Keisha Williams wanted to know. She had cinnamon skin and light brown hair coiled atop her head. She had worked at a childcare business until it closed in April of 2020, during the early days of the COVID-19 pandemic, but could not collect unemployment because her job had been off the books. Her husband, LaChance, was an intense thirty-something man with a goatee and normally a broad smile. He had made a fortune shorting a long list of companies in the stock market twelve years before. He had what some called a Midas touch. He was delighted his wife was no longer working; he had been against her job from the start.

Keisha glanced at her husband, then went on. "You don't think the police…"

"What I'm *saying*," Miz Liz clarified, "is I can't speak for the police. I don't know what they will or won't do, and what they will or won't share with our family. What I'm *saying* is that we are not going to wait on them. We are going to check into some things ourselves. Now, I know Jesse wasn't no angel, so I need to know more about the facts on the ground—who he was with and what he was doing." She looked at Rudy. "And I *need to know* about that poker game."

Rudy looked surprised. "What poker game?"

"Don't you play that with me! Best stay on that side of the room, Rudy Raines, because if I come over there and you're saying 'what poker game,' I can't be responsible for what might happen!"

Rudy cleared his throat. "Oh, that poker game."

A woman with a kind, round face held up her hand. "Miz Liz, I'm Shanice James and I'm here with my husband, Delroy. My husband can explain about the poker game and tell you about Jesse being a part of that and whatever else was going on." She looked at her husband, a heavy man with sad eyes and bushy eyebrows, who was looking at her with an "are you crazy" expression. He wore an expensive leather jacket and black-framed glasses. She nodded to him. "Yes, you will." She looked back at

Miz Liz. "Pretty near everyone who plays in that game is here right now, anyways."

The room was silent for a moment, except for a cry from Samuel and a "hush, Samuel" from Agatha. Finally, after exchanging looks with several other men, Delroy nodded. "We'll get together after, and get back to you."

Miz Liz gave him a severe look. "Get back to you…"

"Get back to you, *ma'am*."

She gave a satisfied nod, then went on. "We need to find some way to stay informed about the police investigation."

"Won't they keep us informed?" Vanessa asked.

"I'm sure—up to a point. I believe we have a good police force here in Beach City, and I believe Chief Stalwell to be a good man. But how much of what's really going on they'll really tell us—that's another thing."

People around the room nodded.

"Mmhmm."

"That's right."

"Truth."

"Truedat."

Miz Liz waved a bony finger in the air. "I don't begrudge them that. They have to run their investigation the way they see fit, and I'm sure leaks don't help, but we want to see my boy's killer caught. We *will* see his killer caught."

"How much do we know?" asked Martine Franklin, a curvy woman with a kind, smiling face, wise eyes, and luscious creamy skin that was the envy of most of her friends. At the moment she looked grief stricken. She had been close to Vanessa since high school. Next to her was her husband Kelvin, who was ruggedly handsome, with prominent cheekbones and watchful eyes. He was a piano player who sometimes played at Rudy's, and more often played for seniors at nursing homes and assisted living facilities, a joyful experience all around. His wife was a project scientist with a master's degree in environmental science, who worked at an engineering company.

Miz Liz shrugged. "You want to take that, Nessa?"

Vanessa rose to her feet. She hated speaking in public and was still reeling with shock and grief, but she understood that her mother-in-law was prodding her to take an active role for her own benefit, to draw her out of a shell that was quickly hardening into intentional isolation.

"We really don't know much," she said, her voice shaking. She touched her hand to the table beside her to steady herself. "He died of …" She swallowed. "…blunt force trauma to the side and back of the head. He was found in the alley behind The Elegant Lagoon restaurant."

"Murder weapon?" someone asked.

"That's all I know, 'cept …when I identified him from the picture, they still had a sheet covering the top and side of his head, because he was…he was…" She began to sob, and Rudy, who was sitting beside her, stood up and put an enormous arm around her shoulders. Vanessa fanned herself with her hand, and sat down.

Dora was sitting behind Vanessa. She put her hand on the bereaved woman's shoulder and leaned forward. "Let's talk," Dora said. She was sitting next to Charlie Bernelli, and noticed that he was saying something with his eyes. "What?" she asked. He nodded toward Miz Liz. Dora understood and stood up to address the room.

"Many of you know me—Agatha does, and Rudy, and now Vanessa. I collect sanitation here in town and was involved in something a little too high-profile for my liking a year and a half ago." She nodded at the many familiar faces around her; some she knew from her sanitation route, a job that was now coming to an end. Others knew her from the publicity surrounding the events of a year and a half before.

"What people don't know is that I gave notice a couple of weeks ago and will be entering the police academy next week. Chief Stalwell came up with the idea." She chuckled, as did Charlie. "Which kind of makes me wonder about him. My point is that I might be able to learn some things. I suspect recruits aren't privy to the details of murder investigations, and I'll be mostly at the police academy, which is over by the Community College."

She shrugged. "They say it's not just a police academy; they've got a whole floor dedicated to the community."

Miz Liz gave a grim look. "And what are we, if not a community?"

At that moment, the two detectives—Ganderson and Mallard—walked in and sat down in the back, surveying the crowd. Ganderson wore his usual cheap brown suit. Mallard wore Armani. Everyone stared at them for a few moments, then continued their conversation and eventually sat in respectful silence until the wake's end.

When the meeting broke up, Miz Liz squeezed Dora's forearm. "Thank you. I'm sure you'll make a good police officer. Lieutenant Hart would be proud."

Dora's eyes filled. She swallowed. "I hope so. I can't promise anything, but I'll find out what I can." She caught Vanessa's eye. "Excuse me," she said to Miz Liz. She gently led Vanessa away from the group.

"Vanessa, last year I lost the love of my life to a violent crime." She grimaced, frustrated by her inability to hold back the tear that spilled down her cheek. "I want to help—not just say, 'If there's anything I can do.' People are always saying that shit."

Vanessa tried to smile. "They mean well."

"I want to do more. In fact, I don't have much babysitting experience, but if you ever need one, I could learn—maybe spend time with your kids, get to know them. 'Course it will depend on the academy, which they tell me is pretty rigorous."

Vanessa looked at Dora for a moment, then threw her arms around the larger woman, who, unaccustomed to public displays of affection, hesitantly returned the hug. "Just that you'd say that… Agatha has hours at the library many evenings, and Rudy's at the bar most afternoons and at night. Consider our home your home. You can study there, work out. Rudy said you train at Shay's MMA?"

Dora nodded. "I do. I want to do more than say I want to help. And I really will work on getting us updates on the investigation."

Vanessa looked grateful but concerned. "Just don't put your new career at risk."

...

On her first day at the academy, Dora considered skipping her morning coffee, then quickly rejected the idea. She needed her focus and whatever little boost of energy the coffee afforded her, despite any additional anxiety and jitters that came along with the caffeine. She often had two, sometimes three cups—sometimes more. She had been told what to expect; in fact, she was aware of much about the academy and "hell week" prior to having any interest in joining. Franny had talked about every aspect of her work, including the training that was its backbone and underpinning.

Once she was behind the wheel of her crimson 2017 Subaru WRX Turbo, Dora was able to relax. Driving her beloved turbo calmed her; it had been a gift to herself several months after Franny's death and the resolution of the Beach City corruption and racketeering case, and Anne Volkov's murder. The purring power beneath her centered her and helped Dora to convince herself that the academy experience would work out, one way or another. She would be okay.

She found herself watching a blonde twentyish woman in a Ford Escape who was driving in the center lane. She noticed the woman because a tractor trailer driver had noticed her too and was playing games. He had maneuvered behind her and was tailgating her. Dora shook her head. Did he think the woman found that attractive? When the woman pulled into the right-hand lane and slowed down to allow the truck to pass, the truck pulled in front of her and hit his brakes. Dora caught a glimpse of her wide-eyed terror.

Enough. Dora pulled in front of the truck and hit her own brakes. If the truck hit her from behind, he would be the cause of the accident. The woman pulled back into the center lane, passed the truck and Dora's turbo, and flashed Dora a grateful smile.

Dora knew she should continue on and leave the truck driver behind. She was, after all, a police recruit now and had a responsibility to the public's safety. But that was just it; her responsibility to the public told her to make sure this asshole of a bully left his bullying days behind him. A small voice in a corner of her mind said, *Don't do it—leave it at that.*

"Shut the fuck up," she muttered to the voice, hoping no instructors from the academy, or worse, Chief Stalwell or Captain Waycrest, were around to see this. She flipped the guy off then slowed to a crawl, and could see his enraged, screaming face on her mirror.

Now he was pointing to the side of the road. She could read his lips. "Pull over!"

Perfect.

He pulled onto the shoulder, and she knew she should probably drive away. Of course, she should. She had open road in front of her, a turbo under her, and she'd already made a fool of this jackass. And yet, she couldn't. Missy had been talking to her about this—developing restraint. She shook her head. Not today.

She pulled onto the shoulder, keeping her tinted windows raised. The truck driver, a burly thirty-five- or forty-year-old in a wife beater, ran up to her car, pointing and screaming.

"Fuckin' pussy! Roll down your window. Get out of your car!"

As soon as she rolled the window down, the truck driver jammed his hand into the growing opening and grabbed a handful of Dora's hair.

Dora clamped her right hand over the truck driver's hand, and twisted it to her right, in what was for him an unnatural direction. He screamed in pain as he caught sight of her face.

She smiled. "Very insightful. I am a pussy, kinda—though you can be more polite than that. I prefer woman. Or lady."

She then employed a trick she had learned at Shay's MMA school. She looked around at the drivers who were watching, some of them filming with their phones, and she began to yell.

"Sir, sir, please leave me alone. Sir! Stop attacking me, sir! Please leave me alone!" Witnesses would register and remember her words and recall an enraged truck driver reaching into an innocent woman's car. What the woman did afterwards would be remembered as self-defense, if anyone remembered it at all.

He had let go of her hair, so Dora let go of his hand and grabbed a fistful of the top of his shirt.

She had been a sanitation worker for six years, lifting and "tipping" filled garbage cans—often with one hand, and carrying all manner of discarded furniture, appliances, equipment, and detritus. She had trained hard and successfully at mixed martial arts, MMA, and dominated at every level, including intramural competitions. She had taken on a brutal, armed enforcer for the corrupt city administration a year and a half prior. But more than any of these, a deep disgust of bullies had been embedded deep in her psyche by long-ago childhood events that never failed to fill her with trauma-fueled rage.

"Come on," she said to the anguished driver. "You can say it. Lady." She pretended to sound encouraging. "You can do it. Lady. Layy-deee."

He snarled something unintelligible.

She wiped her face with the sleeve of her free hand. "Say it, don't spray it." And then she tightened her grip on the front of his shirt and pulled. Hard. Really, really hard.

Her window was still only about halfway open, and she took advantage of that. When during an altercation, someone reaches through an open car window to grab the driver, the attacker may expect all sorts of things—most of them involving being pushed away. The attacker does not expect to be pulled inward, toward the window, but that is what Dora did. She used her lats, her biceps and her weight and heard the satisfying crunch of splintering bone as the trucker's cheek collided with the trim above her door, and he crumpled to the ground. Only then did she drive away, wondering whether she had driven over one of his hands.

"Shit, I shouldn't have done that." She thought about it, then muttered, "My chrome better be intact."

* * *

The academy was housed in a brand-new, enormous, modern facility with great expanses of white floor-to-ceiling windows and steel girders. Dora and the hundred or so other recruits from around the county were told by Police Commissioner Vincent Tanner that they would be studying a daunting array of subjects and skills: officer safety and survival; constitutional, federal, state and local law; the use and safety of firearms; defensive tactics; enhanced driving skills; accident investigation; human behavior and psychology; crime scene management; and interview and interrogation. They could expect to participate in regular simulations reflecting many of the scenarios they might encounter in the field, and would be graded on a combination of written exercises and practical exams.

Recruits, the commissioner explained, should expect the training to be exhausting, stressful, and for some, more than they could handle. Some would not make it, and very likely the reason would be that they would not be psychologically fit for the job. This last bit concerned Dora, though she tried not to think about it. She thought of her psychological/emotional approach to crime as a net positive, though she suspected the academy instructors might not.

"You will learn through repetition and more repetition," the commissioner explained, "until your training becomes instinctive. You will learn and adhere to discipline, and in most cases, you will make myself and your instructors proud."

Dora's thoughts returned to the commissioner's warning about psychological fitness and the many conversations she'd had with Franny about her early life traumas and her anger issues. *We'll see.*

Immediately following the commissioner's speech, the recruits were treated to a series of lectures that further explained what and how they would learn. The classes that would make up the first week included Introduction to Basic Training, Effective Study Habits, the History of Police Work in the United States, Ethics and Morality in Police Work, and Police Officers and the Law.

Everywhere the recruits went during the training day, they were expected to maintain silence. If they wanted to speak, they asked permission. Uniforms were expected to be cleaned, pressed, and worn to perfection. Equipment was to be kept in perfect working order and stored in exactly the manner instructed. Every expectation was backed up with constant ongoing rigorous scrutiny.

A surprise mock shootout with armed robbers was sprung on the recruits that first afternoon, and followed by analysis and correction of mistakes, several hours of instruction on the use of the local police weapon of choice—the 9mm SIG Sauer P226 semi-automatic pistol—followed by firing range shooting instruction and practice.

The day ended with five sets of pushups, sit-ups and a three-and-a-half-mile run, which would be increased to five miles the following week.

The sheer volume of new information, taxing physical routines, and commissioner's warnings left Dora looking forward to getting home, grabbing something from the freezer to heat up, having two beers, and going to sleep.

As she hurried through the sultry summer night toward her car, someone called out to her. "Wait up!" A dark-eyed woman with a thin, vulpine face was jogging toward her. "Hey," she said breathlessly, the sweat on her forehead glistening in the parking lot lights.

"What's up?" Dora asked.

She shook her head. "Just wanted to say hi to another female." She put out her hand. "Tina."

"Dora. Sorry, I stopped shaking hands with COVID."

Tina nodded. "Did you grow up wanting this—being a cop, I mean?"

"Um, not at all. I'm here because of…" She thought for a moment. "…a friend's influence."

"My dad was a cop," Tina said. "He passed last year. He'd love that I'm doing this."

Dora nodded. "I get it."

"Well, I'm over here." Tina waved goodbye and began walking toward a black Crown Victoria.

Dora laughed. "I can see the influence."

• • •

Missy had invited Dora to dinner, but she decided to call and plead exhaustion, which was only part of the truth. The other part was that she and Missy had been circling each other for a year and a half, since the two kisses they'd shared nearly two years before. Dora had been so in love with Francesca, who had been a source of deep healing. Franny's murder had scarred Dora, or perhaps more accurately, had torn and deepened existing scars. Her experience was that those who loved you either hurt you or left you. Her wounds and loss were too deep and fresh for her to consider a new relationship, and Dora was pretty sure Missy understood that. So far, Missy had been patient and kind—a good friend, though Dora had an awareness of her own powerful yearning that bespoke of more than friendship. She was certain that Missy felt the same; Dora was grateful that Missy did not press the issue. Time did heal wounds. All wounds? Dora wasn't sure.

And yet, she deeply enjoyed and appreciated Missy's company. Franny had been wise, loving, and endlessly creative—playing Chopin and Bach on the piano, and giving Dora an education in the arts simply by virtue of their time together.

The love Dora had experienced early in life had been yanked away, and turned against her. For Dora, loving someone and showing vulnerability were difficult. Frightening. She felt she had to always be on the lookout for abandonment, always ready to fight.

Dora didn't know Missy well enough yet to know if she was wise—she certainly had common sense, and as a librarian, she had plenty of book sense. She was also diplomatic; Missy had been gently warning Dora about her penchant for teaching bullies lessons ever since they met—at first half kiddingly and tongue-in-cheek, but eventually with genuine concern. Dora would not have accepted such admonitions from very many people; she had learned as a child to refuse to be told what to do. But Missy had yet to do that directly. Instead, she pointed out risks and said that she would hate to see a good friend suffer. She had a way of asking thoughtful questions that led to Dora sharing Missy's conclusions. Was that wisdom or codependence? Missy was an encouraging, positive, supportive presence, and Dora found it extremely attractive that she was never aggressive, manipulative, or pushy. And yet, Dora was still swimming in loss; her loyalty to Franny's memory meant that Missy would have to remain a friend.

Once in the car, she checked her phone. She had several messages. One was from Missy, asking how her first day at the academy had gone and then asking if Dora was all right. Dora smiled to herself. Vanessa had left a message taking Dora up on her offer of a shoulder to lean on. She needed to find a way to support her children with Jesse gone, and she would need childcare. She knew Dora was busy, so she said it was no rush, though Dora suspected it was.

Dora had seen how much in love Vanessa and Jesse had been, how much and how lovingly they touched one another as part of their natural interaction, which was physical, emotional, and spiritual. Dora had also noticed how they sought one another's input and saw to one another's needs, even with something so simple as what to eat at a dinner party, bringing one another food and saving seats at a party. The joy they took in one another's company extended so naturally to their children, whom they plainly cherished, while they enforced the boundaries and established the consequences children need to grow into responsible adults.

As she drove home, Dora wondered about Vanessa's job skills and what sort of job opportunities a now-single mother of a five-year-old and a toddler would find. She knew Vanessa was studying to be a realtor, and that she wanted to help right the wrongs some in that industry perpetuated around Long Island—particularly the victimization of people of color.

An idea occurred to her. She said, "Hey, Siri. Call Christine Pearsall." She waited. On the second ring, Christine picked up.

"Officer Ellison!"

Dora laughed. "Long way to go before I'm that. How are you, Ms. Mayor?"

"Always work to do, but I'm great."

"And Charlie?"

"Also busy, but good." Christine was engaged to Charlie Bernelli Jr., owner of The Bernelli Group, one of two ad agencies in Beach City.

"C3?"

"Loves his job, lives his job—and as a counselor, he gets to work his program at his job."

"Does Charlie still worry about him?"

Christine laughed. "Always. Charlie could be ninety and C3 could be sixty-five and... Hey, you must be beat, with what they got you going through. What's up?"

"Vanessa."

Christine's manner instantly changed, turning somber. "That poor girl must be on her heels. She's a churchgoer?"

"She is, and she's gonna need it. But what she also needs is work, with two little ones."

"Mmm."

"And a broken heart. Anything for her to do at City Hall?"

"I can look into it. Wasn't she studying to be a realtor?"

"She was."

"Agatha tells me she had ideas of ridding the real estate business of racism. So all realtors would show all homes to everyone, regardless of color."

"Something like that, but that was then." Dora turned off the highway and made the right turn onto Park Boulevard. She drove past the beach clubs, a few of which hosted bands and events from spring through the fall.

"Let me look into it."

"That's all I can ask, Your Honor."

"I'll reach out to you tomorrow. This a good time?"

"It is. You have a good night and say hey to Charlie and C3."

"Roger, Officer."

Dora ended the call and made the turn into her parking lot. It had been a long day.

Chapter 4

The next day was Wednesday, and while only a few people came in during the afternoon wake, the evening shift was filled with many of the same family and friends who had attended the night before. Everyone knew that Wednesday's wake would culminate in a service conducted by Elder Reginald Williams of the Beach City Baptist Church, which both the Beach City and Rockland Township branches of the family often attended before sharing a Sunday afternoon family luncheon at one or the other of their homes, a tradition that went back two generations and had recently been dominated by Rudy and Jesse's barbecuing, watching games and arguing about sports, no matter the season. Everyone knew that Wednesday night was the main event.

Early on, the family and close friends were gathered in the back of the visitation room, with Jesse's casket at the front, next to a tripod that held a picture of him beaming on his wedding day.

"So, tell me. What was my boy up to?" Miz Liz wanted to know. She had worn another of what she called her funeral dresses—black, yet stylish, which, as she was quick to tell anyone within earshot, was an apt description of her as well. She rose to her feet and put her hands on her hips. Though she was barely five feet tall, she seemed to tower over the group. "Don't be afraid to tell me the truth about my son. Nothing you can tell me can hurt me any more than what's already happened, and I'm not looking for who might have influenced his behavior. I just want to know what happened to my boy, and for justice to be done."

"Say hey, he liked playing cards," ventured Little Ru. Eunice, his wife, turned slowly to look at her husband. She had an intelligent, wide face, a powerful nose with permanently flared nostrils, prominent cheekbones, and enormous eyes that took in everything and gave the impression that she knew things she was keeping to herself.

"Who else played?" Miz Liz demanded to know. It wasn't a question.

Winnie May shook her head, which she often did, whether with regret or wonderment.

"I can't say's I know much on the subject," Kelvin Franklin began, "but we need to be careful about throwing stones."

His wife, Martine, nodded. "Who among us is without sin…"

Miz Liz, who had sat back down, slapped the table beside her so hard that she was lifted to her feet. "Who among us has a son in that box in the front of the room!"

Silence — which stretched on for a few long moments. Vanessa looked at each of the attendees, grateful they had come but not possessing the strength to connect with anyone on any level. She was slowly sliding into depression.

Rudy was attending without Agatha, who had taken the night off from the library to watch all three boys. "Well, we smoked the occasional blunt together," he admitted.

"Okay," said Miz Liz. "So, is that what he was doing in that alley? Buying reefer?"

Rudy shrugged. "He had weed. He said something about being out of Sam Adams. Police say it looks like a robbery—his wallet's missing."

Miz Liz looked back at him, unblinking. "But not that fancy Apple Watch, and not his car keys."

Rudy shrugged. "Could still be…"

"We'll see," said Miz Liz, and nodded toward the door. Elder Reginald had entered the room. Everyone turned. Reginald Williams was a head taller than Rudy, who at six four was the next tallest person in the room. Elder Reginald was six eight and three quarters. He was frequently asked if he played basketball, a question that annoyed him a little bit, especially if the asker was white, which was usually the case. The truth was, he had been devoted to Jesus since he learned that Jesus loved him, no matter what, just as he was. He had been a shy child who read constantly and had a speech impediment through high school. To this day, he occasionally lisped slightly when preaching at his full intensity, which was considerable. He felt deeply about the Lord and was powerfully moved whenever he preached.

He nodded to people as he entered, embraced Vanessa, rocking from side to side with her as they hugged, then did the same with Miz Liz and Rudy.

As Elder Reginald approached the lectern, Betty Thomas, who was with her son, Willis, and whom everyone knew as their crossing guard from grade school, leaned toward Miz Liz. "Thing is," she said, "that alleyway where they found him wasn't anywhere near anyplace that sold beer."

. . .

"No temptation has overtaken you that is not common." Elder Reginald's eyes connected with the people before him as though he were speaking personally to each one. "And God. Is. Faithful," he continued, enunciating each syllable with care and precision. "We are all human. We are all sinners. Human nature is sinful, and eternal. Yet, God will not. Let you. Be tempted. Beyond. What you can bear." He spoke slowly, clearly, each syllable ringing out and ringing true—beams of light made of words that pierced Vanessa's heart. She began to cry.

"These are words for us to live by, yet there are many who choose not to live by these words. And their choices can be our undoing. Their choices can lead to tragedy. Their choices can lead to loss—the loss of the righteous. The loss of our children, of our brothers, our fathers. And that is what we are here to mourn today—the loss of a righteous man—a child, a brother, a father."

"Amen, Lord!" shouted Miz Liz, amidst a murmur that fluttered lightly from the lips of some of those assembled.

"God will also provide the way of escape that you may be able to endure. And yet..." He rose up on his toes, as was Elder Reginald's habit when he was coming to his main point. "And yet, all things must pass! There is a season for all things, and for all people. There is a season to live and a season to die—for each of us, and for us all. And so, we are here this evening to mourn the passing of the season of light that was the soul of Brother Jesse Burrell."

The viewing room at Trabor's Funeral Home reverberated with Vanessa Burrell's soft sobs, Miz Liz's murmurs of "Amen, Lord," and the echoes of Elder Reginald's words from the mouths and hearts of those assembled.

...

Dora's second day at the academy could be summed up in a single word: survival—not so much because the classroom, hand-to-hand combat drills or fitness regimens were so challenging, though they were, but because the word was used so emphatically and frequently by her instructors.

"You will survive!" Or, simply: "Survive!" was repeated so frequently that the two-syllable word echoed in Dora's mind for days. She knew others felt the same, because they said so—not in the building, as talking without permission was not allowed, but in the parking lot at the end of the day.

The word was an order; the word was a prediction; the word was the backbone of relationships that would very possibly ensure their survival on the street. Procedures were drilled over and over until they became reflex. Mutual support, despite differences or dislikes, was critical to survival. The officer who saves your life might have the opposite politics, opposite views, and might just be someone you can't stand.

Get over it.

All classroom instruction was conducted by officers with expertise in the content at hand, who were certified as instructors by the Department of Justice. Dress code Class A Uniform infractions were punishable by sets of one hundred pushups for the entire class. Everyone was aware of everyone else's uniform compliance or lack of it.

Day two classroom instruction covered the basics of Constitutional Law and New York State Liquor Laws, Civil Liability, and State Criminal Law. Afternoon Practical Skills covered shooting decisions and the tactical use of weapons, followed by Interpersonal Relations and Stress Management. Dora found these last two courses both annoying and fascinating, for the same reason—they were skills she lacked.

The second day again culminated in pushups, sit-ups, and running. Recruits were directed to their home precincts for a rare evening program—Introductory Criminal Investigation training, including the Principles of Investigation and Crime Scene Processing, subject matter that had been top of mind for Dora, as she hoped to speak with her home precinct instructor, Lieutenant Catherine Trask. Agatha had explained that Trask was one of the initial officers involved in the investigation into Jesse's murder.

When Dora approach Lieutenant Trask and asked if she was in charge of the Jesse Burrell investigation, she was quickly corrected. "That would be Detective Paul Ganderson, with Detective Gerald Mallard second-in-command."

"Thank you for pointing that out," Dora said. "I ask because I'm a good friend of the family, and…"

"I know who you are, Ellison." Trask remained unsmiling.

"The thing is," Dora continued, "his wife and kids are hurting…and hurting for information. They haven't been told anything beyond the cause of death and where he was found."

Lieutenant Trask looked down at the paperwork on her desk, then up at Dora. "Maybe there's nothing to tell, yet. Maybe anything there is to tell might not be tellable to the wife and certainly not to children. As you know by now, an investigation, especially early on, is like a child—delicate—and needs to be handled with care."

Dora nodded. "Understood. Thank you, Lieutenant." She turned and took a few steps toward the door.

"Ellison."

Dora turned back. Lieutenant Trask nodded toward the door. "Close that, come back, and sit down." Dora closed the door and did as she'd been asked.

"First of all, I want to personally convey my condolences to you on your own loss. We all loved Lieutenant Hart, and we know you did too, so that makes you family, in a very real way."

Dora nodded and blinked several times; she tried but could not manage to smile.

Trask's features softened. "We also are aware of the role—I should say *roles*—you played in bringing down systemic corruption, including within our ranks, as well as in the municipal system." Finally, Trask smiled. "No one would say it out loud and I'll deny I said it, but we all owe you. Not just the force, not just the city government—the city itself. Our residents."

"That's ..." Dora shook her head. "No, no—that's..."

"Accurate, is what it is. So, I'm going to..." Her voice trailed off as she looked at her computer screen and hit a few keys. Along the wall beneath the window overlooking the police parking lot, a printer buzzed and shooshed, spitting a piece of paper into a tray. "Would you mind?"

Dora went to the printer, took the paper and examined it. "The police report?"

Lieutenant Catherine Trask grimaced and shook her head. "Don't know what you're talking about, Ellison. Now get out of my office." Her attention returned to her computer screen.

"Yes, ma'am."

As Dora approached the door, she heard Trask's admonishment. "Don't let the Goose and the Gander get to you."

She wondered what that meant.

・・・

It was a Thursday night and Petrocelli's was moderately busy. The restaurant was divided into a takeout and delivery area that specialized in pizza, calzones, chicken and sausage rolls along with the occasional dinner, and a sit-down restaurant with a darkened, upscale ambience—a Sinatra-era music loop, track lighting, and outstanding service.

Dora was seated with Missy, Agatha, and Rudy Raines. They had all received drinks and placed their salad and dinner orders.

Dora was pleased to find that she was not much more tired after this long day at the academy than previous days, probably owing to her MMA training. Being physically attacked during a workout not only increased the cardio but required one to transcend fear and trauma, which added exponentially to the intensity and difficulty of the workout. What tended to be exhausting was the psychological burden—the overwhelm—and she had found herself texting Missy, who finished her library shift at six, and asking her to meet her, Agatha, and Rudy at Petrocelli's. While Dora did not want to give the impression she was looking for anything more than friendship from Missy, and certainly did not want to lead her on, she found the librarian's calm, gentle, supportive demeanor to be exactly what she needed after these stressful days at the academy.

"So, wait," Missy marveled. "You got the actual police report? How?"

Dora shrugged. "Francesca. Magic word. Wherever she is, she's still helping me."

"Nice," Agatha said.

"You sure you're down for this, baby?" Rudy asked his wife.

Agatha nodded. "Got to be. Nessa's not. I'm her eyes and ears for now."

Rudy nodded but said nothing. He sipped a Blue Moon and listened, occasionally glancing at Agatha, while Dora read from the report.

"Cause of death was head trauma and severe loss of blood." Dora looked at Agatha, unsure if she should go on. "You sure?" She held up the sheet of paper.

"I'm sure," Agatha replied.

Dora continued. "The victim was found in an alley behind The Elegant Lagoon, a seafood restaurant in the Beach City business district. The restaurant has a back door into the alley, which lies between the strip of stores and a fence that borders private homes. Residents in two of the three homes nearest that spot remember hearing an escalating argument on Sunday night from that vicinity, and one of those residents looked at her clock, which put the argument she heard at 12:20 a.m. There was little else of interest in the alley, though a detective is still sifting through garbage found in the dumpster there."

"Which detective?" Agatha wanted to know.

"Umm." Dora's finger traced a line from an asterisk to the bottom of the paper. "Detective Gerald Mallard."

Agatha nodded. "That means Ganderson's the lead. The Goose and the Gander—Mallard, the Goose, and Ganderson, the Gander. They're the team that often takes the lead on homicides."

"But are they good?" Rudy asked.

Agatha shrugged. "Good enough to still be leads on the most challenging cases. They're kind of characters. Ganderson's a stickler for rules. Kind of old school. Mallard's a know-it-all. Has theories on everything and can quote from old cases like you wouldn't believe. Some think he's a bit of a quack—hence the name, which is a hybrid of that and his actual name. If they're on the case, it's a good thing but also inevitable, given the size of our police force."

"Cool," said Rudy.

"The other businesses in that strip," Dora read, "are a women's clothing boutique, a women's shoe store, a bank, and a laundromat. All were closed at the time the crime apparently occurred—all except the laundromat, where the person on duty claimed to have heard nothing, due to the noise of the washers and dryers. Let's see." She scanned farther down the page. "Ah, I was looking for this. "The deceased was found without a wallet, cash, or any identification, and may have been the victim of a robbery, offered resistance, and was then killed. He was, however, in possession of his Apple Watch Series 6 and his car keys. His car, a 2019 Prius, was in a nearby public lot, parked legally. None of the residents in the vicinity seem to have noticed his arrival. The victim had a broken ulna bone, which is the outer edge of his forearm, indicating that he may have been defending himself, or perhaps broke his fall with his forearm. No DNA was found under his fingernails."

"Yeah, but what was my brother doing there?" asked Agatha. No one answered.

Dora continued reading. "Responding officers collected two pieces of wood and several stones that were near the victim as potential murder weapons, and sent them to the lab for analysis." She skimmed the rest of the page, paraphrasing. "The ground was wet from an evening drizzle, so the investigation team are using dirt hardener to get prints, though many are partials, since there were multiple sets of overlapping footprints going in every direction; it seems the lot was often used as an exit from the restaurant and dry cleaners, and is also where all of the venues in the strip dispose of their garbage. There are photos of the footprints. Dozens of cigarette butts and several pieces of used chewing gum have been collected and are being analyzed. Multiple fibers from clothing were also recovered and are also being analyzed. Detective Ganderson is in charge of maintaining a crime scene logbook of people who use the alley, including police personnel, and the ME's removal of the body. But an Officer Weiss seems to be the person with that logbook—though it is ultimately Ganderson's responsibility."

Agatha sighed. "Oh, my poor baby brother."

"I thought you were twins," Dora said.

"He's like seven minutes younger—or, was." Agatha looked away. Rudy covered her hand with his.

"There's more," Dora said. "A bit of dark blue cloth was found on a nearby bush, torn from an article of clothing that had brushed against the bush, though it is not known when the cloth was left there. Luminal was used to locate blood spatter on a telephone pole that was adjacent to the body, and secondary spatter, which means smaller droplets—I learned this in class just yesterday—was found on fence poles bordering the area. The location of the spatter indicated that the victim moved around, either fighting back or attempting to flee. We can see from the secondary spatter that the victim was probably next to the fence at one time, perhaps trying to climb over it. There is also the kind of spatter that indicates blunt force—

blood that is propelled away from a body, as well as what seems to be a bloody handprint on the top crossbar of the fence."

Rudy looked at his wife, whose hand was over her mouth, then at Dora. "Maybe you should stop."

"No!" Agatha insisted.

Dora went on. "The precise angles are arrived at by trigonometry. Currently, foot traffic in the area is off limits to minimize new footprints. There was one set of tire tracks in the alley, consistent with a garbage truck. There is also evidence that the area used to be a place where unidentified persons drank alcohol and used marijuana, though there is no indication that the victim or anyone he might have been with was involved in these activities at that location on the night in question. The victim was not found to be in possession of a cell phone. None of the homes in the vicinity have outdoor video cameras. Detective Mallard has videotaped and photographed the scene. A detailed sketch of the crime scene and the victim's position in it has also been made by Mallard. The alley has been divided into narrow numbered blocks, which have been searched, with recovered items labeled as originating from those blocks, all of which are identified by proximity to the victim."

The waiter arrived with the food.

"I keep coming back to—why was he there?" Agatha said, when the waiter had gone.

"I started talking to the guys," Rudy said, "but no one seems to know anything."

"Would they say, if they did?" Dora asked.

Rudy pressed his lips together, thinking. "I guess it depends on how damaging to them the truth is."

• • •

Classroom study the next day focused on Laws of Evidence and Laws of Arrest, both of which Dora found interesting. She was finding that the part of her mind that loved puzzles also enjoyed the nuances of police work, particularly the law. She liked the precision of the law and that it applied to everyone equally, at least theoretically, though history often told a different story.

The afternoon's practicals were First Responder Skills, also interesting, and the Mechanics of Arrest, Restraint, and Control—straight out of Dora's wheelhouse, if anything was. As she exited the locker room, she found herself walking beside Tina.

"Hey," Tina said.

"Hey yourself," Dora answered. "How you liking it?"

"Liking it? Hah. Ten hours of work like hell, four hours of homework, run 'til your legs fall off, then crash—what's not to love?"

"Quiet, girls," said Sergeant Scott Kontaxis, who was leading ARC Mechanics. "Or everybody runs."

The first half of the class consisted of verbal instruction, while the second consisted of hand-to-hand training. Dora had hoped to be paired off with Tina but ended up with Racquel, a tall Latina with big teeth she showed when she smiled, which happened often, along with a sleeve of tattoos. They nodded to one another as they walked toward the mats that were arrayed at one end of the gym.

"Who knew a hippo could be a cop?" someone walking behind them muttered, and Dora stopped walking. The grunt the guy let out as he walked into her was similar to the whispered insult. She smiled to herself.

Today they were learning about Ch'in Na, a system of joint locks used to control the target, or "assholes" as Kontaxis and some of the other police called them. The locks were demonstrated, then each individual was given a chance to practice on his or her partner.

"So, which two of you recruits would like to be our demonstration team?" Kontaxis asked, looking everyone over. Dora put up her hand.

"Whoa," said Racquel as Dora stood up.

"Permission to speak?" Dora asked.

"Granted."

"I'd like to choose my partner."

"You would?" Kontaxis looked amused; he folded his arms. "And who would that be?"

Dora smiled and pointed at the whisperer from earlier. "I choose… him."

Kontaxis shook his head. "I was going to explain that we don't get to choose our partners here, but Aldridge? You're a big girl, but Skinny Aldridge weighs two and a quarter."

"Two fifteen," Aldridge protested.

"Right," Kontaxis said, smiling. "You're serious?" Dora nodded. "Well, in this case, why not?"

"You're crazy," Aldridge said. "But okay." His partner, a grinning, blond quarterback type, laughed out loud.

They began with Dora playing the part of the attacker and Aldridge the arresting officer. Dora swung her arm in the prescribed way, like a looping punch, and Aldridge intercepted the punch, slid his hand to her palm, and attempted to apply the lock.

That's where things went sideways. Dora couldn't help herself. As Skinny Aldridge pushed her palm toward her wrist, she turned her hand, slipped the lock, and found the tip of one of his fingers, which she used to turn his whole body, whether it was 225 or 215 pounds, nearly all the way around.

Aldridge screamed, and the smiling blond started to laugh, then cut his laugh short at a glare from Aldridge, who shook out his hand once Dora let go. "Let's go again," he insisted. They did, with the same result, though out of pity, Dora targeted a different finger.

Five minutes and two tries later, Aldridge had been excused to the infirmary, the fingers of his attacking hand held under one of his arms. Kontaxis approached Dora with admiration.

"I heard about you, Ellison. Those are Wally J small circle joint locks, done really well! Where'd you pick those up?"

Dora shrugged. "Here and there."

"You go to Shay's MMA?"

Dora nodded. "Once or twice."

"Well, if you've been more than once, you must be on her squad. I know how she is."

Dora said nothing.

• • •

After class was a four-mile run, at the end of which the blond quarterback vomited onto his sneakers. Dora didn't dislike him quite so much anymore—pitied him, maybe, but with less dislike.

As she walked to her car, she saw that Tina was parked nearby and was rolling down her window. "What'd you do to Aldridge?"

"Don't know what you mean," Dora said.

"You know he comes from three generations of cops, right?"

"Nope."

"His old man hears about this, he's liable to be disowned."

"Gee, what a shame."

"That was pretty impressive," said someone else. It was the smiling blond. He put out a hand. "Wayne Sylvester."

Dora ignored the hand. "Not since COVID," she explained. "You need to do something about those shoes." She nodded toward his vomit-stained sneakers.

He gave a half-smile. "Yeah, well."

"Dora Ellison." She fist-bumped him.

"I know. I didn't before, but I figured it out. Heard that Stalwell wanted you. Did you really take out Cranky Franky?"

"No, I did not. Did you really attempt to engage in police gossip with another recruit?"

He laughed. "No, I did not!"

Once in her car, she found herself dialing Missy, though until that moment, she would've sworn she had no intention of doing so.

"I thought you didn't want to see me," was the way Missy answered the phone.

"Missy Winters, I never said that."

"I think you said exactly that," Missy replied, teasing.

"I meant I couldn't see you, as in…"

"Stop. I know what you meant. You don't have to explain." She was instantly serious. "I know how you felt about Franny."

"Yeah, well…"

"I know what you need. C'mon over."

Twenty minutes later, Missy was serving an eggplant rollatini she swore had been sitting in the fridge "desperate" for an opportunity to be served.

Comfort, Missy's tiny, chocolate-colored Yorkshire terrier mix, rushed in barking wildly. As soon as he saw Dora, he switched to a multi-syllabic whine that sounded oddly like an attempt at words. "He recognizes you," Missy exclaimed, delighted.

Dora scratched the dog behind his ears, then took a bite of the rollatini and closed her eyes, absorbing the mix of garlic, spices, crispy eggplant, and cheese. "Mmm. Oh my God. Oh my God!"

"So, how's the academy?"

"That's sort of why I wanted to come by. I'm thinking of quitting."

"What? Why?" Missy's fork clattered onto her plate.

Dora looked embarrassed. "I have this thing about being told what to do, and the academy is nothing but that. Maybe I should have thought of this before."

"Ya think?"

"The actual workouts, the training, the classroom stuff is doable, but being ordered around like I'm a little kid…"

"Knowing you, I'm not surprised."

"What's that supposed to mean?"

Missy touched Dora's forearm. "It's supposed to mean I'm getting to know you." She leaned closer to Dora. "I meant it affectionately. Maybe you're jumping the gun—no cop pun intended. Maybe you'll feel better about it in a day or two. Maybe give it a little more of a chance."

"Huh."

"Dora," Missy ventured, "what do you think Franny would say?"

Dora had been looking down at her food, but now her eyes came up angrily. "Now you're playing dirty!"

Missy paused. "So? I'm allowed."

She sounded so much like a little kid that Dora couldn't help but laugh. Comfort had begun licking Dora's hand, which had fallen to her side.

"See?" Missy said. "He knows you just need some love."

...

The following afternoon, Vanessa was scouring listings on the major job websites, social media pages, and apps when the doorbell rang. She checked to make sure that Buster was still napping and Drew was still watching *Karma's World* on Netflix, then went to the door and looked through the peephole to see Detective Ganderson holding out his badge. Detective Mallard stood several feet behind him, sporting salt and pepper hair, a matching mustache, and a bit of a paunch.

"Mind if we come in, Mrs. Burrell?" Ganderson asked as he put away his shield.

"Depends. What's this about?"

"It's about something that might best be discussed in private."

Reluctantly, Vanessa held open the door. "Please keep your voices down. Buster's asleep and my older son is watching TV in the next room."

They sat down in the living room. The TV could be overheard from not far away. Ganderson got right to the point. "There's been an arrest at a local doctor's practice related to the illicit sale of opioids."

"Good, but what's that got to do with Jesse?"

"Well, the suspect gave us the name Julius Burrell. Do you know Mr. Burrell?"

Vanessa's hand went to her throat. "He's Jesse's son by his first marriage."

"Are you aware of his involvement with the illicit sale of opioids?"

"Of course not!"

"Might your husband have been aware of it?"

Vanessa looked steadily at Ganderson. "Do you have reason to believe he was?"

The other detective, who wore a Brioni Double Windowpane wool suit, nodded slowly. "Er, uh…Jesse was found in a location known for narcotics distribution and consumption." His voice had an annoying brassy quality.

Vanessa turned to the second detective. "And you are…?"

He pulled out a shield, held it up, and put it away before Vanessa could read more than a word or two. "Detective Gerry Mallard."

"Where he was found does not prove he was involved with drugs, nor does whatever Julius has been involved in, if he's been involved in anything."

"Well…it does make us wonder."

"Wonder away." She allowed a chill to creep into her tone.

"Let's back up a step," Ganderson said with a glance at his partner. "Might you be willing to tell us a little about your stepson?"

She crossed her arms. "Well, I don't think of him as my stepson, because he's never been a part of this household. He's a grown man now and when he stays with anyone, he stays with his mother, though Jesse sees—saw him now and again. He cared for that boy, and Julius is a good boy, as far as I know."

Ganderson was nodding; he had taken out a pad and pen. "His mother would be…?"

"Laila Burrell-Owens. That's one reason I'm surprised by what you're saying. Laila's a strict, churchgoing woman, but Julius was often at odds with her second husband, Sebastian."

"Sebastian?"

"Sebastian Owens, a white man who produces documentary films and sells them to cable TV stations. Laila left him, oh, a year or so ago, when she found out he was cheating." She shook her head. "Actors and women. Anyway, while married to Sebastian, Laila didn't work—she didn't have to. But after Laila left Sebastian, she starting working at an office—she could type a hundred words a minute—and waiting tables at night, to try to keep up with the rent on her two-bedroom apartment in that converted school in the middle of town, but she couldn't do it and had to give up her place."

"Do you have an address for Laila?"

Vanessa took out her phone and read off an address. "Do you need an address for Julius?"

"We have his address, thank you," Ganderson said, then asked, "To the best of your knowledge, is Julius currently employed?"

"I can't say for sure, currently. He had been selling cars at Beach Valley Ford, but I do know that he hated that job. He thought it was demeaning."

"Mrs. Burrell—" Mallard grimaced and rubbed his stomach, as though he had indigestion. "Aahh, do you mind if I ask who your family physician is?"

"Why do you need to know that?"

"Do you know a"—he looked down at a piece of paper he had taken from a pocket inside his jacket—"Dr. Christian Sahn?"

Vanessa shook her head. "I know that's the name of a doctor's practice here in town. Why?"

"Or a Louise Bradford?"

"No."

"Louise Bradford," Ganderson explained, "is the office manager at Dr. Sahn's practice, which, until two days ago, was the focus of an ongoing investigation into the illicit distribution of pain medication."

"I don't know any of those people." Vanessa furrowed her brow. "You say until two days ago…"

Ganderson nodded. "Dr. Sahn, his office manager, and another person connected with the practice were arrested the day before yesterday at 3:17 p.m."

Vanessa nodded, understanding. "Yes. I read about that online, in *The Chronicle* yesterday."

"Do you know if Jesse was acquainted with Sahn or Bradford?" Mallard asked.

"He was not—not to my knowledge. Did you get Julius's name from one of them?"

Ganderson rose, and Mallard followed him. "We appreciate your time, Mrs. Burrell."

As soon as the door shut behind the two detectives, Vanessa heard Buster over the intercom make his little ecking sounds that were a preface to full on crying. She had a sippy cup with apple juice ready in the refrigerator and brought it into the boys' room, looking in on Drew, who was still engrossed in his TV show in the living room. She changed Buster, singing the short made-up song "This Little Buster" she'd been singing to him since he was a month or two old, and which he had come to expect and love. When she came to his name, she made the usual funny face and her voice squeaked out his name and, as usual, he stopped crying and began to laugh.

Once she finished changing him, she brought him into the living room and sat on the couch with him, where she could keep an eye on both boys. Then she took out her phone and called Laila.

"Hello, Vanessa. I heard about Jesse. I'm so sorry."

"Thank you," Vanessa said, wondering why Laila hadn't called before if she was so sorry. "How is Julius?" *Let's see if she brings up his arrest.*

"Oh, fine."

"Mmm. I heard he was arrested."

"Where'd you hear that?"

Uh huh. "A police detective by the name of Gunderson or Granderson or something like that."

"Julius has never been in any trouble. Someone threw him under the bus."

"What is he charged with?"

Buster had finished his juice and was holding out his sippy cup for more. Vanessa picked him up, cradled the phone between her ear and her shoulder, held him against her chest with a cloth diaper between them, and began patting him on the back.

"He'll be fine. How are you? Do they know what happened to Jesse?"

"Only that he died, not much more."

"How?"

"Blunt force trauma to the head, in the alleyway behind Lagoon."

"Damn."

Vanessa came to the point. "Do you know if Julius and Jesse were fighting?"

Laila paused. "You think my Julius might have had something to do with…?"

"I didn't say that," Vanessa replied. "Did the police ask about Jesse?"

"Well, now that you mention it…"

"So," Vanessa prodded, "were they fighting?"

"No! Not that I know of."

"Mm hmm. So, what was Julius involved with?"

"Nothing. Like I said—other people throwing him under the bus. He's never been in any trouble."

That was true, as far as Vanessa knew. "Did Jesse know Julius was in trouble, even if he was set up, and try to intervene on his behalf—maybe with the wrong people?"

She could hear the impatience in Laila's voice, along with something else. Fear. "Julius is a grown man, living on his own. I can't speak for what he's been doing or who he's with or even if he's seen his father, other than the once-a-month dinners they have."

"When was the last of those?"

Laila hesitated. "Let's see…two weeks ago tomorrow. I know it was a Friday—it's always a Friday. Vanessa, I just want to say again how sorry I am about Jesse. He was a good man—I loved him. We both…loved him." She was starting to cry.

"Laila? Laila?" But Laila had hung up.

Chapter 5

The rain came down hard, splattering up from the road, forming a spray mist about a foot above the ground; it was the kind of rain Dora couldn't remember seeing when she was a child, though she remembered so little of her childhood that she wasn't surprised. She associated this kind of violent rain with Florida, with the tropics. Here in New York, it reflected changes in the climate. The New York area was, it seemed, becoming part of the tropics.

After she got home from the academy and had half of a blueberry muffin and a cup of coffee, she dialed Christine.

"Dora, what a nice surprise!"

"Ms. Mayor! How are you and Charlie?"

"We're great. I'm sorry, I haven't had a chance to look for jobs for Vanessa. Up to my ass in alligators."

"How would you feel if I dropped by?"

"In this rain? Sure, if you can deal with it. In fact, Charlie bought one of these instant pressure cooker pots, and he's obsessed with it. Tonight he made beef stroganoff, and he made a ton of it, so we can both bring it to work. How 'bout joining us?"

Dora smiled. "You know the way to my heart."

"See you soon."

After putting on a sweater, boots, and a rain slicker, Dora took the elevator down to the first floor and headed for her parking lot. She made a quick stop on the way, and minutes later was at the entrance to Christine's apartment building, one of Beach City's most elegant beachfront properties. The lobby was all marble with hanging plants and small statues. The elevator had been upholstered in velour and was lit by soft, violet recessed lighting. The penthouse hallway was carpeted in a similar violet; paintings on the walls were illuminated by violet LED lights, and the ceiling was edged with expensive designer molding.

She rang the bell, and the door was immediately opened by Charlie, who drew her into a hug.

"How's my favorite model? Come on in!"

Dora held out the package she had picked up. "I don't know what this is, but Benny at the liquor store said it goes with beef stroganoff."

Charlie slid the bottle from the bag. "Nero d'Avola. Sounds good to me. Come in. Sit. Chris will be out in a minute."

Dora followed Charlie into the plush sunken living room and went straight to the window. "Wow. That's some view." She watched the rise and fall of the ocean and a handful of surfers. The waters off of Beach City were surfed year-round by locals and visitors alike.

"You'll have to come back on a nicer day. The sunsets from here are gorgeous." Charlie sat down on the couch. "Alexa, play 'Red Garland.'"

"Playing 'Red Garland,'" Alexa said, and instantly the room was filled with sweet, tasteful jazz piano.

Dora sat in one of several upholstered chairs. "Storms must look pretty good. Sunsets must be crazy." She stood up as Christine came in and glanced at the bottle on the counter.

"I see you came prepared."

"Ms. Mayor." They hugged and air kissed, as was Christine's habit.

"Enough with that 'mayor' stuff."

Christine Pearsall had been the mayor of Beach City since the previous mayor, Mark Morganstern, was murdered on live TV, after being accused of covering up the accidental death of Anne Volkov, the daughter of *The Chronicle*'s former editor, Tom Volkov and his wife Irene, who pulled the trigger that killed the mayor. Their daughter Anne had died during a sexual liaison with Mo, Mayor Mark's son, a teen at the time, twenty years earlier. The death had been ruled a case of manslaughter, for which Mo Morganstern was still serving time.

Christine was thirty-seven, with medium-length reddish brown hair and a friendly smile. She had been in love with Charlie Bernelli since they had been an item twenty years before, when they were in their teens. He had been her first and only. She thought of herself as old fashioned and conservative in a very good way—a churchgoing girl, and yet she made allowances for modern challenges, one of which was her fiancé. Charlie had finally popped the question six months prior. He had long struggled with alcoholism, and though he continued to drink, he kept it to wine and beer and, on the rare occasion, a single scotch—a single very good scotch. Christine had made it clear that his drinking was his business, as long as he kept it under control. During what she called his "dark years" Charlie had been a nasty, abusive drunk, and while he had to take responsibility for his behavior, drinking or not, Christine blamed herself for not setting and maintaining strict boundaries.

She was not shy about sharing that once they were married, in early 2022, she planned, and expected Charlie to plan with her, to have children.

"Oh, I forgot," Dora said, putting a hand to her mouth. "Was I wrong to bring alcohol?"

"Not at all," said Charlie. Dora looked at Christine, who shrugged.

"It's fine," said Christine. "As long as this boy behaves."

"I've been behaving," Charlie insisted. "Besides, you're confusing me with my son." Charlie's son, Charles Bernelli III, or C3 as he was known by family and friends, had been in detox and rehab several years before, but was now more than a year sober and the proud owner of a CASAC degree, which won him work as a drug counselor at a local counseling center, a job he found immensely gratifying.

To Dora, Christine appeared tolerant yet dubious—with a coy smile. "How 'bout we save the wine for dinner, shall we?" Christine sat next to Charlie on the couch, a palm on his knee.

Dora was in a comfy recliner. "How cool is this? We haven't had a chance to really talk since…"

"Right?" Charlie agreed.

"So, what's it like going from city clerk to mayor?" Dora asked.

Christine laughed. "Traumatizing! At least in this case."

They all laughed.

"Honestly?" Christine continued. "It's not all that big of a change, really."

Dora didn't believe that. "Come on."

"I'm exaggerating, but there's truth in what I'm saying. Before, the clerk sort of ran the city—not that I ran the departments, but everything ran through me, and as we know now, the mayor wasn't exactly straight with the public."

"Or anyone," Charlie added, scoffing.

"In my case," Christine went on, "the mayor's actually running the city."

"Imagine that!"

"So, um, some issues came up that were both on the police radar, so to speak, and in *The Chronicle*. I was wondering how well you know Sarah Turner," Dora asked.

Charlie rose. "How 'bout we continue this conversation over some serious beef stroganoff and vino?" He headed for the kitchen.

"Sounds good to me." Christine stood up, as did Dora, and they made their way to the dining room table.

The dining room was done in white—white stone tabletop, white ivory chairs with white seats and back cushions, and a sparkling chandelier that refracted the white light of its bulbs and sent colorful shadows playing over the walls and guests.

"Is it okay if I sit here?" Dora asked. "So I can look at the ocean while we eat?"

"You read my mind." Christine waited until Dora was seated, then turned to Charlie. "Can I help you serve?"

He shook his blond head—he had the same lion's-mane, swept-back blond hair as the last time Dora had seen him, a year and a half prior, only now it had begun to sport a few wisps of gray. "No, you cannot," he said to Christine. Charlie brought over the casserole dish, laid it on a wooden rack, and spooned generous portions onto each of their plates.

Once the main course was served, Christine turned to Dora. "I know Sarah better now than I did before. We're in similar situations, really—women running the show where we were worker bees before."

"And I know Sarah to the degree C3 allows me to," Charlie explained. When Dora looked confused, he added, "they've been seeing each other for about six months."

"Eight months," Christine corrected.

"Really. How old is she?" Dora asked.

"Ten years older," said Charlie. "I know, but wait 'til you have kids and you try telling them what to do."

Dora nodded, understanding. "How does *The Chronicle* compare to when Tom was running the paper?"

Christine exchanged a look with Charlie. "Tom was pretty good, actually."

Charlie gave a hearty laugh. "Except for the fact that he'd been blackmailed into not reporting a very major segment of the news for well over a decade."

Hiding a smile, Christine gave a quick nod. "Right. Except for that." They all laughed. "Wine?" She had already opened the bottle. Dora held up her glass.

"Just one. Driving."

"Right," Christine agreed, pouring Charlie's then her own wine. "We don't want one of our police recruits getting a DWI after leaving the mayor's apartment, do we?"

"Nah," Dora agreed. "Not tonight."

"But really," Christine continued, "*The Chronicle* was never a bad paper, on the face of it. Tom had just made the transition from print to online when the fallout from poor Annie's death hit the fan. From what I know, they maintained their circulation, ran stories on all sorts of topics…"

"Except one," Charlie added. "And they sold their share of advertising, which we bought at least some of."

"And now?" Dora asked.

"Well..." Charlie shrugged. "Jeremy Anderson picked the wrong horse. Now I produce just about all of Sarah's ads—at least those her clients can't produce. She can't really afford a production department, and I give her a volume discount."

"Really?"

"Mm hmm. She farms out whatever she can. We do her ads and she has a freelancer..."

"Contractor," Christine corrected.

"Right, contractor—she doesn't like the term freelancer. She has a contractor sell her advertising."

Dora was surprised. "I didn't know that."

"Tom did the same thing," Christine explained, "and he would have been more upset than Sarah for you to know about it."

Charlie nodded. "He had this vision of himself as a cross between Hunter Thompson and Tom Snyder."

Christine shook her head. "Cooler—Jann Wenner. Or, even better—Ben Franklin."

Charlie laughed, trying not to spit out his sip of wine. He covered his mouth with his napkin, his eyes tearing up. "Oh, Chris. Ben Franklin! Spot on, ego-wise. Mr. Gravitas magazine magnate. I mean, c'mon. He let himself be blackmailed over the death of his fucking daughter, by her killer's father! Are you kidding me!"

"Kind of Shakespearean in a Hamlet-Lear sort of way," Christine mused.

"If you mean sick and twisted, then yeah."

Dora held up a "calm down" palm. "You guys are getting a little above my pay grade."

Christine turned serious. "Sarah's doing a good job. The paper's editorial standards have probably improved, and she's found ways of making it work business-wise, by aligning with chambers of commerce and running co-op ads. She really works at it."

"And our Beach City Tourism ad campaign is in its third year and doing better than ever." Charlie was particularly proud of this accomplishment. "It's a three-way deal, between the city, my agency, and *The Chronicle*."

"It's because you had a great model for the ads," Christine said, looking at Dora, who had been that model in a Rosie the Riveter-style campaign.

"Rumor has it you have an 'in' with the city," Dora said, looking soberly into her food.

Charlie nodded. "Um, well..."

Dora smiled. She really liked them both, and she liked so few people. "So, when are you guys tying the knot?"

Christine looked at Charlie. "That's what I want to know." When her fiancé looked hurt, she waved her ring finger, which sported a large diamond on a platinum band.

"This probably bought him six months. He asked two months ago, but we haven't set a date yet."

"Congratulations!" Dora exclaimed, clinking glasses with Christine and Charlie. "Do you guys know what happened to Mrs. Volkov?" she asked. "What was her name?"

"Irene. She's in a facility. A sad story. As far as she's concerned, her daughter's still alive."

Charlie nodded. "Anne's death broke her heart."

"No—her mind," Christine corrected.

Dora sat back. "So, you like your job?" she asked Christine.

"All those years I saw the way the city was run and knew the way it should run. Now I can make that happen."

"To a degree," Charlie said, raising an eyebrow.

"Right, but I have a lot of say. Ultimately, of course, it's up to the voters. I get to build or contribute to building the departments we always should have had. I pick the department directors, and there's no one better informed to do that."

"Including the public." Charlie nodded.

"Well, yeah. They picked me. I'll work in their interest, best I can. But enough about us—tell us how you're doing at the academy. I've gotta tell you," Christine said, leaning conspiratorially toward Dora. "Knowing all I do about you and your past, well, you know—this took us by surprise."

"Why?" Dora asked.

"Let me rephrase." Christine spoke with exaggerated care. "You might not be the first individual to come to mind when I try to imagine a municipal employee whose job it is to hold us all to the letter of the law."

"All right, all right." Dora shook her head and tried not to look hurt.

"So?" Charlie waited.

"It's okay." Dora shrugged. "But the discipline's a bit much."

"See?" Christine turned toward Charlie.

"The academics are hard because it's not all necessarily common sense, and I'm not the best book learner."

"Like a lot of cops," Christine suggested, shrugging.

"True," Dora agreed. "And the physical stuff's fine. The pushups, sit-ups, running—I can keep up. They have to make it so all sorts of people can pass."

"And the hand to hand?" Charlie asked. "Bet you gotta tone that down."

Dora nodded slowly. "Yeah. I've never been a big rule follower, and there are things I don't love." She rolled her eyes. "We'll see." She looked at them both for a moment. "I wanted to talk about what's going on now. You guys are close with Agatha. Has she talked to you at all about what happened to her brother?"

Christine and Charlie shook their heads. "She's pretty private," Christine said. "And when I was clerk and she was on the council, we didn't really run in the same crowds, you know?"

"Yeah, well, whoever killed Jesse's still out there, so I'm not sure it's the right time to be private, at least about the criminal aspect of it."

"What can we do?" Charlie asked.

Christine nodded eagerly. "How can we help? The police are handling it, no?"

"They are. I don't know. You're two smart, good friends and…it's all so awful and overwhelming for everyone—Vanessa especially, but Agatha too and oh my God, the kids!" She gave a long exhale. "Vanessa really could use a job."

Christine and Charlie exchanged a look.

"My shop could always use a proofreader," Charlie offered.

"Really?" Dora asked, then mused, "She'd need someone to watch the kids. I already told her I'd be interested."

Now it was Christine's turn to look surprised. "You?"

"What, kids can't have a gay babysitter? Charlie, what would the hours be?"

"Are you serious about this?"

"Yes, I am. I can't say what she'd think, but she does need to feed those kids, and I don't know what the school district or the teacher's union will do for Jesse's family. I don't know if he had tenure…"

Charlie nodded. "Let me get back to you."

"Is what happened to Jesse connected to the oxy and fentanyl busts going on now?" Christine asked. "Did Jesse have a drug problem?"

Dora looked at them both. "The answer to both those questions is…we don't know. I'm sure the police asked his wife, but I'm not sure Vanessa would open up to them about something like that."

"Are you friends?" said Charlie. "Maybe you could ask."

• • •

After dinner, Dora got into the Subaru and yawned. She had one more stop to make before turning in for the night. "Siri," she said, "call Sarah at work." She waited.

"*Chronicle,* Sarah speaking."

"Hi, Sarah. Dora Ellison here."

"Dora—oh, hi! How are you?"

"I'm okay. You?"

"Busy, but good."

"Too busy for a short visit?"

"Never. You know where my office is."

"Sure do."

Ten minutes and a fun ride later, Dora was climbing the familiar, narrow, aging white stairs to *The Beach City Chronicle*'s office, which was technically a suite—two tiny rooms off a slightly larger common room that was a combination office, tech area, and waiting room, depending on the situation. The offices were more brightly lit than Dora remembered and had been painted a light beige over their ancient, original dirty white. Framed front-page headlines and stories adorned the walls. The waiting area had a long table on which sat two MacBook Pros; both offices had similar computers.

Dora knocked on the open outer door. Some kind of rock music from about ten years earlier was blasting beyond it. She knocked again. A woman's head peeked out from one of the offices, and immediately the music's volume was lowered.

"Sarah," the woman called. "Someone here to see you." She smiled—a beautiful, warm smile. "I'm sure she'll be right with you."

Sarah emerged from the other office. "Oh, hey!" She was a youthful thirty-six, with short brown hair cut in a purposely messy bob that looked as though she'd just fallen out of bed—a look that probably came with significant cost, not unlike distressed jeans, Dora mused. As usual, Sarah was dressed entirely in black—black knit sweater, black slacks, black neck gaiter, and black shoes.

They hugged briefly. Dora had eschewed hugging and shaking hands since COVID, but so many people had offered her hugs lately that her resistance was wearing down. She was vaccinated and hugs were nice, after all.

"Dora, this is Esther—associate editor. Esther, Dora." Esther, a dark-skinned Black woman, nodded and smiled again. "Great to finally meet you."

"Same."

Sarah glanced toward the doorway from which she had emerged. "Lemieux—come out here. I want you to meet someone."

The man who emerged from the second office was tall, thin, and balding. He waved. "Hallo."

"Dora," Sarah said. "This is Lemieux—reporter and chief of IT."

He nodded. He had a fringe of black hair, pale pink skin, and blue eyes. "And sometimes ad sales associate, sometimes floor sweeper, toilet cleaner, hanger and framer of pictures, phone answerer…"

"And extreme wise ass," Sarah finished.

"Pleasure," Dora said, exchanging nods with Lemieux. "Is that your first or last name?"

"No one knows," Lemieux claimed, mysteriously.

"His first name is Yves," Sarah said.

"Please, call me Lemieux," Lemieux insisted. "Otherwise, it sounds like you're making a nighttime date."

"Okay, Lemieux." Dora smiled, then looked at Sarah. "Can we talk for a sec?"

"Use my office," Lemieux insisted. "I have to reboot the server. Incoming."

Sarah nodded toward one of the computers on the nearby table. "That's our server. Where the photos, ads, and, particularly, videos come in. We use lots of bandwidth."

"Ah," said Dora, and slipped past Lemieux and into his office. Sarah followed.

"Still the same old place," Dora mused.

"We're hoping to get out of here into someplace nicer, and bigger," Sarah said. "A lot will depend on the winter—especially holiday ads."

"So, you're the boss now," Dora said as they both sat down.

"Livin' the dream. Coffee?"

"Too late for me."

"You don't mind if I—?" Sarah looked at Dora as she poured from an industrial-sized coffee pot.

"How do you sleep?"

"Haven't since 2012."

"Ah—Hurricane Sandy."

"More or less."

"So, I guess you like the business?"

Sarah gave a half smile. "I guess I do. Was kind of running the news end all along, with occasional help from a stringer reporter, Charlie Bernelli's graphics guy and his video person—who uses an iPhone on a little gimbal, believe it or not. We all do a bit of everything around here. Oh, and I have someone selling advertising, but that's always been the case. Good to keep advertising and news separate. And how do you like the police academy? Is it like the movies?"

"Um, no. The training has its ups and downs."

Sarah waited, but Dora had nothing to add.

"So, what's up?"

"What's your relationship with the police?"

"We have a working relationship. We're a city news source. A lot of our news is about police-related activity or issues. And they want us to be friendly to them, tell the truth, not skew things in any particular way. They like us; we like them. I mean, we all want a safe city and we work together toward that end."

"So, you know about Agatha's brother."

Sarah nodded. "Well, I know the basic facts—we ran them. We know he was found beaten to death in an alley. Doesn't sound as though he was killed somewhere else and moved there."

"And the relationship between his death and the police fentanyl and oxy full court press?"

Her brow creased. "I don't follow."

Dora shifted in her seat. "Are the police pushing you to connect Jesse's death with an uptick in recent drug-related deaths?"

Sarah shook her head. "Not any more than I would otherwise. I'm not aware of any facts that directly link the two. Circumstantial, yes, but not facts on the ground. Mentioning a trend in drug-related deaths along with a somewhat high-profile murder in circumstances that may be drug-related—nothing wrong with that. As long as we're clear with the facts."

Dora sighed softly. "The man left two babies."

"I know. I'm sure it's rough for his wife and family."

"Sure is. I was hoping we could put our heads together…"

Sarah pressed her lips together. "I don't think I have any special insight to share."

"You know about his son, Julius?"

"It'll be in the paper this week."

"Well, I came because if anyone can see patterns in any of this, it's you, Sarah, and you're privy to information the rest of us don't have—on a timely basis."

"I want to help. I just don't know what I can do. I like Agatha, I care about you, and I care about this city. So, if there's something I can do, information that comes my way, and sharing it doesn't jeopardize some situation, story, or relationship that's on my plate—I'm here to help."

Dora rose. "That's all I can ask. Thank you, Sarah."

• • •

Once back in her apartment, she opened a can of beer, sat down on the couch, and turned on the TV. She drank the beer, went back to the kitchen and opened another, but knew she wouldn't finish it. She'd eaten too much of Charlie's outstanding beef stroganoff.

Once in bed, Dora turned over on her right side. "Hey, Babe." She had saved some of Franny's clothes, kept them unwashed, and piled them under the blankets next to her in a shape approximating her beloved girl. She rolled toward the clothes, burying her face in them and inhaling what was left of Francesca's smell. As they did every night, the tears came.

• • •

The next day brought new classroom and practice experiences at the academy, including Handcuffing, Defensive Tactics, Police Baton Training, and an interactive Engaging the Public class. This was followed by an introduction to Juvenile Offenders and the Law, which was taught by an extremely bureaucratically-minded Sergeant Gary "Re" Morse, whose answer to many issues seemed to be "there's a form for that." Dora decided that his goodwill might be worth cultivating.

When she stopped at her locker midday, she noticed there was a message on her phone from Sarah, but knew she couldn't listen to it or return the call until the end of the day.

To date, all of her classes were interesting from the point of view of a recruit eager to join the force, yet Dora felt as if she were going in the wrong direction. She could feel her hackles rising, her resistance to being told what to do increasing, and she didn't know what to do about it. She talked to Franny about it every night—which for Dora was a form of prayer.

The early afternoon brought a subject that caught her attention: Modern Police Science and Substance Abuse, taught by a Lieutenant Heather Fulman, a fit woman of mixed race, with short curly hair and warm brown eyes. She was one of very few women, Dora noticed, who were teaching at the facility.

"Tens of thousands of deaths each year are attributable to opioid addiction," the instructor explained. "When dealing with addiction—say, a heroin addict, or someone who is high on heroin—what is our job?"

Tina put up her hand, and Fulman called on her. "Protect the public—make the arrest if there's possession or sale. Administer Narcan, if necessary."

"Okay," Lt. Fulman agreed. "How do we prevent recidivism?"

"Lock 'em up," said Kenny Moore, a hefty recruit with frizzy reddish hair—a nice guy, in Dora's experience, but a little too cocky.

"Give me thirty," the instructor ordered.

"Sorry," Moore offered, and raised his hand, realizing he should have done so before answering, but it was too late.

"Fifty," Fulman said. "Want the class to join you?"

Moore began doing his pushups, slowing noticeably at thirty, and paused, arching his back and holding the up position to rest on the last five.

"Anyone else know how we avoid recidivism?" Fulman scanned the room. Either no one knew, or they were afraid to answer.

Dora put up her hand, and when the instructor widened her eyes and quickly nodded, she said, "Teach them to quit."

"Okay, good! But how?" She looked at Dora, who didn't answer, then around at the rest of the classroom. "The day you arrest a heroin addict, the day you Narcan someone and maybe save their life, may just be the worst day of their life." She looked around. No one said a word. "It's an emotional day. Their best friend, the drug, has deserted them. And understand this: they may not want their life to be saved." She began walking up and down the silent aisles. "But there's teaching potential in that moment. When are you most likely to be willing to learn a difficult skill? C'mon. You guys are in that boat right now."

A hand went up. "Skinny Aldridge."

"When you're on a career path you've always dreamed of?"

"Really? Well, okay, you guys are learning skills in which you are emotionally invested. But that's not when you're at your most motivated."

Another hand went up.

"Racquel?"

"When your life's on the line."

"Ahh!" A small smile crept onto the instructor's face. "What's my job?" She nodded at Moore, who was still red-faced and breathless.

"Police instructor."

"True. Think of the subject at hand. Eve?"

A woman with a thin nose, deep-set gray eyes, and a bit of a smirk answered. "Drug counselor."

"Good guess. Close—social worker." She let that sink in. "My job includes identifying and engaging members of the public who have substance abuse issues, are in need of treatment, and…? Anybody? What's the most important criteria for quitting alcohol and drugs?"

Dora knew this; she had heard C3 talk about it many times in the past. She put up her hand. "The desire to quit."

"The desire to stop drinking or drugging. We—some of us, anyway—are here to help those who really want to stop. But first, we have to understand addiction—how the brain can be taken over by substances and behaviors that feel good, especially when the life of the person in question does *not* feel good."

Dora heard the words and thought about Jesse, but the description did not seem to fit the man she had met at the party at Agatha and Rudy's house. She had to remind herself that addicts can be difficult to spot, even by those who know them best.

...

Dora found she looked forward to the workouts at the end of her day and especially the hand-to-hand combat. Just about everyone, including her, had lost weight. Waistlines were trimmer, muscles firmer. Everyone had a new spring in their step. The combat was like visiting an old friend—a little different from what she had been used to at Shay's MMA and her training the previous two years, but in the same wheelhouse. The focus at the academy was less offensive, since whatever the media might say, police are rarely on the offensive. Rather, the focus was on using the attacker's weight and energy against him, or her, or them.

Once in her car, she felt refreshed. She looked at her phone, remembered Sarah's call, and called her back without playing her message.

"Hey," Sarah said. "So, interesting bit of information. The cops are squeezing Julius Burrell and he gave up a name. I received a call about it late last night. Guy's in my database. A bad dude."

"The guy who called?" Dora asked.

"The name he gave up."

"Okay, what was the name?" Dora asked.

"I'll tell you, but I suggest you talk to the police—the Goose and the Gander—to learn more, seeing as how I don't really have anything but a name someone they're squeezing gave up and not a whole lot of context. I would really rather you didn't say this came from me."

"So, where would I have learned this? They're gonna want to know."

"Someone at the academy? Something you overheard? In my business, we don't share our sources."

"I'll deal with it," Dora said.

"Guy's name is Vincent Doyle. Not a nice man. Julius was in there sans lawyer, and apparently admitted to dealing drugs—claiming it was to earn money to help his mom, who's been on the balls of her ass since she threw her husband out."

"His mother is Liz?"

"Liz is his grandmother. His mother's Laila."

"Oh, right. I was told that her son had been selling cars or something, and he said he hated it."

"I heard that too."

"So, what about this guy, Doyle?" Dora asked.

"I don't know much, but I know this. He's the kind of guy you might run into in an alley where drugs are being used, and you might not come out. What if Julius was involved with him—sinking in the deep end of the pool...?"

Dora finished Sarah's thought. "...And he reached out to his father, who did what dads do. Yeah. Thank you, Sarah."

"Well, your timing was good."

• • •

Dora had to think about how to approach the detectives working Jesse's murder, but again, luck was with her. That night, at ten thirty, as she was watching a comedy on cable to try and lighten up her day and soften her evening, her phone rang and she saw Beach City PD on the display.

"Hello?"

"Ellison? Paul Ganderson. I'm working the Jesse Burrell investigation."

She paused. He sounded downright friendly. "Yes, hello, Detective. How can I help you?"

"I'm glad you asked. Would you mind coming to the station in the morning?"

"I'll be at the academy…"

"I've already cleared it with your instructors and Sergeant Morse."

"Sure. Of course."

"7:30?"

"Great. I get to sleep late."

"Make it seven."

"Gee, thanks."

"See you then."

・・・

The following morning, Dora did sleep late—she awoke at six, made herself scrambled eggs and toast with a little jelly and a big mug of coffee. Then she took the turbo out, tooled around the highway for a bit, and headed to the police station.

Despite the early hour, the station was bustling with activity. Officers were hard at work at desks, on phones, and clustered in little groups. Several looked up when Dora asked for Detective Ganderson at the front desk. Before Sergeant Morse could call for him, Ganderson approached, stopped a few feet from Dora, caught her eye, and waved her inside.

"Coffee?" he called over his shoulder.

"Sure."

He indicated a table with an urn and fixings. "Self serve."

Once she had her coffee, he motioned for her to sit next to his desk. "So, what can you tell me about a Vincent Doyle?"

"Nothing. Don't know him."

This didn't seem to surprise Ganderson. "To your knowledge, did Jesse Burrell—or, any Burrell, for that matter—know him?"

Dora shrugged and shook her head. "I wouldn't know. You're asking the wrong person. What's his connection to the case?"

"I'll ask the questions." He softened his tone. "He's someone with a history of drug involvement in the vicinity. Has an arrest record but has been on the street for about a year. Burrell's son, Julius, gave up his name."

"Okay," Dora said, wondering where this was going and hoping to learn more. "Not sure I can help, though."

"I think maybe you can."

"How?"

Ganderson smiled, showing a lot of teeth. "You're friendly with Mrs. Burrell. I'm not sure how…forthcoming she is with us." He held up both palms. "And I understand that. Tragedy like this, it's time to circle the wagons, protect the kids."

"Two little boys just lost their daddy, and she could use a job."

Ganderson seemed to consider this, then went on. "If she were talking to someone she really trusted, I wonder what she might say—about her husband's associates, the places he frequented, the things he might have done, and why he did them." He looked Dora in the eye, making his point with eye contact. He raised his eyebrows. "Might be a useful conversation—if such a scenario could be put in place."

Dora smiled a little. "You want me to pump a friend who just lost her husband for information?"

Ganderson looked insulted. "Not what I said. Not what I said."

"I think it *is* what you said."

"Well, I would never put it that way. That's movie talk! Come on. You're a police officer now—well, almost. Think about what would be helpful—to Mr. Burrell's memory, to his family, to society."

"To closing your case," Dora finished for him.

Someone at the next desk laughed; Ganderson turned to them. "Hey!" He turned back. "Maybe I'm off base here. If I am, I'm sorry. I don't want to impose on what I'm sure is an important friendship."

"Sure you do," Dora argued.

Ganderson couldn't help but smile. "Yeah, I do." His smile faded. "But it's for a good cause. Listen." He leaned forward. "This guy Doyle—he does business in schoolyards. I mean, schoolyards! And listen to this—he somehow finagled himself a job as a security guard at the catholic school."

Dora found this hard to believe. "Why would they hire him? And if you told them about him, assuming they didn't know already, why would they keep him on?"

"All I can do is pass along the information and make suggestions. At a private institution, there's nothing I can do if they go about their business within the confines of the law. And hey, it's a terrific school. My kids went there and they did great. They were taught discipline and…"

"Okay. I understand."

"And you'll see what you can find out?"

Dora gave a half-hearted nod.

Ganderson grinned. "You're gonna make a great cop someday soon." He turned serious again. "Now, I'm trusting you with this information, which is confidential." He paused, held up a warning finger. "In the wrong hands, my telling you this could jeopardize a court case. So, we never spoke."

Dora gave a little smile. "I don't even know who you are."

...

Vanessa had to think about how she would coordinate this trip. Drew was in pre-K but she had Buster with her, and Buster demanded her attention or he could start to scream. And once that started, it would grow in decibel and pitch and ruin most outings and many people's days. What usually kept him happy was singing to him, as long as he knew she was focused on him. The challenge was, this trip was built around his grandmother, Miz Liz, or GranLiz as he called her.

Liz had another doctor's appointment—she'd had one several weeks earlier with a different doctor—and they seemed to be growing more frequent. Miz Liz refused to discuss them. Vanessa had no idea what the appointments were about and, frankly, she was focused on her own problems. Besides, Miz Liz was a woman of great dignity who believed in keeping her medical details private, even from her own daughter-in-law, who was now doubling as her chauffeur.

Liz had begun using a travel chair—a light, easily folded wheelchair that Vanessa was able to use by putting Buster into a Snugli baby carrier that held him against her chest in his preferred position, leaving her arms more or less free. This could work for a while, as long as he was in a happy mood, and today he was.

Unfortunately, his grandmother was not, but her moods were expressed at lower decibels than those of her grandson. In fact, Miz Liz communicated her unhappiness on this day via intransigence and silence, which suited Vanessa just fine. Navigating Miz Liz and Buster into their respective wheelchair and car seat and then into the doctor's office was a complicated and stressful production, but somehow, Vanessa managed it.

Once they had completed the front desk sign-in and insurance process, Vanessa wheeled Miz Liz over to an empty seat. She lifted Buster out of his Snugli—he was fast asleep—and held him to her with one arm while taking out her phone with the opposite hand. She glanced at Miz Liz, who seemed also to have fallen asleep, or was resting with her eyes closed. One never knew with Miz Liz, who was apt to startle awake at any given moment and, despite what one might think, demonstrate she'd heard every word of a conversation.

Vanessa saw she had a message from Dora, who had contacted Charlie Bernelli about a job. She also had a message from Charlie, asking if she would be interested in a second shift proofreading job. *Yes! Yes! Yes!* She hoped she would be able to afford a babysitter on whatever the job paid.

Once the doctor was ready for Miz Liz, Vanessa wheeled her into the medical area, then returned to the waiting room and called Charlie Bernelli to accept his offer.

...

"I'm so glad I could help," Dora said, and obviously meant it, when she got off from her day at the academy and returned Vanessa's call. "How's Miz Liz?"

"Who knows? You'll never get her to admit there's anything wrong. The only reason I know was because I was her ride. I guess the answer would be she's tired. She's tired whenever I see her."

"She's been through a lot—you've both been through a lot. Would it be a terrible inconvenience if I stopped by for a few minutes?"

"It's fine. Buster doesn't go down for an hour and Drew for an hour after that."

"Can I bring anything?"

"Nope."

"See you soon."

"Yup."

While Vanessa was waiting for Dora, she read a children's book to Drew—she suspected he would be an early reader—while she held Buster, who pretended to read along. Halfway into the book, her phone rang again.

"Hi, Mom."

"Tell me something."

"If I can."

"Why don't we have more information from the police about Jesse?"

"Investigations take time."

"But shouldn't they give us progress reports?"

"I wish I knew."

"Well, I wish I knew too! I'm here all alone and whoever killed my boy is out there somewhere, doing who knows what!"

"I think I might have a job. Charlie Bernelli, who owns an ad agency in town, offered me a proofreading job in the evenings."

"Well, all right. But who'll watch the boys?"

"I guess I'll get a sitter for early afternoons, and Dora said she might be able to help out in the evenings, after her classes."

"I'll take the afternoons and early evenings until she gets there. I can take the Senior Ride over, meet Drew's bus, and keep Buster in the stroller."

"Mom, no. You had trouble getting out of the car today. It's too much. I appreciate the thought, but…"

"I know my body!" Miz Liz's voice was firm. "And no buts about it. I let myself rest today because I was going to the doctor. Doctor days take a lot out of me. My grandbabies will give me energy, not drain it. Those boys energize their GranLiz."

The downstairs buzzer sounded. "Someone's downstairs. Let me get back to you. Love you, Mom."

"I love you too, Nessa."

The buzzer sounded again. After confirming the visitor was Dora, Vanessa buzzed her in and was holding the apartment door open when Dora stepped out of the elevator.

"So, you heard from Charlie."

"I did. Not sure what I know about proofreading, though." Vanessa led Dora into the living room, where Drew was building a tower out of multi-colored blocks. Buster stumbled around and ran right into it, toppling the tower and scattering the blocks, which his big brother patiently rebuilt, and the process began again.

"Hey, guys. Whatcha building?"

"A tower for Buster," Drew answered without looking up.

Dora looked impressed. "That's a pretty good brother."

"Right?" Vanessa agreed. "Teamwork."

They sat down on the floor a few feet from the boys. "I'm sure Charlie will show you whatever you need to know about proofreading. I did some work with him on an ad—you know, the first Beach City tourism ad, the one I was in. Pretty sure it's just reading really, really carefully. I looked at some of the ads as they were in progress. There are symbols—proofreader marks—I guess you need to learn, and I'm sure you will."

"So, are you interested in watching these boys in the evening? I'll pay you, of course."

Dora took a deep breath. "Aw, I'm not worried about that, but I might have to sleep here, given my academy homework."

"Your bed." Vanessa made a voila gesture toward the couch. "It pulls out, and I've got sheets, pillow, pillowcase, blankets. And…you will never hear the end of my gratitude."

Dora smiled. "My new home away from home."

"Think you can deal with these two?" Vanessa looked at the boys; Buster was now attempting to help Drew build his tower, taking time out now and then to gnaw on one of the blocks, which Vanessa gently removed from his mouth. "Not in your mouth, Buster."

"What about diapers?"

"Want to learn?" Vanessa ventured.

"Guess if I can learn to catch criminals, I ought to be able to change a diaper, right?"

Vanessa laughed. "Guess we'll see." She stood up and fetched the younger of her children, holding him against her with her forearm, while pulling the waist of his diaper away from his behind and peering inside. "Great timing, Buster." She looked at Dora. "Ready?" She carried Buster into the boys' bedroom, trailed by Drew and Dora, then called over her shoulder. "You do know he's named for what he does to diapers."

Five minutes later, they returned to the living room with Buster newly changed.

"What do you think? Could you do it without me here?"

"Like you said—guess we'll see." Dora's expression turned serious. "I want to ask you about something. Ever hear the name Vincent Doyle?"

She nodded. "He's a friend of Rudy's."

Dora raised her eyebrows in surprise. Vanessa continued with a shrug. "Just someone that comes into the bar. All sorts of people come into Rudy's."

"He's apparently a major part of the local drug scene."

"Is this something to do with what happened to Jesse? I'll bring it up to Rudy, if that's okay. Why do you ask?"

"Julius gave his name to the cops."

"As what? Someone Jesse knew?"

Dora shook her head. "Someone involved in the local drug scene—heavily involved."

"Well, I don't know anything about him except that he comes into the bar. He's a customer and his money's green. That's what Rudy'll say. I'm still not hearing the relevance to what happened to Jesse."

Dora chewed on her lip for a moment, considering. "Do you think that with all the customers that come and go and with the poker game and such —maybe Rudy knows some things that could bear on Jesse's death?"

Vanessa shook her head. "He would've said. Instantly. He would never hold anything back that had anything to do with what happened to Jesse."

"Right. But that's assuming that he knew...that he knew something of value."

"What do you mean?"

"He knows a lot of people—who they are, what they do. But he might not know that some of those facts connect to what happened to Jesse."

Vanessa frowned. "So...how are we supposed to find out if Rudy knows something or someone involved in Jesse's murder, when he doesn't even know it himself?"

Chapter 6

On Monday morning of the second week at the academy, equipment was issued, including pistol belts, holsters, magazine holders, handcuffs and handcuffs cases, portable radio carriers, keys, baton rings and eighteen-inch batons. Bulletproof vests, a.k.a. body armor, were also issued and were expected to be worn every day. Because of recent budget cuts, each student was expected to purchase his or her own vest or return their vest at the end of the course of study. The vest's price was affordable for her, so Dora purchased her vest.

Demerits were given out for just about everything—uniform or equipment that was anything but perfect, talking, lack of perfect attitude—even failure to acquire demerits brought on demerits.

The afternoon class was Interviewing Techniques—which included maintaining safety, establishing rapport, and reading body language. The class was conducted by Sergeant Rick Edwards, who was graying, forty-something, and had surprisingly long hair, a trimmed mustache, and silver-framed glasses.

What Dora learned surprised her. "Seat your interviewee near the door to establish psychological comfort. Despite what you may have heard or seen on TV, there are no direct indicators for deception. Everyone is different. Looking to your left, coughing, blinking—these may indicate discomfort, even distress, but not necessarily deception." *Interesting.*

About a half hour after the class began, there was a knock on the classroom door. Detective Mallard stuck his head in and crooked a finger toward Edwards, who went over to see what he wanted, then turned to the classroom.

"Ellison. You are wanted in the hallway."

Both Mallard and Ganderson were waiting for her in the hallway. Ganderson motioned for her to follow him into an empty classroom, where Dora sat down and the detectives sat at nearby desks.

"So? Doyle?"

"He's a friend of Rudy Raines."

"Did he know Jesse Burrell?" Ganderson wanted to know.

"No idea," Dora said.

"So," said Mallard, crossing his arms across his chest, "Burrell goes out after a house party, ostensibly for beer…and ends up deceased in an alley with a blow to the head. His son Julius is named by one Louise Bradford, office manager of one Dr. Christian Sahn, as being involved in the illicit sale of opioids. Julius Burrell names Vincent Doyle as central to such activities in the vicinity, and now we learn that Doyle is an acquaintance of Rudy Raines, who is the late Jesse Burrell's brother-in-law." The detective raised an eyebrow, cocked his head to one side, and held out a hand, palm up. "Where there's smoke…"

"Yeah, well, in keeping with your metaphor," Dora said, "you're the firemen."

"Well, answer me this," Mallard continued. "Why would Julius make a call to his father just prior to Jesse heading out that night? Hmm?"

"Really?" Dora said. "Phone records?"

"Really," Mallard answered.

"The answer is, I don't know, and if I don't get back to class," Dora said, "I might miss something and get a demerit, so I'm going, okay?"

As they left the empty classroom, Ganderson gave Mallard a stern look. "Not sure she needed to know that."

• • •

Dora was intrigued by Detective Mallard's rundown of the case thus far, and decided to keep an eye on Vincent Doyle herself. While he was a school security guard at a local parochial school, Dora knew better than to skulk around schools on school days. Foot surveillance had been touched on at the academy the previous Friday, and Dora decided to put what she had learned to use.

Stay close, but not too close, she reminded herself, *and pay attention to what the subject is doing during the surveillance. If he rounds a corner, don't rush up to the corner to see where he went. Don't draw attention to yourself. Don't make eye contact. In fact, don't look directly at the subject at all.*

She noted that Doyle was about five seven and in his thirties, with short, dark hair and a way of leaning forward, hunching at the shoulders—both while stationery and when walking.

Doyle left his residence at 3:30 in the afternoon on Saturday and drove to the mall, parking in several different spots, where individuals approached his car for what looked like drug buys.

He then proceeded back to his residence, where he parked in his driveway. This was at 4:15. Just after 4:30, a Jeep SUV parked in front of the house next door to Doyle's. Two young men got out, went to Doyle's door, and were let into the residence. They came out after fifteen minutes. A similar sequence of events occurred an hour later.

Still later, Doyle drove to a park along the bay, where families were strolling. Several men, three teens and one woman were fishing, and kids were riding bikes and skateboards. Doyle walked along the water and into the park, around the basketball courts, and proceeded through the playground. On several occasions, individuals who seemed to know him approached him and shook his hand in what Dora thought was a suspicious way.

Soon afterward, he approached a black Escalade, which rolled down a rear passenger window as he approached. Doyle then got into the back seat of the Escalade, and it drove off.

As Dora was about to turn toward her car to follow, a hand grasped her shoulder from behind—an incredibly strong hand. Before she could grasp that hand and spin, as she'd been taught, the cold steel of a gun barrel pressed against the space just below her right ear.

"Why so interested in Vinny Doyle?" The voice was male, reedy, as though its owner had a cold in his throat.

"Who? What are you talking about?"

"You got no reason to be anywhere near Vincent Doyle."

"Don't know anyone by that name. You must have me mixed up with—"

The gun barrel pressed harder into her neck. "You're a wannabe cop. And if you wanna stay a wannabe cop and not be a dead wannabe cop, you'll stay away from him. Got it?"

"I heard you."

"Good." He gave her a slap to the temple with the gun barrel, a slap that would have knocked down most people and knocked out many, and Dora did indeed drop to the ground, but not from pain or concussion. She dropped onto her right hip, slapped the ground as she landed with her right hand to break her fall, and in a scissor-type motion, swept the man's legs out from under him with her left leg, forcing him backward and tripping him over her right leg.

He cursed as he found himself looking up, his gun having skittered several feet away. Dora retrieved the gun. Now the man, who was short, muscular, and swarthy with a five o'clock shadow, looked afraid.

"Hey," he said. "Just doin' what I'm told."

"Look," Dora said, trying to salvage something from this situation. "You've got me confused with someone else. Yeah, I'm a police recruit, but I'm not interested in anyone or anything but a nice day at the park. I look at the scenery, the birds, now and then at this person or that person—but that's it. Seriously. Now, I'm taking this thing off your hands. You might hurt somebody." She noticed several people were watching, and raised her voice. "You had no right to attack me, sir. Now, I'm leaving and I'm asking you to please leave me alone!"

• • •

Two days later, Wednesday afternoon, was Vanessa's first day of proofreading for The Bernelli Group. Her shift was from 3:00 p.m. to 11:00 p.m.

Miz Liz had said she would watch her grandsons, Vanessa's sons, until 7:30, when Dora would come directly from the academy and bring her books and a change of clothes with her. Vanessa had left a Tupperware container of spaghetti and meatballs that was left over from the weekend for Dora to have as much of as she wanted. Apparently, spaghetti and meatballs was one of three staple meals at the Burrell household—the others being pizza, and hamburgers with fries, smothered in ketchup.

"Hello, Mrs. Burrell," Dora said when Liz answered the door.

"Miz Liz will do." The barely five-foot tall, white-haired woman turned and headed back toward the living room, where Drew was looking at a picture book about astronomy. His younger brother was looking at another book about farm animals. When he pressed the buttons on the book, they emitted animal sounds.

"How are the boys, Miz Liz?" Dora asked.

"They're just fine. Two gentlemen." Liz sat down at the dining room table and covered her face with her hands. "We need more like them."

"Are you okay? Can I get you anything?"

Liz lifted her head and looked Dora in the eye. "A new body," she said wearily. She looked at her watch. "I'd better get going if I want to catch my bus."

"Are you sure you don't want to stay a while? I was wondering if you were teaching the boys to sing."

Miz Liz stopped what she was doing and frowned at Dora. "Now why would I be doing that?" she asked, her tone severe.

"Oh. Well, I ... Vanessa told me how beautiful your singing voice was."

Miz Liz shook her head. "*Was* is right. That girl talks too much is what she does." She continued muttering to herself as she let herself out of the apartment without as much as a goodbye to Dora or her grandsons.

Dora wondered if perhaps she shouldn't have raised the subject, though singing seemed a pretty benign topic. The woman had just lost her only son, Dora reminded herself.

After helping herself to a plate of spaghetti and meatballs topped with parmesan cheese, Dora sat down on the living room floor.

"Would you boys like me to read to you?"

"Da!" Buster cried, toddling over to her.

"Pastrami!" Drew exclaimed.

"Pastrami?" Dora echoed, and Drew promptly ran from the room and returned with his book.

Dora smiled. "*Astronomy*! Sure. Come sit down beside me, boys."

She read several books to the boys before she realized it was time for them to be changed, which she managed rather clumsily but without any major mishaps. Then she helped them brush their teeth and change into their pajamas. In Buster's case, she did most of the brushing and had to wipe quite a bit of toothpaste from his face afterward. Both boys went to bed willingly enough, though Buster insisted that she stay in the room for a while, so Dora sat in an armchair she supposed was in the corner of the room for that very reason, and went over her academy notes. Once she was sure both boys were asleep, she moved to the living room, making sure their monitor was on and working.

She was startled awake by the sound of keys in the door, looked up at the clock on the living room wall, and saw that it was half past eleven.

"How were they?" Vanessa asked, then, without waiting for an answer, peeked into the boys' room.

"Guess they decided to take it easy on me the first night," Dora answered when Vanessa returned. "How was proofreading?"

"Pretty much like you said it would be. Not too hard, but you've got to focus and be meticulous, and I got taken to school by Luis Martinez, who oversees Charlie's production. How was I supposed to know that quotes go outside the punctuation or that there are hyphens, en dashes, and em dashes?" She seemed to see Dora for the first time. "Oh, let me get you some bedding for the couch."

"Thank you."

"Spare toothbrush in one of the drawers under the bathroom sink," Vanessa called over her shoulder, as she brought supplies for the sofa, then headed into her bedroom.

As Dora stretched out on the couch, she wondered if it was her imagination or if Vanessa was a bit less friendly than usual. She noticed the same trend on the second night she watched the boys, and so on the third, she decided to ask if something was the matter.

Vanessa pressed her lips together. "Well, since you asked. Using your friendships with our family for a police fishing expedition is not..."

"Whoa—what? Fishing expedition?"

"Vincent Doyle. You asked me about him and I told you he was someone Rudy knew, and now the police are leaning on Rudy and Agatha about their relationship with Doyle."

"Okaaayy," said Dora, nodding and thinking about it. "Yes, I did that."

"Yes, you did. And I need you here with the boys, or you wouldn't be here right now. I wasn't going to say anything—"

"Hang on. Yes, I did that, but it wasn't a fishing expedition. You're saying it like I used you."

Vanessa looked hurt and angry. "Didn't you?"

Dora held up her hands. "I'm a friend of your family—a genuine friend—who happens to have a police-related connection. All I want is to see whoever killed Jesse caught and for justice to be served. Using you would be a personal gain thing, and there's nothing like that here. Things you and your family know might help the investigation and bring Jesse's killer to justice. I'm just trying to connect the dots. Isn't that what you want—what we all want?"

Vanessa nodded slowly, still looking at Dora from the sides of her eyes. "Mm hmm."

"Something else," Dora said. "Is Miz Liz okay? She doesn't seem quite herself."

Vanessa sat down next to her and nodded. "I know. I wonder that myself, but I figure Jesse's death is wearing on her. It sure is wearing on me.

She loved that boy. Loves Agatha too, and the grandkids. But that's her firstborn son." Vanessa's eyes filled. "Oh, I loved that man. I miss that man."

She clenched her arms against her sides, balled up her fists, grimaced, and began to cry. After a few moments, Dora put an arm around her shoulder and pulled her close, so she rested her head on Dora's shoulder. They sat that way for a while—Vanessa sobbing and Dora holding her. Finally, Vanessa disengaged, got up, took several tissues from a box on the kitchen counter, and blew her nose.

"I just don't get it. Jesse was the sweetest man. I just don't get it."

"You don't think he was mixed up in—"

"No. Other than the occasional joint with Rudy or one of his friends, he did nothing. He liked to play cards, he liked his Sam Adams, but that's it, really. Really! He was a nerd, truth be told. Know where he went in his spare time? The library. Really. The library. Said he liked the quiet. That sound like a drug dealer?"

· · ·

Classes at the academy the following day included Admissions, Confessions, and Criminal Statements, followed by Fingerprinting. Dora had the misfortune of making mistakes in each—mistakes that were not in and of themselves much of a problem. Nor were the demerits a problem; she was a student and students made mistakes. They were part of being a newbie, a recruit. She also knew that treating students badly, borderline hazing, was common, and supposedly part of teaching future policer officers to develop thick enough skins to be unaffected by the occasional moody superior or coworker.

That part did bother her—she knew it shouldn't, but it did. She had never grown accustomed to being treated badly—an old issue for her. Tolerating extreme criticism that bordered on verbal abuse was a challenge, one she had taught herself need not be tolerated, and yet here she was, in a situation where achieving her goal required exactly that. It was all she could do to keep from inviting one of her instructors to go ahead and try to speak to her that way again. She realized that the best she could do would be to continue to remind herself to put up with it, that the goal was important to her and tolerating the occasional dressing down was part of the package.

That night at Vanessa's, she read again to the boys, and together they looked at star charts. She then brought them to their room, turned the light off, and sat with them at the window—Drew standing and Buster on her knee. Together they found the constellations. Then she asked if they would like to sing. She didn't think Buster understood, but when she began singing "I've Been Working on the Railroad," she was surprised when Drew joined in and Buster did his best to sing as well. She wondered whether it had been Miz Liz who taught them to sing.

Once they were changed and settled in bed, she called Missy, hoping that she would be home from the library.

"Hey, schoolgirl!" Missy sounded too cheerful.

"Hey."

"What's wrong?"

"That obvious?"

"Yep."

"School."

"It's just one day."

Dora smiled. "How is it you manage to always say exactly the right thing?"

"No mystery there. You're my friend and I care about you."

"Tell me something. You know what Jesse Burrell looked like?"

"Yeah, pretty much."

"Ever see him at the library?"

"When?"

Dora considered the question. "Well, in the weeks before he died. Relatively recently."

"Hmm. I might have. Not sure. Why?"

"Vanessa said he used to hang out at the library a lot. Asked me if that sounds like a drug dealer to me."

"Well, maybe. If he was selling to kids who hang out at the library. Might be a clever cover. Counterintuitive."

"Yeah, well. I told her it doesn't."

"Doesn't what?"

"Hey, keep up—sound like a drug dealer to me."

"You're probably right. Listen, you don't sound so hot. Why don't you come by tomorrow? You don't babysit on Saturdays, do you?"

"No. And sure. What do you have in mind?"

"Don't know," Missy replied. "Something to cheer you up."

Dora wondered what that could mean, but was sufficiently impressed with her friend's ability to cheer her up to give her the benefit of the doubt and see.

A half hour later, Vanessa let herself in, and unlike the previous evening, she was in a good mood—more willing than the previous nights to discuss the police investigation. "Dora, have the police mentioned anything to you about Jesse and his son Julius being together the night that....on the twenty-second? You know, Julius was his son by…"

"I know. And no, they didn't. What they did mention was a phone call between them, just before Jesse went out."

"And you were planning to tell me this when?"

"I figured you knew. Why would the police tell me but not you?"

"Mm hmm. I don't suppose they told you what Jesse and Julius spoke about, or if they met up?"

"No. That's what they were asking me. And no. I don't have an answer to either of those things."

• • •

Dora explained to Vanessa that she wouldn't be staying over. Instead, she drove over to Missy's apartment.

"So, Jesse Burrell gets a call from his son Julius after the party at Agatha and Rudy's," Missy began. She was lying on her back on the couch in her apartment, bare feet up on cushions and iPad in hand, doing a Sudoku puzzle.

Dora finished the thought. "Then he goes out, and gets himself killed at a known drug hangout."

"And with no hard evidence of a drug deal gone wrong," Missy continued.

"Looks like your basic robbery where the guy resisted and the asshole—that's what we call them at the academy—picked up a rock or something and beat him to death."

Missy gave her a look. "I'm a librarian—I do read."

"Okay. Okay. Just sayin'." She was lying on her back on the floor, a half-done puzzle depicting Sedona, Arizona, beside her, and Comfort dozing with his chin resting on Dora's left wrist, which inhibited her work on the puzzle.

"Well, if Jesse went out and it had nothing to do with that call, it's a bit of a coincidence, wouldn't you say, Miss Almost-Police Lady?"

"No such thing, Sudoku Girl," Dora replied. "I think he had said something earlier about wanting more of whatever beer he drank."

"Right. Ooh."

"What?"

"Oh. Nothing. I just got a number I've been trying to figure out in this puzzle. So, Julius was picked up because someone who was arrested for selling oxy…?"

"Opioids of some kind, anyway—out of a doctor's office," Dora explained as she rubbed the scruff of Comfort's neck. "The office manager was arrested and gave up his name—Julius, I mean. So, the cops picked Julius up and put pressure on him, and he gave them the name of this guy, Doyle."

"So, we don't know if these drug sales—"

"Alleged, at this point."

"Right—we don't know if these alleged sales, whether we're talking about Doyle or Julius Burrell, had anything to do with Jesse's death." She sat up and leaned forward. "I mean there's nothing pointing to Jesse selling or buying drugs at that moment in time—that night, behind The Elegant Lagoon," Missy said.

"Correct," Dora agreed. "But there *is* evidence of a phone call between father and son, and the general rep of that spot."

"Maybe the kid was in trouble and needed help."

Dora sat up and leaned on her forearm. Comfort reluctantly lifted his head, opened his sleepy eyes and began licking Dora's hand. "Could be."

"What if," Missy began, "someone made Julius make that call?"

Dora pressed her lips together and shrugged. "Could also be. We need more hard info."

"So, how are you feeling now?"

Dora shrugged again, sadly this time. "Kind of beat up. Kind of confused. I don't know what I want. Or, more accurately, I want several conflicting things. And my instructors were all over me today, treating me like a kid. Did I mention that I followed Vincent Doyle a few days ago?"

"Wait, what? You—really? No! How did you find him?"

"White pages, online—double checked via similar sites, of which there are many."

"So, what happened?"

"Someone wasn't happy I was watching him."

"Someone as in him? And…?"

"Not him. Some other guy. And…I had to defend myself."

Missy got up off the couch and sat down next to Dora on the floor. Comfort was now resting his chin on Dora's ankle. "What? Are you okay?"

Dora smiled. "That part was kind of fun."

"How's the other guy?"

Dora didn't answer. She sat up, next to Missy. Comfort had begun to lick the cuff of Dora's pant leg. She laughed. "Dude, that's cloth, not food!"

Missy shook her head. "Everything's food, in his world. So, what do you want to do? I'm sure students, recruits make mistakes all the time, and they're taken to task for it."

"They are. Look, I know I'm a little—what's the word?"

"Mercurial."

Dora laughed. "That's a polite way of saying it. I was going to say sensitive, thin skinned—even immature."

Missy shook her head. "I wouldn't call a grown-up who gets upset when she gets scolded immature. But that sort of thing *is* part of the culture."

"It's part of the deal, yeah. The fact that I'm a grown woman means I've gotta be able to take it, and that's just not my strength. Has to do with my past, I guess. But you know what—at lots of jobs, women have to take a lot of shit." She pointed a finger. "And that's not right."

"But here, everyone has to take it. It's not necessarily sexist. Hey," Missy said, looking at Dora. She quickly leaned in and gave her a peck on the cheek. Dora looked startled, then Missy stood up, reached a hand down and pulled Dora to her feet. "Alexa, play Playlist One."

"Playing Playlist One."

A driving beat suddenly filled the room—bass, drums, guitars, and two women singing. *"I was sitting near the phone. Nobody was home...!"*

Missy was suddenly dancing to the beat—leaping onto the couch and down again, surprising Dora with her lightness on her feet and the joy with which she danced.

"Come on!" she encouraged.

"Wait. Who is this?" Dora wanted to know. She hesitated.

"Who cares? Come on—you'll feel better. Dance with me!"

And so, she did, abandoning her hurt feelings—paving them over with joy, with dance steps, with motion—losing herself in the music.

They danced to four songs, after which Missy brought them both ice cold lemonades.

Dora was shaking her head. "I can't believe you got me to dance."

Missy shrugged and grinned. "It's a gift."

Chapter 7

It was late Thursday night of her third week at the academy, and Dora had just come home from babysitting Vanessa's boys. Tonight, as she did now and then, she had opted to come home, pop open a beer and read *The Chronicle* online. She clicked on the lead article, read a sentence or two and just stared at the words on the screen. Half a dozen people in Beach City had been arrested for heroin and fentanyl trafficking the previous week, including Vincent Doyle, who had been arrested for distribution near a school—presumably Beach City Catholic. According to the article, school authorities knew nothing of Doyle's criminal record and explained that two sources—a science teacher and a teacher's aide—had recommended Doyle for his position, from which he was now terminated. Both the science teacher and the teacher's aide denied knowledge of Doyle's previous arrests for similar offenses. The school's communications department was bracing for a backlash from angry parents.

She called Vanessa.

"Hi. It's Dora. Have you seen today's *Chronicle?*"

"I try to stay away from the papers nowadays."

"Well, I came home and happened to click on today's news and saw that Vincent Doyle's been arrested for selling drugs by the school."

"I guess that's a good thing, right?"

"If he was doing what he's accused of, which from what we know, he probably was. What it means as far as what happened to Jesse is anybody's guess."

"I wonder if he'll say anything about Julius."

"You don't know anything about their relationship?"

Vanessa sounded unsure. "I've always been out of the loop as far as Julius is concerned. Whatever I know came through Jesse. Julius is his son with Laila, so, you know, I stay out of it. Hang on. Someone's banging on my door."

Dora overheard Vanessa saying, "Hey, stop that banging! I'm coming."

And then another woman's voice. "You need to help me, Vanessa!"

"Help you? How am I supposed to help you? I don't even know what you're talking about! You can't just show up, banging on my door, and telling me what I've got to do!"

Vanessa picked up the phone. "Gotta go. Laila's here."

Dora heard the other woman's voice. "Who's that on the phone? Who you tellin' I'm here?"

• • •

Vanessa hung up and turned to Laila, who was still standing in her open apartment doorway. She took a deep breath, got her bearings, walked past Laila and closed the door.

"Now, what's this about?" Vanessa walked back into the kitchen, with Laila in tow. Vanessa had never seen her anything less than perfectly put together, and couldn't help but feel a little satisfaction that the woman her ex so often compared her to—usually unfavorably—was looking less than her usually perfect self. Her normally flawless braids were a scraggly mess, her brown eyeliner was smeared and tear-streaked, and she needed a shower.

"They're going to charge Julius with murder!" Laila moaned and looked heavenward. "Lord, why are you doing this to me?" She began to wail and threw herself into Vanessa's arms, and it was all Vanessa could do to hold the near hysterical woman at arm's length to keep from staining her work clothes.

"Shh, Laila! The boys are asleep. I just got in from work fifteen minutes ago."

This took Laila by surprise. "Work? Where are you working?"

Vanessa shook her head. "I got a proofreading job at a marketing company called The Bernelli Group. Now, I need to know—did they charge Julius with Jesse's murder? Is that what you're telling me?"

"Not—not as of yet, but they said they were going to." Now that Vanessa was not embracing her, Laila stood up straight, blinked a few times, and sat down heavily on a kitchen stool. She looked around the apartment and nodded, her devastation waning. "This place ain't bad. Good for you."

Vanessa closed her eyes for a moment, then opened them. "Julius. What's going on with Julius and the police? He's at the station now?"

Laila picked up crying where she had left off. "Vanessa, you have no idea! Julius was working. He had a good job—he was helping to support his mama. He's a good boy."

Vanessa frowned. She was afraid to sit down, as Laila might be encouraged to stay. "So, it sounds like you're saying you're afraid that if Julius is charged, he might not be able to continue helping you out."

Laila instantly stopped crying. "I wouldn't put it that way, no. I'm afraid because the police are threatening to charge my son with murdering his own father! Ohh, ohhh!" She began to sob, her head lurching forward with each exhale.

"Listen to me, Laila. Listen. Where did you hear this?"

"From Julius."

"And where was he when he told you this? Was he with you?"

Laila thought for a moment, then shook her head.

Vanessa spoke as though she were speaking to a child. "Was he on the phone? Did Julius tell you this over the phone?"

Laila seemed to take on the little girl role. She nodded, wide-eyed.

"Okay," Vanessa said. "And where was he at the time? Where did he make the call from?"

Laila looked to either side, as though the answer might come in through one of Vanessa's west-facing windows or through a picture frame on the east wall of the room. "His apartment."

Vanessa nodded and smiled. "Okay. Good! So, Julius was home, then."

Laila nodded.

"Well, there, you see? Julius is not under arrest for murdering his daddy."

"But they're gonna, they're gonna—" She was going to cry again.

"You don't know that, Laila. Could it be that the police were trying to scare Julius? Kind of leaning on him to get him to say something—admit to something?"

Laila shrugged. "Mmmaybe. But admit to what? He didn't do anything! And the police took some of his clothes. Why would they do that? And... how am I going to live?"

Vanessa had no patience for this. She had lost her husband, pulled herself up by her bootstraps, despite being emotionally on the floor herself, and now this woman who had no place in her life had barged into her apartment on a weeknight, trying to dump her problems on *her*?

"Here's what I suggest. Julius is not under arrest today, right?"

"Well, not yet."

"And your needs are met today, right?"

"Well..."

"You have food in your refrigerator, and your bills are paid?"

"Well, my Mercedes lease payment is—"

A piercing shriek emitted from the monitor, and Vanessa went into panic mode. "That's Buster. He knows there's someone here. If anything goes on around here without him being in on it, he feels left out and he will let you know it!"

Laila's mood instantly shifted. "Ohhh, Buster! Can I see him?"

"No you may not. If he sees you he'll want to play and he'll keep me up half the night."

"Ohh." Laila sounded deflated.

"Laila, I'm sorry. I've got to see to Buster. You are okay. Trust me, you are okay, and Julius is okay and it's all going to be..." She shooed Laila toward the door. "Okay. You just hang in there." Laila's momentum carried her to the front door, which Vanessa opened, and Laila stepped through and into the hall.

Vanessa closed the door and leaned back against it. Had she just apologized to Laila?

She hurried in to Buster, but he must have sensed that their company had left, because Vanessa found him sound asleep. "Well, thank God," she breathed.

Her cell phone rang. She looked at the caller ID and answered.

"Mrs. Burrell? Is this a good time to talk?"

Was he kidding? She put on her sweet voice, realized she couldn't manage that, and switched to the civil voice with firm boundaries she used at retail stores. "Detective Ganderson."

He didn't wait for an answer. "I wanted to update you on the progress we've made."

She waited for him to mention Julius.

"We have lab results from fibers found at the scene, and we are looking at the clothing of individuals who may have been present."

"Okay." That fit with what Laila had said.

"But there's something else. You say you hosted a barbecue earlier on the day of Jesse's death?"

"No. His sister did."

"Agatha Raines."

"That's right."

"I see, and Rudy. They hosted the barbecue?"

"Yes. They're married. Why are you asking—?"

"Can you give me an idea of what food was served at the barbecue?"

"Well, barbecue—ribs, burgers, hot dogs. And some rice, and coleslaw, and beans and some greens, and let's see. Chocolate cake…"

"Was there lobster?"

"Lobster? No."

"Or fish of any kind."

"No, detective. There was no fish. This was a barbecue celebrating my nephew Samuel's first birthday."

"Might Jesse have had fish earlier in the day?"

"No, I can say for sure that he did not. He had eggs earlier in the day. Scrambled eggs, toast with butter and jelly, bacon…"

"And Samuel would be Rudy and Agatha's…"

"Son, yes. Why are you asking about lobster and fish?"

"Because the contents of your husband's stomach included lobster and another kind of fish—possibly snapper. Both of which are on the menu at The Elegant Lagoon restaurant."

Chapter 8

"Hi, Dora. Do you have time to come by my place? There's something we need help with."

"Sure, Christine. Half hour okay?"

"Fine."

When Dora arrived, she found Christine, Charlie, Luis Martinez and Missy Winters arrayed in a semi-circle in Christine's living room, facing an empty chair. At the far end of the circle sat a middle-aged man with carefully combed hair in a yellow collared shirt and brown slacks.

Dora found a spot between Missy and Luis and sat down, touching Missy's hand.

"We're waiting for C," Charlie said.

"His birthday?" Dora asked.

Christine looked at her. "Intervention."

Charlie nodded toward the man in the yellow shirt. "This is Dan Michaels. He works with C3 at the counseling center."

Michaels nodded and smiled. "I've explained to everyone here that we need to support Charles, and stay away from blame. We don't want to drive him further into his addiction."

The room descended into silence and stayed that way for twelve minutes.

The doorbell rang.

"Showtime," Charlie muttered.

Christine opened the door, and C3 followed her into the apartment, his blond hair bleached by the sun. He wore a blue polo shirt and jeans and was smiling.

Dora marveled at how the young man had filled out and cleaned up in the two years since he had been in prison. Whatever the current issue was, it had yet to take much of a visible toll.

"I don't know when my father will…" He walked into the living room and stopped when he saw everyone arrayed there.

"What is this?"

Charlie stood, went to the single chair in the middle of the room, and grasped the chair's back. He slapped the cushion twice.

"You know what it is."

Dan Michaels rose and walked slowly toward the center of the circle, but remained slightly off to one side so he could address C3, who was in the center chair, and everyone else at once.

"Your friends and I have joined you here today, Charles, because we love you and we want to be here for you."

C3 appeared to be barely paying attention. His expression had turned sullen, disinterested—even surly. "Really? That's why you're here?"

"Yes, it is!" his father exclaimed, emphatically.

"We want to see you get the help you need, so you can get back to work, and back to being the son, friend, employee, and coworker you've always been."

"Not always," C3 argued.

"But for quite some time. Years—good years," Charlie Jr. said.

"I have no plans to do or be anything else. Why would I? Why not let me get back to it? Why blame me?"

"This is not about blame, Charlie," Christine began.

"Sure feels like it."

Dora could not help but sympathize with C3, as she felt echoes of her own long ago battles.

"Addiction is not a person's fault, but getting clean and sober is their responsibility," Christine continued. "How many people have you said that to?"

C3 stared at his father, but said nothing.

"You have pills in your bathroom at home," Charlie said, and Michaels held up a hand for him to stop.

C3 continued to glare at his father, and then began to yell. "I should never have given you a key!"

"That's not the point," Charlie Jr. argued, his own voice rising.

C3 paused, gathering his strength. "Like you're not having your scotches before dinner! You hypocrite!"

Michaels stepped into the space between them. "You know how this works. This is about you, no one else, Charles. If you want to keep your job, you'll get help and stick with the program."

C3 looked each of them in the eye for a long moment—waging individual miniature battles. But he'd lost the war, and he knew it.

His gaze returned to his father and, for a moment, his anger burned brighter, then faded to raw pain. Dora wondered if everyone present could see the young man's wounds, which were so obvious to her.

"What brought all this on?"

Charlie and Christine exchanged a look. "It's been brewing for a while," Charlie explained, "but the final straw was when the police reached out to me."

"To you?" C3's brow furrowed in confusion. "About me?"

"Yes, to me. The police have been keeping an eye on your friend, Vincent Doyle, about…an unrelated matter, and happened to see you stopping by his apartment. I run a business in this city, and they were doing me a favor, giving me a chance to straighten you out. And by the way, your buddy Doyle's at the county jail."

...

When Dora arrived back at her apartment, it was late—just enough time for her to change, make herself a cup of tea, and read one of her Kindle mysteries before going to sleep.

Just as she settled in under the covers and began reading, the apartment buzzer sounded. She thought about pretending she wasn't in, but then it sounded again, and before she could think about it, she had bounded out of bed to the intercom.

"Who is it?"

"Rudy Raines."

"Is this an emergency? It's late!"

"I wouldn't be here if it wasn't important."

Five minutes later, she had put on a robe and was sitting in her living room in her comfy chair. Rudy was on the couch and they were both sipping chamomile tea.

She waited. Neither of them spoke.

"Agatha closed the library tonight," Rudy said.

Dora nodded, waited. Eventually, she said, "Listen, I have to be up early."

Rudy looked at his hands, which were clenching and unclenching. He scratched his head. "Ags and I are concerned about your interaction with the police."

"Concerned about—? What do you mean, concerned?"

Dora could see how uncomfortable the man was, and wondered if this meeting had been someone else's idea—Agatha's, perhaps, or Vanessa's, or even Miz Liz's.

"They've asked us to come downtown a bunch of times and when we get there, they lean on us like we've done something wrong."

"Okaaayy. And what does this have to do with me?"

The big man grew even more agitated, pressing his lips together until they disappeared. He stood up and walked to a small breakfront along the north wall of her apartment and seemed to examine some of her old CDs and books. The content she consumed nowadays was all digital.

"I can show you my Kindle or Spotify," she offered, "if you want to peruse those."

He blew out a breath. "You've talked to the police about our family, and that's blowing back on us."

She grimaced and shook her head, not understanding. "What do you have to hide?" She could see he was annoyed and trying to keep his temper in check, but so was she.

"Why not let the police do their jobs?" he suggested.

"You think I'm standing in their way?"

"I think you're not a police officer—yet, and maybe you're not ready to investigate a crime of this…"

She crossed her arms. "Why don't you tell me why you're really here?"

"I'm here because the police stopped by to see me, asking why they saw me at Vincent Doyle's apartment."

"Ahhh. And?"

He shook his head but still wouldn't look at her. "He's just a guy who comes into the bar now and then, like a lot of guys—women too," he said. "And I know him a little bit—no crime in that." He walked over, took a final sip of tea, and stepped to the door. "Thank you for your time, Dora."

She shut the door behind him, then went to bed, tossing and turning for nearly an hour, trying to figure out what Rudy was trying to hide.

• • •

The group met late on a Saturday morning at Rudy's, before the bar opened to the public. The two televisions were tuned to ESPN, where talking heads were talking college football. The place smelled of bleach and stale beer. Miz Liz was there, along with Vanessa. Many of their friends had joined them, including Delroy and Shanice James, and both Big Ru and Little Ru, but their wives, Eunice and Nia, had gone shopping together. That made the Ru brothers nervous, as their wives loved to buy shoes—expensive shoes.

Rudy was also there with Agatha, who had brought the boys and agreed to keep them off to one side, away from the discussion. Dora had showed up as well, without Missy; she was working at the library for the afternoon.

The card players were laughing raucously at, or perhaps with, Delroy.

"Riiight. And four of a kind beats a straight flush," teased Little Ru, laughing so hard he was having trouble catching his breath.

Delroy held out a hand as a stop sign. "Okay, now. That was a long time ago."

"Doesn't matter, Del. We're never gonna let you forget it," said Ferret Wallace. He had been working for Lenny Altamont's business, Lenny's Auto Repair, since getting out of prison several months before; he also gardened a few hours a week, again for Lenny. He was teased about his appearance—small, darting eyes, pointy face, twitchy nose—hence his name, but he took the teasing well and had an ability to laugh at himself and was accepted by the rest of the friends, all of whom had cars that occasionally needed repair.

"Five to one we don't forget it," said Big Ru.

"I'll take that bet," Delroy said, taking the ribbing rather well.

Miz Liz was at the front of the room, hands on both hips, her elbows out like wings. "Excuse me, everybody! I appreciate you all coming out and giving me some of your Saturday afternoons. We have learned some things and I want to share them with you. Since my husband, Mr. Burrell, passed, I have worked as hard as I could to raise my twins right, and I believe they turned out just fine, so I am personally insulted by anyone saying or implying otherwise." She looked around, as though daring anyone to disagree, then seemed to lose focus, wrinkled her nose a few times, and went on. "I feel stronger knowing that Jesse's and Vanessa's friends are with me, and I want to keep you informed as much as possible. They say that Jesse ate at The Elegant Lagoon that night, after he left the party at Agatha and Rudy's house. Anyone have any knowledge about why he did that, if he did that?"

"Why would he?" asked Little Ru, whose name was actually Clevon. "He ate at the party, right?"

"That's right," said Rudy. "So it's a little hard to believe. You eat barbecue, Rudy style, you're done eating."

"Rude!" Agatha's whisper was loud enough to carry across the room. Rudy turned, saw her sternly shaking her head, and bit his lip.

"While he may have eaten at the restaurant," Levi Cohen ventured, "he was probably there for some other reason." Levi was a lawyer who offered his services at a discount to many of the friends.

"Care to speculate?" Dora asked.

"No, I would not."

"The other thing is Julius." Miz Liz frowned and stopped speaking, her attention turned inward. She grabbed the edge of a nearby table and lowered herself into a chair. "Excuse me." She sat silently for a moment, then looked up. Her forehead glistened with sweat. "The other thing is Julius. He believes that the police want to charge him with murdering his father."

A ripple of surprise went through the room. Levi stood up.

"If they had sufficient evidence to charge him with that or any other crime, they would have done so, Miz Burrell. I suspect they are pressuring him for information. My understanding is he has already given them a name."

Miz Liz nodded. "I know all about that. Vincent Doyle. Known for selling narcotics. What do you all know about this Doyle, and how is he connected with my Jesse?"

No one answered.

"Come on. I know some of you have knowledge of that world. Stella?"

Stella Malone, who had dyed black hair and heavily applied eyeliner, looked surprised. "Why do you say that?" She made a living dealing pot, which was becoming a problem for her because it was so readily available at such reasonable prices that she was being pushed out of the market. Several people in the group bought from her, but she was primarily there for Vanessa, who had been her friend since grade school.

"Don't answer that," advised Levi Cohen.

"You know why." Miz Liz glared at Cohen, then at Malone. She turned to Ferret Wallace. "You fixed my son's car at one time, is that right?"

Wallace glanced quickly to either side and wrinkled his nose. "Yes, ma'am."

"And I'm told you have ties in that area," she continued.

"Don't—" Cohen began.

"It's okay." Wallace smiled at Miz Liz. "Yes, I was in prison once upon a time, but I'm out now. I've done my time. And I'm working for Mr. Altamont, at Lenny's Auto."

She held Ferret Wallace's gaze for a few moments, then pushed herself to her feet. "I want to thank Dora Ellison for learning what she could through her connections with the police."

Dora nodded and ventured a smile. "I want to make sure, Miz Liz, that you know that Vincent Doyle's been arrested for distributing narcotics on school property."

"'Bout time someone did something!" She gave an emphatic nod in Dora's direction. "Does anyone else have anything to add?" Miz Liz paused, her eyes scanning the group. "If not, then, Rudy, please take me home. I need to take a nap."

"Can I ride along with you two?" asked Vanessa. Agatha, who had brought her own car, was going directly from Rudy's to the library, where she had to work the afternoon shift in Reference.

A slight crease of confusion touched Rudy's forehead, but he nodded. "Sure thing."

• • •

Vanessa waited in the car while Rudy walked Liz, her arm through his, to the front foyer of her apartment building. He kissed her and watched her let herself in and disappear into the lobby. Then he returned to his car.

"Why did you want to ride with me?" Rudy asked Vanessa as he got back in the driver's seat. "I'm taking you back to the bar, right? To get your car?"

Vanessa's lips were a thin line. "How 'bout you telling me the truth about your involvement with Doyle?"

"What're you talking about, Nessa?"

"I know you know him. I know you spent time with him. But mostly, Rudy, I know you. You like to party and you like your weed. And that was Doyle's thing."

Rudy shrugged. "It's also Stella's thing."

"So, you bought from Stella? That's what you're saying? Not from Doyle?" Rudy didn't answer. "Jesse was my husband!" Vanessa was furious, but also starting to cry.

"And besides being my brother-in-law, he was my best friend." Rudy gripped the steering wheel. He was driving too fast—something he did when he was angry.

"And now they're trying to put Jesse's death on Julius, and that's hard to believe. Can you honestly believe that boy killed his father?"

Rudy didn't answer. He was struggling with a decision. "I'm going to tell you something, but you've gotta keep it quiet."

"I'll decide that for myself."

He took a deep breath. "Yes, I was with Doyle recently. I was trying to run interference for Jesse."

"What the hell does that mean?"

Rudy glanced at Vanessa, then back at the road. His tone was pleading. "I was trying to protect him. I still am."

"Protect him—from what?"

"Mostly, from himself."

Vanessa clenched her teeth and glared at her brother-in-law. "I don't know much about this, but I know a line of bullshit when I hear it."

"It's not bullshit, Nessa."

"Then explain."

"I know—I knew Jesse was doing some things."

"What things?"

"I can't say."

"Well, it can't be because you're trying to protect Jesse—he's dead. And anyway, if you were trying to protect him, you obviously failed."

Rudy swallowed, and his eyes filled with tears. "I know it. I did. I failed my best friend. This is on me."

"You'll get no sympathy from me, Rude. I'm going to ask you again to tell me what is going on. He was my husband and I have a right to know."

"Nessa, there are some things I just can't get into—for your own protection."

For a moment, Vanessa didn't answer. Then she exploded and tried to grab the steering wheel, but Rudy blocked her with an enormous forearm. The car swerved hard to one side, then back again.

"Pull over, Rudy. Pull over, damn it—let me out of this car!"

Instead of pulling over, Rudy kept driving. "Let me take you home, Nessa. You can be as pissed as you want, but let me take you home."

Vanessa didn't answer and retreated instead into sullen silence.

• • •

After dropping Vanessa off at her apartment, Rudy drove to Dora's, calling to tell her he was on his way. Rather than let him in, Dora came down to the front door. "Now what?"

"We need to talk."

"Well, how 'bout we go for a walk?" she suggested.

"Sure."

The heat of the day had not yet dissipated, and the air was heavy with humidity. Fireworks crackled from a block away. Cars, trucks, and motorcycles from the main road could be heard in the distance.

"What did you want to talk about?" Dora asked.

"Jesse did know this guy, Doyle, but he wasn't really involved with him. They were aware of one another."

Dora considered this. "So, you're saying Julius gave the police his name so they'd back off."

"I honestly don't know. Could be."

"Was there a connection Doyle had with Julius that had something to do with Jesse's death?"

"Not that I'm aware of."

Dora stopped walking. "So, what are you aware of? Why are you here?"

Rudy stopped a few steps ahead of Dora and waited while a girl in jean shorts and a light blue t-shirt walked a dachshund slowly past them in the opposite direction.

"Doyle's connection to this had nothing to do with Julius—at least, I don't believe it did."

"Okay."

"Jesse knew who Doyle was the way a lot of us know who's doing what around here. It's a small town, Dora." She began walking again and caught up with Rudy.

"No one knows that better than me. Everything that went down a year and a half ago taught me all about the sick connections people have around here." She glanced at two teenage boys on motorized skateboards who caught up to them in the street and passed them. "So, what was Jesse's connection to Doyle? Did he buy from him?"

Rudy didn't answer.

"You want to talk to me or to Detective Ganderson? The Goose and the Gander are shot out of a cannon about this—with the publicity about this and the drug busts, the opioids, the fentanyl. They're feeling the pressure downtown, and they'd just love to spread it around."

"I get that," Rudy said. He hesitated, his jaw tight. "Jesse didn't buy from Doyle. He went to him because he needed help."

"Help with what?"

Rudy shook his head. "Can't say."

"Can't or won't?"

"I'm just not saying, is all."

"You know the Goose and the Gander are going to be all over you about this. And they're going to really lean on you."

Rudy gave her a hard look. "Yeah? So, who's going to tell them?"

Chapter 9

After Rudy left, Dora felt too restless to go back to her apartment, so she called Missy, who said that she could meet Dora in fifteen minutes. Dora suggested the boardwalk at Beach City Boulevard.

"Better yet," Missy said, "let's take a walk on the beach."

A full moon had risen over the water, its light glittering on the waves crashing against the jetties. Dora waited at the entrance to the beach—a doorway that led beneath the boardwalk to the sand and, eventually, the ocean. She could hear people walking and talking on the boardwalk above her, and the low *clickity-clack* of bicycles on the boards. The boardwalk had been destroyed in Superstorm Sandy, and rebuilt Smarter, Stronger, and Safer, according to the local government. Much of the city had been rebuilt—homes, including Agatha and Rudy's, had been gutted and lifted; storefronts had changed hands and emerged as new incarnations with new owners. While Sandy had not been forgotten, and the possibility of future storms doing even greater damage was ever present, many of the city's residents, including Dora, had resumed their lives and were obsessing less about hurricanes and climate issues and more about current crises, like the COVID pandemic.

Because she was in the shadow of the boardwalk, she saw Missy, who was approaching on the red cobblestones under the streetlights, before Missy saw her. She stepped into the light.

"Oh, I didn't see you," Missy exclaimed.

Dora smiled but didn't answer. She led the way through the beach entrance and into the dark shadow of the boardwalk.

"Hang on." Missy stopped, gripping Dora's shoulder and leaning against her as she slipped off her water shoes and dug her toes into the sand. "Mmm. Just love cool sand on a hot night."

That sounded good to Dora, so she followed Missy's example. "Ooh, you're right."

Now Missy led the way toward the ocean and the packed sand just above the water line, where they walked together, side by side. "How's the academy?"

"I guess I'm…sorta getting used to it. Still don't like the way they treat us sometimes."

"Who, specifically? What class?"

"Guy named Kontaxis—Sergeant Kontaxis. Bit of a hardass, and yeah, I know it comes with the territory."

"I wasn't going to say that."

"What were you going to say?"

"I was going to say that's gotta be pretty challenging."

"Yeah, well, he doesn't like me because I guess I'm a little insubordinate."

"Hah! You?"

Dora reached a hand toward Missy then stopped, and let her hand fall back to her side. "And this guy Re Morse. His bureaucratic obsessiveness is killing me."

"No, it's not."

"It is."

"It's not killing you."

"You're right. It's not killing me."

They walked together in silence, their fingers occasionally brushing. Lights from fishing and party boats winked off shore, and the waves lightly sprayed their faces with a cool, salty mist.

"About two years ago," Dora began, "Franny made me a video for my birthday. It's just a thing she made with her phone of her singing me this little song and telling me she loved me."

"Nice," Missy said. They continued walking in near silence.

"I watch it every day, and I talk to it like she's still here."

• • •

A Gathering Storm David E. Feldman

Dora had forgotten how much she hated school. She supposed she had what was called ADD nowadays—or maybe it was ADHD. She didn't know and didn't have the attention span to think about it. She only knew that classroom learning bored her. Life was interesting; books she wanted to read for her own enjoyment were sort of interesting. Dry, abstract classroom learning was not, and so much of the academy course work was classroom learning she was expected to learn, remember, and be able to apply. Lives depended on it. She wasn't at all sure she was cut out for this.

Search and seizure required an understanding of the Fourth Amendment and how to effectively and legally navigate a course between the rights of the public against unreasonable searches and seizures, and the police officer's duty to protect the public and keep people safe in situations where searching individuals and possibly seizing dangerous possessions were deemed necessary.

In the course of day-to-day police work, Dora suspected that she would be able to apply the information she gleaned from her classes, but listening to hour after hour of lectures was driving her stir crazy.

Her job would be to protect the public while taking care to avoid violating the rights of an alleged perpetrator or person of interest. Not only was the subject boring to her, but she would just as soon go well beyond the careful application of what was being taught. She preferred to be absolutely sure the assholes were neutralized, and if they got a little banged up in the process…oh well, they started it.

She was expected to memorize and be able to apply in extremely stressful situations decisions about how to apply force—including deadly force—how to protect the public in a range of situations, and how to deal with the aftermath of the use of force, applying proper procedures and related policies, safely securing suspects, and having an awareness of what the police officer could and could not do when laws were broken, along with possible litigation issues and protocols.

Her job would ostensibly be to apprehend an alleged perpetrator and secure him or her safely so that the individual could be tried for the crimes for which they'd been arrested.

Ugh.

Dora understood violence. She knew how to handle herself in violent encounters, and her go-to process had always been to bring so much force to bear that the target would be overwhelmed and utterly neutralized, likely incapacitated. Now she was expected to navigate nuance.

She hated nuance.

She could hear Missy in her head: *You can do this.*

Ugh. Missy—get out of my head.

She had experienced and mastered violence, but she had never expected that violence would be her job.

• • •

That evening, she sat at Vanessa's living room window with Drew and Buster, looking up into the clear night sky. The moon was still aglow on the other side of the horizon. She drew a curling line in the air for the boys with her finger, then held Vanessa's iPad up to the window with the constellation app open.

"This constellation is called Draco."

"Deeka!" cried Buster.

"What is Draco?" Drew wanted to know. "What's the story of Draco?"

Dora searched her memory. "I think that in the myth, Draco was a dragon who guarded golden apples for Hera, queen of the gods."

"Ohhh," Drew marveled.

"Appaws! Appaws!" Buster cried, pointing toward the kitchen. "Kai have appaw?"

"Let's do another constellation, then we'll do appaws." She wasn't sure if the child understood, but Buster didn't add anything and seemed to have settled back to listen for the time being.

"This one, just below Draco, is Hercules." She held the iPad up to the window. "See? The triangle is his head, and his arms are up like he's fighting and his legs are running." She showed both boys, who looked at the app, then at the sky, then back at the app.

"What he do?" Drew asked, pointing to the constellation.

"Hercules was very strong. The strongest of the gods. And he had to fight giants!"

The boys were listening, wide-eyed and rapt.

"But these giants were also very strong, and there were two of them."

"So, what he do?" Drew wanted to know.

"So, Hercules prayed. He prayed to Zeus, who was the king of the gods, and he won!"

"Yayy!" Drew cheered, both hands in the air.

"Appaw! Now appaw!" Buster insisted.

Dora laughed. "Okay, now appaw." She led the boys back in to the kitchen, where she cut up an apple for them to share. She had offered to care for these two little boys to help a friend in need, a friend who had endured a terrible loss—one which Dora understood only too well. But she had never expected to fall in love with them.

• • •

Sarah looked around. She had instructed Esther to temporarily shut off all the phones, and set up the three lights they used for interview shoots in front of the green screen. It was late in the day, giving today's guest a chance to fulfill her work obligations before her interview. Four lights would probably be optimal, since the green screen had to be lit independently, along with a key light, a fill, and a back light, to light the backs of everyone's heads. But Sarah was fine with three, omitting the fill light. The only people who would notice enough to say anything about it would be the videographers in the audience. Criticizing *The Chronicle*'s shoots, their little pissing contests, made them feel better. Sarah thanked them for their help and went on doing things her own way.

Lemieux handled the camera, which was an iPhone, and the program that keyed out the screen. Sarah was the "talent." The subject tonight was the apparent recent uptick in crime, opioid, heroin, and fentanyl sales and use, along with what appeared to be the related murder of councilwoman Agatha Raines's brother Jesse.

Christine knocked and waited politely at the door to the stairs. She wore a simple navy-blue dress with sleeves that ended at the elbow, and a single strand of large South Sea pearls.

Sarah and Christine air-kissed; they were not quite friends but more than acquaintances. Sarah was wearing her usual black—though she wore both a skirt and a sweater for the occasion, rather than a long-sleeved t-shirt and sweats.

Esther had put two bottles of water, labels removed, on a round table at which they would both sit, along with a small vase containing a single yellow orchid. It was important that Lemieux be careful with his keying program, so as not to key out the flower, as yellow is related to green, but he knew to do that, and of course, everyone knew not to wear green.

Christine took a small mirror from her pocketbook and checked her makeup and hair, then settled into one of the sand-colored tufted linen chairs, and crossed her legs. Sarah sat in the other chair. Both Esther and Lemieux were focused on Sarah, who would give the go ahead for the interview to begin, as well as a cue to stop taping. The questions had been sent to Christine beforehand.

"Do you need anything from me?" Sarah asked.

Christine shook her head with a small smile. "Fire away."

"Okie dokie." Sarah gave a barely perceptible nod to her assistants, and a TV screen along the wall running from the main stairway entrance to the window opposite the offices flickered on, displaying Sarah and Christine in what appeared to be a modern TV newsroom, courtesy of Lemieux's keying program. Sarah smiled into the camera.

"Welcome to *Chronicle Today*. I'm your host, Sarah Turner." She turned to Christine. "With me today is Mayor Christine Pearsall. Welcome Ms. Mayor."

"Thank you, Sarah. It's a pleasure to be here."

"Let's jump right in. We're here to examine the recent spate of drug-related arrests, including one at Beach City Catholic—"

Christine interrupted. "I've got to stop you there, Sarah. The arrest you reference was not at Beach City Catholic, but off the grounds in the vicinity of the street parking between the school and the boardwalk."

Sarah paused. "I stand corrected, but would it be fair to say that the individual arrested, one Vincent Doyle, was selling drugs to students at that school?"

Frowning, Christine spoke with the gravitas the subject deserved. "Well, I only know what the police tell me. Apparently, this gentleman allegedly—"

"Gentleman?"

"This…guy…was arrested for allegedly distributing illicit drugs onsite. I'm not entirely sure he was arrested for sale to minors or for selling on school grounds."

"Okay. Fair enough. Let's switch gears. Is it fair to say that this arrest is part of an unfortunate trend? An increase in the use, or let's say arrests for the use and sale of narcotics."

Christine let out a long sigh.

"Long day?" Sarah smiled.

Christine shook her head. "You have no idea. But we all have long days, don't we? Let me answer your question. There has been a tragic trend for quite some time—not just in Beach City, but nationally—in the use, sale, consumption of and overdoses from opioids, heroin, fentanyl, and so forth. It's awful. I am not a parent, but I do have someone, a young person I am very much like a mother or perhaps big sister to, who is struggling in his own way. I'm not at liberty to say more, except that I sympathize, I empathize with, and understand the pain of the parents out there, and those who are addicted." She looked directly into the camera, holding the eyes of the viewers with hers. "I empathize with you who are addicted. Addiction is not your fault—not your fault." She rapped her knuckles on the table with each syllable.

"Now, is Beach City worse than other places? Is there a local epidemic of narcotics consumption or sale or overdoses? We throw those words around a lot. They sell advertising, Sarah. You know that's the truth."

Sarah gave a half smile. "I'm not going to apologize for my industry. We have a job to do and we do it, and that has a cost — hence, advertising. We are ad driven, and I'm not going to get into a debate about the relationship between news and advertising. As far as I'm concerned—and I've said this to advertisers—as far as I'm concerned, there is none."

Christine snorted a laugh. "Really?"

"Ms. Mayor…"

"Look," Christine said, folding her arms on the table before her, "the facts are more or less true—but I don't believe they represent any increase or uptick or trend, as you seem to suggest."

"You're splitting hairs."

"No. I'm serving the public. I'm doing my job. Your job is to spotlight these things—you report on, talk about a thing, note what appears to be a trend, though it's all in how you spin it—and then, this is my favorite—you do stories that are essentially, 'Do you know what that *means*?' That's what at least half of the news is nowadays—commentary on some other story. Such and such happened today—do you know what that *means*?" She shook her head, disgusted. "We have good police officers, led by Chief Stalwell, who are doing a great job, a hard job—and sure, it's your job to criticize and to, from your point of view, make them better. But I'm going to defend my police, my departments. Look at what we've seen happen in this city in recent years—in prior administrations."

Sarah waved a hand. "I know. I know. It happened here at *The Chronicle* too."

"Yes, it did. Suffice it to say that this Doyle character will be investigated and prosecuted to the fullest extent of the law, whether he sold drugs in the street or on a school's property." She looked into the camera again. "And to all the parents of kids at Beach City Catholic, your kids are safe; those grounds are safe." She looked back at Sarah. "Now, as to your second topic, I can't really talk about what happened to poor Mr. Burrell, because I honestly don't know."

Sarah looked at the camera. "Councilwoman Agatha Raines's brother."

Christine looked into the camera. "To all of the Burrell and Raines family—our sincerest condolences for your loss. I'm told that Mr. Burrell was a wonderful teacher, a husband, a father to two little boys, a son to a woman many of us know and love, and of course, the twin brother of our own Councilwoman Agatha Raines." She turned to Sarah. "To anticipate your question—no, we are not prepared to label this a drug-related murder. We don't yet have all of the facts and we are not prepared to draw conclusions until we do. Look, Sarah. I know something about the press. I ran a campaign. I work with you. And something I can say without reservation is that when there is a tragedy—and what happened to Mr. Burrell is nothing less —then, it is held under a microscope by the press."

"As it should be," Sarah pointed out.

Christine tipped her head forward and to one side, and flicked her auburn bangs out of her eye. "But that attention may give the appearance of a trend. The media's attention increases our awareness and increases the size of the issue. Yes, these are big issues, but your attention makes them feel bigger. As news consumers, your coverage fills up our consciousness, and that feels like a trend."

Sarah sat back, impressed yet dubious. "Well, that's an interesting take."

Christine held up a finger. "I'm serious about this. These are genuine problems. Whether statistics say they are worsening or not, we have to deal with them. So, what I am prepared to say is that we will not rest until Mr.

Burrell's killer is caught, and our streets, schools, and city are as safe as safe can be."

After a pause, Sarah nodded to Christine with a thin smile. "Thank you, Ms. Mayor."

"And…we're out," Lemieux said, and everyone relaxed.

Once Christine had left and the equipment was put away, and as Sarah was preparing to leave the office for the evening, her cell phone rang.

"Hiya, Charlie."

"Sarah. I'm calling about my son."

She snorted—half laugh, half derision. "I would never have guessed."

"Are you sure you won't put him in a halfway house?"

"Charlie, I'm not putting him anywhere. He's a grown man who can make his own decisions about where he wants to be."

"That he's staying at your place is really your decision at least as much as his."

"I guess that's true. He does have my permission to stay with me. He got sober once, he's been through detox, and I believe he'll get sober again and will, ultimately, stay sober. He knows what he did wrong."

"And what was that?"

"He picked up. If you don't pick up, as they say, you won't get high. Charlie, you of all people should understand."

"Oh, I do understand. That's why I advocate for tough love."

"And yet you still have a few, now and again."

"Because I can keep it to that. C3 can't."

"We'll see. I hope you're wrong."

"How is he?"

Sarah blew air out between pursed lips, puffing out her cheeks. "He seems fine—like his old self."

"The calm before the storm."

"I believe he needs love, Charlie."

"And I believe real love for an addict is tough love."

"We're going to have to agree to disagree."

"Sarah, I truly hope you're right and I'm wrong."
"G'bye, Charlie."
The line went dead.

Chapter 10

Vanessa Burrell arrived at the police station the following morning before work. Miz Liz had not been up to babysitting, so she'd arranged for one of the babysitters she knew from networking with the local moms to stay with Drew and Buster.

Detective Paul Ganderson had arranged for them to meet in a conference room. He waited at the door while Vanessa came in, offered a small smile, and sat down.

Gerry Mallard had arranged for a pot of coffee, three mugs, sugar, sugar substitute, and half and half to be brought in from the lunch room.

"Please, help yourself," Mallard encouraged her.

"No, thank you," Vanessa answered.

"I hope you don't mind." Mallard reached for a mug.

"Not at all."

He added sugar, half and half, and poured some coffee. "Can't let coffee sit around in this place, or someone'll dive for it." He chuckled.

Ganderson waited for Mallard to finish with his coffee and stand off to one side. Vanessa was already seated at the head of the table. Ganderson then sat at a right angle to Vanessa.

"Thank you."

"You're welcome." Ganderson's tone was more ingratiating than his usual terse candor. He placed a photo in front of Vanessa.

"Do you recognize this man?"

She examined the photo's subject: a bald, overweight, white man with a grey goatee who looked to be in his mid to late forties. He was wearing a loud, turquoise Hawaiian shirt, bright with printed green leaves and yellow pineapples, tinged with sunset magenta. Despite the shirt, which was open at the collar, the man did not look easygoing, but stared back at her as though challenging the camera.

Vanessa shook her head. "I don't think so."

"His name is Corb Egar," Ganderson explained.

"And you think he had something to do with Jesse's...?" She didn't finish the sentence.

Mallard had begun to pace along the wall at the foot of the table. "Wouldn't be surprised. We believe he's been involved in multiple homicides around this area, along with many other crimes."

"And he's never been caught?" Vanessa asked.

"He's been arrested and tried several times," Ganderson explained, "but never convicted."

"He's fat, but slippery," Mallard offered. "Drives a Lamborghini Countach in road rallies around the East Coast."

"Those are illegal races from one city to the next," Ganderson explained. "When you see these luxury sports vehicles flying in and out of traffic on the highway, they're often in a road rally."

Mallard exhaled a laugh. "Don't know how he gets shoehorned into that little car. The guy lives in an apartment filled with automatic weapons and bodyguards—that's when he's there. Spends a lot of time at restaurants and after-hours clubs."

Vanessa looked from one detective to the other. "I think I'll have that coffee, if you don't mind."

"Of course," said Ganderson. "Allow me." He poured. "Cream? Sugar?"

"Cream. Splenda, if you have it—two."

"We do."

Once she had her coffee, Vanessa sipped and looked again at the picture.

"What does he"—she indicated the picture—"have to do with Jesse? You think he was at The Elegant Lagoon that night?"

Ganderson nodded. "We've interviewed all the employees we could get a hold of, but no one is saying a word—about Egar or about Jesse."

"So, how...?"

"A neighbor," said Mallard, who had stopped pacing. He put the hand not holding his coffee into his pants pocket, and was bouncing up and down on his toes. "She thinks she saw and heard his car hauling around late that night. Heard it, looked out the window, and thinks she saw it."

"But it was dark," Ganderson added. "And the car is black."

"And she doesn't know much about cars," Mallard finished. "Could have been a Corvette—something sleek and low to the ground."

"So…you have nothing?" Vanessa asked, disappointed.

"What about this guy?" Ganderson put another photo in front of her, this one of a swarthy man with a stubbly beard. Vanessa shook her head.

"What about him?" The detective set a photo down of a man with a much thinner face, a bony nose, and small eyes that were close together and charged with menace.

"Now he looks familiar."

The detectives remained silent, allowing her to examine the photo and ruminate.

"Any idea where you've seen him or with whom?" Ganderson asked, after a few moments.

"Or when?" Mallard added.

"Do you think Jesse knew him?" Ganderson asked gently. "His name is Charles Wallace."

"I just don't know." She shook her head, biting her lip. "I can't say for sure, but he does look familiar. It might be he looks like someone I know, but isn't that person. He looks familiar but something about him looks … off."

The detectives looked at one another. Ganderson sighed. "Okay. That's okay, Mrs. Burrell."

Mallard sat down, so Vanessa had a detective on either side of her at the head of the table.

"Part of why we called you here is because Julius has been released. He's with his mother."

"Has he been charged with anything?" Vanessa asked.

"Not at this time," Ganderson answered.

"But we're keeping our options open," added Mallard.

Ganderson continued. "Julius did give us some interesting information. He told us that Jesse did in fact want to purchase drugs, but that for some reason Doyle could not meet his needs."

"I find that hard to believe — that he was looking for street drugs, other than marijuana, I mean." Vanessa was biting her lip.

"Supposedly, Doyle bumped him up the ladder to this guy, Egar." Mallard was up again and pacing, which appeared to Vanessa to annoy Ganderson, though he didn't say so. "We do know that Julius and Jesse spoke that night," Mallard explained. "But Julius wouldn't tell us what was said."

"A kid talking to his father, was how he put it." Ganderson sat back and folded his arms across his chest. "What light can you shed on any of this?"

"We want to catch the guy who killed your husband," Mallard said. "And put him away—keep him from hurting anyone else."

"I know it. I want that too. I'm just not sure I—" Vanessa shook her head and held her hands out in frustration.

"The contents of his stomach circumstantially put Jesse in that restaurant, and we have"—Mallard held up a palm and tipped it to either side—"so so evidence that Egar was there too."

"So, Doyle's out of the picture?" Vanessa asked.

"No one's out of the picture."

"Well, for now we're focused on this guy and what drugs he could get your husband that Doyle could not," said Ganderson.

Vanessa slapped the table. "That's what's so confusing! Jesse didn't do drugs! Oh, he smoked a little weed, but that's barely a crime nowadays. And he drank beer."

"I don't think we're talking about marijuana."

"It just doesn't make sense," Vanessa insisted.

They sat in silence for a few moments.

Finally, Mallard spoke up. "Doyle did say he knows Julius Burrell, but not Jesse, and that Julius had contacted him on behalf of someone else, possibly his father, who was looking for drugs, only they were something he could not procure for this person. So, the person Julius knew was put in touch with…" he pointed to the pile of photographs.

"Colby," Vanessa said.

"Corb. Corb Egar," Ganderson corrected. He ran a palm through his slicked-back hair, and Vanessa made a mental note to avoid shaking his hand—though truth be told, she had been avoiding handshakes whenever possible since COVID.

"And Egar has an alibi for that night," Mallard added. "He was at another restaurant and after-hours club, but his associates, those providing the alibi, are of questionable character."

"You think they're lying?" Vanessa asked, sipping from her coffee.

"These are individuals," Ganderson said, "who are not known for their honesty."

"And yet you believe what they're saying about Jesse wanting drugs."

Ganderson shrugged. "We do have Julius as a source on that."

"Did Doyle say anything else that could shed light on what happened to Jesse?"

The detectives glanced at one another. "He said, 'If this guy knows I gave up his name, he'll chop me into little pieces. And he'll get to me at county and he'll get to me in the upstate penitentiaries…'"

Mallard nodded toward the photographs. "And the shoe fits."

Vanessa shook her head, exasperated. "So, what do you have—a lot of little pieces but not a whole picture."

"I'd say that's pretty accurate," Ganderson agreed.

"And what are you doing about it?" she demanded.

"Everything we can, ma'am," Mallard answered. "We're combing the murder scene and vicinity for a weapon for one thing."

"But so far, the stones and pipe pieces we found in the area show no evidence of being involved in a crime," Ganderson said. "And we have fibers but nothing to match them to—Laila gave us a jacket of Jesse's—"

"Two, in fact," said Mallard.

"One was a hoodie," Ganderson said, "but nothing matched. We also have phone records."

Mallard put a hand on the table and leaned toward Vanessa. "And we're interviewing everyone with any connection to Jesse, Julius, or Doyle."

"But really, you've got nothing."

"To quote Chief Stalwell, nothing *actionable*," Ganderson answered.

"Yet," Mallard added.

• • •

Sarah Turner arrived home exhausted. Interviews were fun, but they were intense. They required focus. She had come to love her job—to love being paid for staying abreast of current events, for translating them into consumable bites, for writing and editing, and for interacting with policy-makers and business shakers downtown. After a lifetime of being treated as a second-class citizen because of her gender, she valued being appreciated as an equal, and speaking up and ensuring her voice was heard when she wasn't. Of course, her job also required attention to advertising, though not, thank goodness, to ad sales. She did have to focus on sports, store openings and closings, and on funerals and obituaries.

She was surprised to find C3—Charles, as she called him—wide awake and sitting in a kitchen chair doing nothing at all when she arrived home.

"You're up late," she mused.

"Can't sleep."

"Lie down and rest."

"Tried that. Can't."

She went to him and put her arms around his neck. She brushed his long, blond hair back with her fingers. "Aww. It'll pass. You'll sleep, eventually."

He reached for her, pulled her close, his head against her breast. "I don't think so. It doesn't feel like I'll ever sleep. Honestly?" He looked up into her eyes. "I want to get high."

Sarah pressed her lips together.

"What?" he asked.

She didn't answer.

"Why are you looking at me like that?"

"I'm trying to decide if your father was right. That you won't make it without really, really tough love."

C3 dropped his hands, pushed Sarah away, and went to the window, which overlooked the busy nighttime street. "My father. My father! My father was no better than me. He just has a successful business, so no one can tell him what to do."

Sarah didn't answer.

"What?

"Was the detox enough?" she asked.

C3 took a deep breath and exhaled with a whoosh, then nodded. "It has to be. I can do this."

"Okay then." She went to him, took his hand, and led him into the bedroom.

• • •

The following afternoon, Miz Liz came by early to stay with the boys, and Vanessa went to the library and found Agatha in the children's section, reading to a group of seven-year-olds—some smiling and eager, others distracted by the colors, sights, and sounds around them; one sullen and defiant.

After the reading, when the children had all gone home with their parents, Vanessa approached. "We need to talk."

Agatha put a finger to her lips and walked to the book stacks. Vanessa followed.

"I had a long talk with the police today, and it seems there's evidence Jesse was involved with drugs."

"Involved how?"

"Trying to get them—and whatever he was using, he had to go up the ladder"—she checked herself—"or down the ladder, I guess, to get them."

Agatha nodded and looked at the floor, but didn't answer.

Vanessa narrowed her eyes. "You knew about this?"

Agatha turned away. When she turned back, she was near tears. "Yes, Jesse was involved with drugs, but it's not what you think."

Vanessa's answering whisper was harsh. "What the hell does that mean?"

"Shhh." A librarian at a desk beyond the stacks sent Agatha a warning look.

But Vanessa raised her voice. "I need to know what he was into and why everyone is keeping it a secret."

Agatha leaned close. "I can't."

"You can't—fuck you can't."

Agatha's shoulders sagged. "Nessa, this is a library, so please keep your voice down. And there's an aspect to this…I, we can't talk about."

Vanessa was done whispering. "Do you know who killed my husband?"

Agatha shook her head. "The drugs aspect…I can't say, but it's nothing to do with you, and it doesn't shed any light on who did this."

"What the fuck, Agatha! What is it with you and Rudy? Are you into something criminal? Were you involved with drugs with my Jesse?"

Agatha grabbed her sister-in-law's upper arm and held it tight. "Do we get to know every aspect of your life with Jesse?"

"But he's dead, Agatha. Murdered—and he was my husband. If you know something about that, I deserve to know!"

・・・

Vanessa left the library angrier and more confused than when she had arrived. She took out her phone.

"Laila? Nessa. Is Julius with you? I'm getting the runaround from just about everyone, and I'm hoping he can clear some things up about his daddy."

Laila answered, her voice steady and firm. "Julius is done talking—done talking to everyone—to cops, to so-called friends, to so-called family."

"C'mon, Laila! We were both married to the man. Don't you want to know—"

But Laila cut her off. "Why should Julius talk to you? You have no idea what he's been through, the pressure the cops have put on him—implying, even accusing him of murdering his own father! Are you kidding?" She was shouting now. "He's out. He's free. We got him out. And yes, his father's dead, and you know what? There's nothing anyone can do about that, so the only thing I have to say is—see ya!"

There was a click as the call was disconnected. Vanessa looked at her phone in disbelief.

• • •

By popular vote, the friends and neighbors of the Burrell and Raines families decided to begin holding regular meetings at private homes. Many agreed that, while Rudy was only too happy to provide free drinks and finger food for everyone, the meetings were an imposition. No one mentioned this to Rudy, lest he take offense and insist on continuing to host the get-togethers.

The first meeting outside of Rudy's was at Lenny Altamont's home on a Sunday afternoon. Lenny owned the auto repair shop where Ferret Wallace worked. Lenny was a cheerful old man with close-cropped reddish hair and skin the color of cherry wood, who appeared to be always on the verge of laughing. His lips were tight, as though holding back a guffaw; his cheekbones were pointed, and his eyes crinkled at the corners with laughter. He and Ferret were like two peas in a pod in that they were upbeat men who enjoyed their work, good food, drink, and the company of friends. Nearly everyone in town brought their cars to Lenny, since he was known for being unfailingly honest in his dealings with customers, often telling them their cars were just fine and not in need of repairs at all—the best possible advertising.

Lenny also loved to garden; his yard was a riot of flowers—crimson dahlias, pink and white roses, and multi-colored lilies, all edged with kale and filled out with tall Queen Anne's lace, whose tiny white flowers looked like nighttime stars. Because he had experienced, able, trusted employees, Lenny could often be seen in his yard at home, tending his flowers, his tomatoes, or peppers, but today he wasn't gardening. He explained that he had offered to host the meeting because he knew Jesse Burrell, as he was the only local mechanic who could work on a Prius, and Jesse had brought his car in on the rare occasions it needed work. Lenny supplied tacos, burritos, iced tea, and beer and sat at the edge of the group, politely listening as updates were shared.

Miz Liz was not present. Except when watching her grandchildren, she had taken to staying at home, resting, and going to her doctors' appointments. Losing her son has devastated her and seemed to have affected her health. To Vanessa, she appeared to have aged ten years in just these last few weeks.

Vanessa was the first to arrive, followed by Agatha and Rudy. She did not speak to them. A barrier seemed to have risen between them, and she felt as though they knew more about Jesse's death than they'd been letting on. Vanessa had no choice but to be confused and upset about this. Instead of talking to them, she strolled around the garden and patio, where the meeting was to take place. Lenny had beautiful stone pavers throughout his yard, surrounded by black mulch and, of course, his manifold flowers and vegetables. The yard was filled with the subtle yet pungent smell of tomato plants.

People had begun arriving, and Vanessa nodded and did her best to smile at them all. She had a stressful moment when Ferret Wallace arrived—a deja vu of sorts. She thought that she had seen him somewhere else, but upon thinking about it she realized that no, she was mistaken. The face she associated with him belonged to someone with longer hair that was parted in the middle and a facial expression so different she was sure it was a different person.

Just then, Charlie Bernelli Jr. arrived. He and Vanessa hugged and shrugged at one another's hesitation, a common reaction nowadays thanks to COVID. They were both vaccinated and were comfortable hugging despite the minor risks. Next to arrive was a surprise—Sarah Turner. Vanessa supposed she was there in her professional capacity as a journalist. She wondered whether those attending would be as open to discussing whatever they knew about the case with Sarah there. She also wondered who had invited Sarah and why.

Dora arrived with Missy, and after greeting everyone, they walked around Lenny's garden, marveling at the beauty and variety of his flowers.

Big and Little Ru arrived, this time with their spouses. Vanessa was delighted to see Dora—they, too, hugged. Elder Reginald Williams was another surprise. He arrived with Willis Thomas, followed by Kelvin and Martine Franklin.

A pleasant, handsome young man with a smooth complexion and puppy dog brown eyes named Teófilo was bringing around a tray of crudítes. Unfailingly polite, he waited to the left of each guest until there was a natural break in their conversation, when he quietly offered his hors d'oeuvres.

Beyond her general level of exhaustion and devastation, Miz Liz's absence on this particular day was for two reasons—she was watching her grandsons, and now that there was confirmation or, at least, strong suspicions that Jesse was involved with drugs beyond marijuana, and was probably dealing with Corb Egar, nobody wanted to burden Miz Liz with what could be even more painful yet unverified information.

Vanessa took charge of the meeting, as she was determined to do as often as she could. She was making a real effort to motivate herself, to go on her errands, to go for walks, to spend quality time with the boys, to work. To stave off depression.

Once she welcomed everyone and thanked Lenny for hosting, she got right to business.

"Does anybody know this Corb Egar? The police showed me a picture—he's a big, bald white guy with a grey beard."

Lenny put a hand up. He was sitting at the far edge of the group. "And a lot of money. He brings his Lamborghini in before he goes on his road rallies. I don't know anything about the drugs, but the man has some serious cars—he's a good customer, too. Nothing bad to say about him."

Willis Thomas had taken off his prosthetic leg and leaned it against his chair. "I heard some things about Egar, but to be honest, I don't want to talk about him out of school. Don't feel it's my place and I don't want to stir the pot."

"I understand," Vanessa said, "but anything anyone knows—you don't have to say it here, but there are channels, private channels." She looked over the crowd before continuing. "There's something about this I just don't understand. I've been led to believe that there was an aspect to my husband's involvement with drugs that is none of my business." She looked at Rudy and Agatha. Rudy tipped his head back and looked at the sky, then clasped his hands together behind his head. Agatha looked away.

"Would anyone care to comment, or to further enlighten us?" She waited, looking at Rudy and Agatha all the while. "I figured. Well, to set the record as straight as I can, I want to say that to my knowledge, my Jesse was not a hard drug user, yet the police and some others seem to be trying to tell me different. I knew my husband. We shared everything. Again, can anybody here tell me different?" She waited. "Well, then. I would like to say a public thank you to Mr. Charles Bernelli for giving me a job and teaching me about proofreading, a skill I'm actually learning and sort of enjoying."

Charlie waved her off. "You're doing a great job. I needed a good proofreader, and now I have one—you're on your way to being a really good one."

Vanessa managed a smile, then grew serious again. "So, what are we going to do about this? Dora, what are the police doing?"

Dora stood up to address the group. "It might sound silly, but they're doing police work, which can take time. They're analyzing all sorts of things that were found in that alley, talking to anyone with any connection to Jesse, scouring the local drug world."

Vanessa looked frustrated. "Well, how 'bout we all try to see what we can learn about this Corb Egar and anything my Jesse had to do with him? Anyone can contact me privately at any time, and I will keep the communication quiet. No need to say anything now."

Ferret Wallace and Teófilo, the waiter, were off to one side, talking quietly; Vanessa gave them a hard look and they stopped.

Again, from the sidelines, Lenny put up his hand. "I just want to respectfully suggest that from the little we've learned here, Egar sounds more dangerous than I was aware of, so I want to urge everyone to be careful."

Elder Reginald Williams stood and addressed the group. "Something we can do is to support this young lady here, and support one another as friends, and as a community. Wouldn't hurt to come to church and pray and give thanks for what we have now and then."

Then Rudy stood up. "I'd like to say that Kelvin and I are putting together a fundraiser to donate to Vanessa and Jesse's boys' college fund."

Vanessa was suddenly in tears. "No! I don't want no charity."

"Believe it or not, we all want to help—if not for you, for your boys, Jesse's boys."

Vanessa began crying harder. She turned away, and Lenny drew attention away from her by beckoning everyone to a large table that offered a spread of tacos and pulled pork sandwiches. The tension soon dissipated, and the meeting became a social gathering.

Chapter 11

The day at the academy had started badly and gotten worse. The morning class was Suicide Ideation Management, a subject that interested Dora, but for some reason the parking lot had been full, so she'd had to find street parking. She wondered if there was a program or presentation in the building, but she didn't wonder for long, because the parking issue caused her to be late to class, a fact that immediately drew her instructor's attention and ire.

She had brought a cheese sandwich for lunch—Swiss and lettuce with a bit of mustard—and as she sat down to eat, she noticed a spot of mold on the bread, which disgusted her and ruined what little respite lunch offered.

Afternoon was O.C. (Pepper) Spray Training, but her instructor, Captain Jason Taub, noticed a few wrinkles in her pants. Dora hated ironing. She thought it was a stupid waste of time. Of course, Taub picked Dora to be his partner and managed to spray her with pepper spray. She was certain he did it because of the wrinkles.

On the way home, she decided to stop by Laila's to see if she could ask Julius about Corb Egar. She texted Vanessa for the address, ignoring the little voice in her head that warned her against such direct involvement with the case.

As she arrived and began looking for parking, she saw a black Mercedes pull up and stop in front of Laila's building. The rear door of the car opened, and Julius got out. Miz Liz had shown Dora his picture on several occasions; she was always showing off her grandbabies, as she called them. Dora's car was in front of the Mercedes, so she could see the driver's face in her rear-view mirror. A hefty-looking bald man with a grey beard. She dismissed the idea of approaching Julius and demanding to know why he was driving around with Corb Egar, and decided she should probably go on to Vanessa's and attempt to speak with Julius another time.

She arrived at Vanessa's apartment to find it in disarray—children's toys were everywhere, and Miz Liz was on the couch, her legs folded beneath her, snoring softly, while the boys played on the floor with model cars and trucks. Liz looked tired and, once awakened, was eager to leave and go back to her apartment, so Dora jumped right in to playing cars and trucks with the boys, trying—but not too hard—to teach them a children's version of the rules of the road.

Dora gave the boys their dinner—chicken with vegetables and rice that had been prepared the prior weekend for Drew, and applesauce for Buster, who was going through a phase where he would eat very little besides applesauce and certain breakfast cereals without milk.

Both boys insisted on staying up to be tucked in by their mother, but Drew faded while Dora was putting on a puppet show with a Kermit Muppet. Buster, however, was another story.

"Gamaliz sunshine!" he crowed, as the puppet show ended.

Dora had no idea what this meant and realized that this was a "be careful what you ask for" moment. She had asked to be a detective—well, here was something to detect. What did Buster want? How could she placate this adamant if exuberant child before his exuberance turned to frustration and then to something many decibels louder?

"Gamaliz sunshine?" Dora repeated, tentatively.

Buster brightened and repeated the phrase several times, then said, "Tashuns! Tashuns!"

Dora thought about the things the boy loved to do—his toys, his bedtime process, and what he might be asking for if not demanding.

"Tashuns. Tashuns..." she ventured, then remembered she had been told the boys loved to sing Motown hits with their Grandma Liz.

"Ohhh." She smiled at Buster. "Want to sing 'Temptations'?"

"Tashuns! Tashuns!"

This took at least as much courage as anything at the academy—she hoped the toddler was a gentle audience, as she took a deep breath and sang the first phrase.

"...sunshine...on a—"

"...kow dee ayye!" He was even on key.

Several minutes later, Dora heard the rattle of the key in the apartment door, followed by a long sigh as Vanessa dropped her keys on the kitchen counter, opened the refrigerator, took out a beer, and popped it open.

"Maaaa!"

Dora walked from the boys' room down the little hallway into the living room, where Vanessa was standing and looking through the day's mail.

"Maaa!"

Vanessa and Dora made eye contact and smiled, each recognizing the other's exhaustion. Vanessa started toward the boys' room and held up a finger, indicating that she would be back and for Dora to wait.

"Busterrrrr!"

Dora took a beer for herself, something Vanessa often insisted she do, and sat down on the couch to wait, listening to the music of mother bonding with son through bedtime singalong. After a while, Vanessa returned to the living room and sat on the couch next to Dora, her smile fading fast.

"How's the proofreading?" Dora began.

"That, actually, is pretty good, but it's the only thing that is." Vanessa let her head loll back and looked at the ceiling, then allowed herself a small smile as she looked at Dora. "I've gotta say, I'm learning a skill that maybe I can make a living at, and Charlie Bernelli is a freakin' saint."

Dora smiled and nodded. "He is a good guy."

Vanessa's little smile disappeared. "But otherwise?" She groaned. "I can't do this anymore!"

"Do what?"

"All of it. Manage the boys on my own, deal with Miz Liz, who is pushing, pushing—always pushing for more information. I mean, I get it. But I don't have information to give her, so maybe she should push the cops, not me. And the cops...they aren't getting anywhere... And what I really can't do is put my head on that pillow without my sweet Jesse looking into my eyes and telling me he loves me like he did every night we were together."

"I get it."

"No you don't—" Vanessa paused, looked at Dora. "Yeah, maybe you do."

"I do. I sleep with a pile of Franny's clothes that still smells a bit like her."

"How do you do it? Tell me."

"A minute at a time. Crying, praying, screaming, failing…" Dora turned her body so she was halfway facing Vanessa. "Let me ask you something—you believe in God, right?"

Vanessa rolled her eyes. "Don't start with God. I already have Elder Reginald pushing God on me. God's not going to bring him back. God's not going to make this pain in my chest I have to live with every day go away. God's not going to raise those boys!"

"I hear you. But please answer my question."

Vanessa couldn't help but laugh. "What was it again?"

"Do you believe in God?"

"Well, I was raised to."

Dora nodded. "I wasn't raised to believe in anything, and in a way, I think it's kind of an advantage. I didn't have a lifetime of sermons staring me in the face when the shit hit the fan."

"What do you mean?"

Dora could see that Vanessa was listening. "When you're told that God heals everything, then something comes along that's so wicked painful that you're like—okay, heal me—and you're not, like instantly healed—that can be daunting. See, we're not told how or when the healing will work. We're not told how long it will take—at what rate we will heal. So, when we're kicked in the gut by life, we look up and say, 'Okay, God. I'm here. Do your thing.' And it doesn't really work like that."

Vanessa was looking at her and nodding. Then she shook her head and half smiled. "Ooh. Now, I feel better."

Dora gently touched Vanessa's arm. "Well, hang on. Because on my darkest day when my sweet darling Francesca was gone and my heart was broken and I was crying in bed, I decided, you know what? God either is, or God isn't."

Vanessa was listening.

"This has nothing to do with anyone else," Dora cautioned. "This is not about what I think you should believe. This is to do with me."

"So, what'd you do?"

"This is what I did. I said, out loud—God I need your help. I don't need a bolt of lightning. I just need you to hold my hand."

"What happened?"

"Not a whole lot."

"So, what's your point?"

"The next day."

"The next day...what?"

"Somehow, the next day I found the strength to put one foot in front of the other again. Just for that day, and I keep doing that."

They sat together in silence for a few long minutes.

Vanessa spoke first. "You think...God was holding your hand?"

Dora looked back at her friend, raised her eyebrows, and shrugged.

• • •

When her academy classes let out the next day, Dora saw that there had been a call from Rudy. *What now,* she thought as she dialed him back from the parking lot.

Rudy answered right away. She could tell from the background noise that he was at work, and she hoped that would keep him from being able to talk—she didn't really want to talk to him. But instead, he told her to hang on while he found a place, probably the back room, where he could talk.

"What?" Dora said, when he came back on.

"I've gotta try one more time to get you to stop what you're doing."

"What are you talking about? What do you have to hide? Come on—we're friends, or we were!"

"It's not about hiding. Someone's going to get hurt."

"So…you're threatening me now? Are you kidding?"

"I'm not saying that."

"I think you are. You're saying I'm going to get hurt."

"I didn't say that."

"You know I like puzzles and riddles and shit, but how 'bout being straight with me."

"That's the problem. What you're trying to find out, it's not something you need to find out. It's not going to help Jesse. What it will do is hurt people."

"Try me. Come on, Rudy. Your wife feels this way too? She was acting as weird as you at that Altamont guy's house."

"Dora, she's with me. Agatha feels the same as I do. You do not know what you're messing with. We're with you as far as solving the murder, but you don't want to know what Jesse was involved in, because it's going to hurt people."

"So, tell me this—the people it's going to hurt…you're not talking about me?"

"Correct."

"Huh. So…is it going to hurt you?"

"No more than it already has."

"And Agatha?"

"This isn't a question-and-answer game. This isn't a game at all. Let me tell you something. This isn't just about Jesse—he's gone. There's other people here."

"You mean his kids, right? And Nessa?"

"You know I love you, Dora, right?"

"Actually, no. I did not know that, but it's good to know, I guess…"

"Well, one of my favorite qualities in you is that you have only two gears—one and a thousand."

"Yeah, that sort of is me, I guess."

"Well, not today."

"What do you mean? You're going around in circles when all I'm trying to do is solve Jesse's murder. There's nothing else, zero, I care about here."

"Now is not the time for going from one to a thousand. You're my friend. You've gotta trust me. Back. The. Fuck. Off. People you care about will be better off. And if you don't, you'll be hurting them. It'll be on you."

She was about to answer him, but Rudy was gone.

Chapter 12

C3 was on his way to the taxi stand to apply for a job. He had been thinking about driving Uber but wanted to see what the taxi stand offered, so he could compare. He had loved his job—he knew only too well about addiction, so being able to put that knowledge to use helping someone was a marvelous thing that helped him, the other person, and society at large. Unfortunately, he was at least temporarily unable to work at the counseling center, having been told that if he stayed clean for a while—the timeframe was not discussed, but he suspected they meant a year—he might be able to regain his job.

Meanwhile, he did his best to think of other things. He was relieved that Sarah continued to support him and allowed their relationship to remain. She offered a simple explanation: she loved him. Losing his job and Sarah would have been too much. He hoped he would prove worthy of her trust.

He parked on the street around the corner from the train station and went over to the little hut used as a taxi stand. An old acquaintance named Freddie was working at a desk.

"Hey now!" Freddie exclaimed, with his trademark vigor.

"Whatsup, Fred?"

"Looking for work?"

He nodded, then was surprised to hear himself ask, "Can you get?" *Where did that come from?*

Freddie answered, "Depends what you want."

"Oxys." His mouth seemed to have taken on a life of its own.

"Maybe."

"Are they real?" C3 asked.

"Oh, yeah! Listen, come back to the train station during rush hour, and you'll see a guy playing a guitar for money, with the case open. Tell him Freddie sent you. He'll know."

"What's his name?" C3 asked, having forgotten about the possible job.

"Kelvin. Kelvin Franklin."

A Gathering Storm   David E. Feldman

...

The entire week at the academy had been dedicated to a wide range of police procedures, some of which overlapped. Lessons were taught, studied, and practiced over and over, including Policing the Community, Domestic Violence, Crimes in Progress, Dealing with Animals, Motor Vehicle Law Enforcement, Radar Operation, High and Low Risk Vehicle Stops, Gang Violence, and Accident Investigations.

By the end of the week, everyone was relieved and looking forward to the weekend. Parking lot socializing at the end of each day had grown friendlier as the cadets bonded over their shared sense of overwhelm and accomplishment. The little cadre that had met because they parked in the same area that first day had begun to grow as friends, and Dora had come to look forward to seeing Tina, Racquel, and Eve, and sharing their observations about the classes, instructors, challenges, and other recruits. Most of the bullying and sexism had grown out of the discomfort and anxiety of some of the less secure among the cadets—some of whom seemed to have matured and grown out of that phase, while a few, like Kenny Moore, decided not to continue with their training and left the program entirely. Nearly everyone developed a shared sense of responsibility for the public's safety and well-being.

Skinny Aldridge had lost the spare tire around his middle, and the wise guy grin of "Smiling" Wayne Sylvester had all but disappeared.

Dora had been walking with the other three women and sharing their anticipation of hell week, which would be the following week. As she pressed the key fob and approached the turbo, a thought occurred to her, and she turned.

"Wait up."

The women had begun to go their separate ways, but now stopped and turned. "Have any of you ever heard the name Corb Egar?"

The friends looked at one another—all shook their heads.

"My mom shops at Egar's Meats in Hempstead," Eve volunteered. "Do you think it's the same Egar?"

"Only one way to find out. Thanks." Dora got into the car, started the engine, and headed toward Hempstead.

Egar's Meats was a small store that sold a variety of deli-style meat, prepared meat products, canned goods, fresh pastries, and beverages. Dora went in and bought a six pack of Rolling Rock for later that evening. She did not see anyone who could have been Egar there, but there was a young man behind the counter who looked like a younger version of the man—he had the same heavy brow and dark eyes, but had hair on his head and a brown rather than gray beard.

Later, when Vanessa returned home from work, Dora explained what she had seen. "Thanks for checking him out," Vanessa said, as she took her phone from her pocketbook and pressed a number. "Hi, Detective? Vanessa Burrell. You've said if I ever wanted to talk … Well, I'd like to come by in a little while."

She hung up and turned back to Dora. "I'm going over to talk to the Goose and Gander about this guy. I'll try not to wake you when I get back."

・・・

Fifteen minutes later, Vanessa pulled into a parking space on the street alongside the police station, went inside and explained to the officer at the front desk who she was and why she was there.

"Yes, Mrs. Burrell. I remember you." Sergeant Morse smiled and picked up a phone, then nodded to her. "Detective Mallard will be right out."

"Thank you."

After a few moments, the door from the lobby to the police station's interior was held open by Detective Mallard, who led Vanessa to his and Detective Ganderson's desks. Ganderson looked up, smiled at Vanessa, and stood.

"Can I get you coffee, Mrs. Burrell?"

She shook her head. "Not at this hour, and anyway, I can't stay, but I wanted to pass along something."

He beckoned her to the conference room. Mallard followed.

Once she was seated, the two detectives took their seats. "What have you got?" Ganderson asked.

"This Egar guy—does he have anything to do with Egar's Meats in Hempstead?"

Ganderson nodded. "He owns it. Difficult business to run with all the competition from supermarket deli departments nowadays."

Mallard grinned. "Unless you're a violent criminal—a fact that makes competition"—he made a "poof" gesture, opening the fingers of both hands—"disappear, like magic."

"Have you spoken to him?"

The detectives looked at one another. "We will deal with him if and when the time and circumstance are right," Ganderson answered.

Vanessa took a deep breath. "So, what have you been doing about solving my husband's murder?"

Mallard sat back in his chair, tipped his head back, raised an eyebrow, and began counting off on his fingers. "We've spoken to everyone who was at the family party, quite a few people at your late husband's job, including both teachers and students, a number of his acquaintances on social media, and we've questioned everyone who works at The Elegant Lagoon—including a few people with priors. We obtained a search warrant and searched the premises, and we've received the lab reports for many of the items removed from the crime scene."

Vanessa held out a hand, palm up. "And?"

"If you really want to know—there was some blood on a fence post and two stones we retrieved, but we have yet to find a murder weapon."

"Have you looked beyond the crime scene?"

"We have and we're still looking."

"Let me go on," Mallard insisted, still counting on his fingers. "We've scoured the neighborhood for video from that night—and no, we did not find any. We've also looked into delivery people at the restaurant, and cross-referenced them with associates who work for or had occasion to know Mr. Egar—both professional and personal."

"And?"

Ganderson answered. "When we have something definitive to share with you, Ms. Burrell, we will give you a call."

"Mrs. Burrell. Mrs."

"I apologize. Mrs. Burrell."

Now it was Ganderson's turn to elaborate. "There's something else. While Egar is a step up the criminal food chain from Doyle, he's not at the top. While he may indeed have had the answers your husband was looking for, and he may prove to be his killer or to have ordered his death, we believe that there is someone above Egar who would have had to sign off."

"Sign off?"

"To kill someone or to have someone killed would have required approval from upstream, if not their actual involvement."

"So? Who is this person … upstream?"

"We don't know."

She shook her head, grimacing. She could feel the tears coming, as they so often did. "Haven't you gotten anywhere?"

Mallard continued for his partner. "We've been trying to catch and convict Egar and to find out who his superior is, as well as who that don's Luca Brasi is, for quite some time."

"Actually, Mrs. Burrell," Ganderson said, more gently now, "we've been able to learn a few things from employees at the restaurant who have criminal records."

"And who are on parole, in fact," said Mallard. "Amazing how forthcoming and helpful some people can be when you point out a thing or two." He grinned at Ganderson, who nodded.

"Right, when you point out what's in their best interest."

"So?" Vanessa said.

"We've confirmed that Jesse was there, and that he ate a small meal with Egar, and that he exited through the front—"

"Not the back, into the alley?"

"Through the front, where he was met by another individual, we've been told, with whom he argued, and who then followed him around back and into the alley."

"He argued with someone? Out front? And there's no video?"

"Not that we've identified," said Ganderson. "But we believe that person to be the don's personal killer—someone expert in multiple methods of murder."

"The restaurant's cameras are not working at the moment, and we have found no cameras from neighboring businesses that show The Lagoon's property."

Vanessa was shaking her head. Her lower lip curled and she blew air upward, fluttering her bangs. "So, none of the cigarettes or beer cans or whatever else you found in that alley tells you anything?"

"There's DNA there, but we have nothing to match it with at this time," Ganderson explained.

"None of the DNA belongs to Egar?"

"No, ma'am, but the investigation is ongoing," Mallard said, with an air of finality.

• • •

When people wanted to buy drugs in Beach City, unless they knew someone with whom they could deal directly, either at that person's home or via delivery, they went to any of several street corners around town. Alleys like the one behind The Elegant Lagoon, which was now off limits, were the rare exceptions because they lacked escape routes. The alleys were more often used for drug consumption and drinking, especially for those who were under age, who could not use drugs or drink at home.

C3 met Kelvin Franklin under a large oak tree on a street corner in a part of town well known enough for drug-related activity. A person could go there and have a reasonable expectation of finding what they wanted. He handed over his money, was given a vial containing ten pills, and the transaction was complete. He took two of the pills, each of which were five milligrams of oxycodone, with water in his car, and drove back home.

Sarah was sitting on a chair in the living room, staring sadly at the door, so she was the first sight he saw when he came in. He walked right past her, went into the bedroom, and closed the door. He knew that she knew, and that he knew better, but the lure of the pills was too strong. He would make up his mind to stop, but when confronted with his own craving, he inevitably gave in. The addiction was stronger than him. He knew that from his years spent working in the field. He had tried to go back to his meetings, but his pride got in the way. Those people thought of him as a success, as a drug counselor, as being clean and sober and having a deep knowledge of the steps and traditions of twelve step programs. They thought of him as a model of recovery, and he was anything but that—and that awareness was crushing him.

He was a failure. He knew it, and he was sure others did too, and this knowledge drove him further into the disease. He suspected his father was right—he needed tough love. He needed boundaries. He needed to be locked away until this thing passed. Quite possibly, he needed to die.

Who was he kidding? He had no idea what he needed. His ideas about what he needed were what had gotten him into this mess. He lay on his bed, covered his face with his hands, and moaned.

He heard the door open and felt Sarah's weight on the bed. She tried to pull his hands away from his face, but he resisted. He didn't want to look at her. He didn't deserve her.

She lay next to him, rubbing his arm with her hand.

"I'm not leaving you. I'm staying. You're a wonderful man—you're my man, and I love you."

• • •

Miz Liz had practically ordered Vanessa to call a meeting of the friends at her home. LaChance and Keisha Williams were there, both Big and Little Ru were there sans spouses, along with Lenny Altamont and Ferret Wallace, and the Franklins—Kelvin and Martine—though they arrived late, as they were bringing food—roasted chicken, gravy, biscuits, and sweet potatoes. Dora was there; Missy was not, as she was subbing for Agatha at the library. Agatha had come, but Rudy was absent, as he was home with Samuel.

There had been discussion about finding someone to watch Drew and Buster, but everyone agreed to do their best to talk around the details of the meeting so as to shield the boys from the awareness that the meeting was for the purpose of finding out who murdered their daddy.

Miz Liz was furious, something of a relief to the family and friends, as she had recently seemed so beaten down by Jesse's death.

Last to arrive were the two detectives, and if looks could kill, Miz Liz would have been arrested for murder. Vanessa had asked them to come without seeking Miz Liz's permission, hoping to provide the group with some answers.

"Why don't you all take some food and find seats before we begin," Miz Liz suggested, and for ten minutes people busied themselves doing exactly that.

"Now then," she began, once everyone was seated. "I see we have our two detectives joining us. I just want to say, for the record, that I don't believe you folks are doing enough to catch my boy's killer. I think you all are stonewalling. So, now that you're here"—she cast an angry eye at Vanessa—"why don't you tell us what you're doing, if there's anything to tell."

"Happy to," said Mallard as he rose to his feet, followed by Ganderson. They made their way between knees and backs of chairs to the front of the room.

Mallard started pacing and bouncing on his toes. He was wearing what looked like a new, beautifully tailored, green three-piece suit with a yellow tie. "The main thing we're doing is pounding the pavement," Mallard began. Miz Liz scoffed. "Whatever you think, and whatever you've seen on TV, that's what real police work is about. Hard work. We talk to everyone in the neighborhood and at the restaurant, and find out what they have to say and what they heard."

"What'd they say?" Little Ru asked.

Ganderson stepped forward. "Two people say they heard an argument—someone pleading—at about midnight, though they could not be certain of the time."

Miz Liz shook her head and muttered something unintelligible.

"Takes two to argue," said LaChance Williams.

"Well, that's as much as we know about what was said. Loud voices, was the way it was described, and pleading." Ganderson took a step back and clasped his hands behind his back.

"Someone reported seeing what they thought was a Lamborghini, which actually makes us think Egar was not responsible," Mallard said.

"Why is that?" Miz Liz demanded. "He owns one, doesn't he? Who else around here has one of those?"

"Well, that's just it," Mallard explained. "You're right, ma'am. No one else around here owns one, and that's a pretty noticeable car. Would you drive one to a planned murder?"

"Maybe it wasn't planned," said Big Ru.

"Maybe he was on drugs and wasn't thinking straight," Liz continued. "That's Egar's thing, right? Drugs?"

Ganderson stepped forward. "We are considering all possibilities, but a claimed sighting of a car doesn't—"

"And let me ask you this." Miz Liz stood up, pointing a finger at the police officers. "Why don't you compare fingerprints from that alleyway to fingerprints on the dinnerware at Lagoon?"

Ganderson kept his voice level and deliberate. "Cops on TV apparently have unlimited budgets, and I suspect they wash the cutlery at the restaurant. And anyway, we can't just examine everything we find for forensic evidence."

"Well, then," Miz Liz continued, "prints belonging to the suspects."

Ganderson remained expressionless. "We are currently working up and vetting a list of suspects."

"Ha! You don't have suspects!"

Ganderson's expression hardened, his lips pressed together. "We can't fingerprint everything belonging to everyone indiscriminately."

"Maybe if they were white…"

"Nothing to do with color. No, ma'am, and even if we did—there's a wait to do such extensive forensics, and when we do—when they do—it's going to take a few days. We rely on out-of-town labs to supplement, when the requests are this extensive."

Mallard nodded. "And do you know what causes the backup at police labs? Drugs. Pills, OxyContin, Percocet, fentanyl, crystal meth, heroin, morphine, PCP, angel dust, ecstasy, MDMA…"

"And if we have to wait to examine forensic evidence, the sample can be degraded, or it might be handled improperly. It's not the well-oiled machine you see on TV. More often than not, it's a shitshow."

Miz Liz gave a bitter smile. "Whose fault is that?" She shook her head, sat down, and turned away. "Excuses…"

Big Ru spoke up. "Want to get things done and done fast at the police department? Go to traffic division—they have the clout. They bring in the money."

"Now you're talking sense," Liz said, still facing away.

• • •

The next day at the police academy, Dora learned about and practiced with a security holster, which made taking the weapon from an officer all but impossible. Upon placing the weapon in the holster, the device automatically locked the weapon inside. Releasing the weapon required only the pressing of a lever on the inside of the holster, where it faced her body. She and the rest of the class practiced holstering and unholstering their weapons several dozen times, until the process was intuitive.

The class was also taught to use a universal speed loader that made loading the 9mm SIG Sauer P226 much faster and easier and reduced finger soreness. Technique, consistency, and, of course, speed were markedly increased with the device, which would naturally lead to greater effectiveness and safety in the field.

During the hand-to-hand part of the afternoon, the class was taught to use mini flashlights for pain compliance. These little devices were slightly longer than a roll of quarters, and were used in much the same way. They were grasped in the fist and their weight was added to the strike. Because they were longer than a roll of quarters, they protruded from Dora's hand, though not the hands of some of the larger men—and could be used as striking implements. The larger mag-type lights were also used for striking, though these were not part of the day's lesson.

She learned to test for alcohol consumption using the person's horizontal gaze nystagmus (HGN), a standard field sobriety test in which the individual was asked to track the movements of a light shone in their eyes. Jerky motion of the eyeball indicated a degree of alcohol consumption.

In the parking lot at the end of the day, each of them shared a similar story.

"You guys up for hell week next week?" Wayne Sylvester asked.

"Does it matter?" Dora answered.

"Did they tell you we have to allow ourselves to be pepper sprayed in the eyes?" Racquel wanted to know, looking at each of them. Everyone nodded.

"Shit," Dora said. She was concerned about her ability to self-govern her reactions to attacks, something that had been a challenge in the past. She had overcome childhood trauma by going right at it, with extreme intensity, often violence. If someone was foolish enough to attack her, all bets were off. She had always been willing to risk arrest or injury when acting in her own self-defense. Overcoming that instinct and allowing herself to be attacked with a weapon she knew to be incapacitating would be a challenging test of her willpower. There was no point in worrying about it now, though, as hell week was next week, not today.

But on Monday of the following week, there was no apparent indication that the week would be any different from any other week, except that Ganderson showed up with Lieutenant Trask and explained to Dora's first instructor, Lieutenant Fulman, that Ellison would be returned as soon as they were done with her.

Dora followed Ganderson and Trask to an empty classroom, where they sat down at a computer. Trask logged into the system and brought up a somewhat blurry video of what appeared to be the interior of one of the major chain drugstores.

"Tell me what you see," Ganderson instructed, as Mallard arrived wearing a Burberry wool mohair suit that was probably a size too small. He flexed his shoulders as Ganderson asked, "Did you take care of—"

"Done," Mallard confirmed, rolling his shoulders back the other way.

They watched the video together. It was shot from above and appeared to be of an empty, darkened store.

"Wait for it," Trask advised, as she sped up the video. In the background, flashes of light and shadow danced across the screen until a shape darted into and then out of view.

"There he is," Ganderson said.

"Got it," Trask agreed, clearing her throat, and reversed the video and replayed the segment, which showed a masked person, with a body shape that appeared to be male, walking into view and glancing at the camera. The video was black and white and not very clear, and the person was wearing a hooded sweatshirt, dark pants that might have been jeans, boots, and gloves.

"Okay, now back it up," Ganderson said. "That's it, a couple more frames. There—freeze it. No, you went too far, back it up. Okay. Stop! Good." Ganderson stepped back, giving Dora room.

"Tell me what you see."

Dora scanned the image. "Well, a burglary obviously."

"What else?"

"I think it's at a drugstore—a closed drugstore."

Trask coughed as Mallard explained. "It seems to be one of a series of drugstore burglaries that have occurred in the southwest part of the county during the last, oh, five or six weeks. We have other video, but this is the best of the bunch."

Ganderson was riveted to the screen. "What else?"

Dora shook her head. "No way to tell who this is. Guy in a mask, a sweatshirt…"

"Ah! Ah! Trask—zoom in on the left chest."

They waited.

"A logo," Dora said. "Something with a C. What is it?"

"Increase zoom." Ganderson turned from the screen to Dora. "What's it say?"

She looked more closely at the blurry image. She wanted to be sure before she spoke. Finally, she was. "Columbia."

• • •

After leaving the academy that evening, Dora mulled over whether or not she ought to call Vanessa. Finally, she dialed. Jesse was gone. What was to be gained from keeping her knowledge of this video from Vanessa?

"Dora?"

"Hey. I have some information. I hope you're sitting down. You're not going to like it."

"Tell me. What difference does it make if I like it?"

"The police think that Jesse might have been involved in at least one recent drugstore burglary."

"Burglary? First drug deals, now burglaries? Seems like now that my Jesse's gone, his reputation is getting worse every day."

"Let me rephrase. Today I saw a video of a drugstore burglary, and the police are wondering whether the burglar is Jesse."

"You saw the video—was it him?"

"The guy was wearing a mask."

"Why do they think it was him?"

"Well, they're considering the possibility, since they have information that he was searching out drugs beyond what's available on the street."

"Uh huh. Pretty flimsy reason."

"So, let me ask you—did Jesse go to college?"

"He did two years at Nassau Community."

"Not Columbia?"

"Columbia? God, no."

Dora frowned. "What about his teaching master's?"

"He did the New York Teaching Fellows program—where you go to school while you start teaching. You get a job and a more or less free education."

Dora's eyebrows rose. "Wow. I didn't know about that."

"Why do you ask?"

"The burglar was wearing a Columbia jacket."

"Ah, well, no—he did not go to Columbia. Listen, Buster's yelling for me. Got to go. There's probably applesauce all over the kitchen by now."

Chapter 13

As luck would have it, on Tuesday at 5:30 a.m., when Dora was leaving for the academy, the temperature had already reached 92 degrees. That day and those that followed were filled with pushups, sit-ups, squat thrusts, and running. Lots and lots of running.

Hell week had arrived

Dora was accustomed to punishing her body and was confident that she would not only survive hell week, but excel. And she did. Her training at Shay's MMA had prepared her for extreme physicality and cardio—there is nothing like the extra level of intensity that comes from having to move on your feet while actually fighting another human being. Running and moving around a ring require fitness, but when the fight element is added, the adrenaline rush of fear—fight, flight, or freeze—the extreme stress, the cortisol that pours into a person's system, quickly leads the uninitiated to exhaustion.

Dora was used to that. She *enjoyed* that, and now that Franny had been killed, this kind of violent physical exertion was a kind of comfort, a distraction, perhaps even a dissociation, that allowed her to engage with life without the extreme grief that so often overwhelmed her. She didn't have to consciously dwell on Franny's death—the grief took her over and filled her up. It came looking for her and found her—she didn't have to go looking for it.

The running, the physical exercises, were not a problem. But something else was.

Hell week included an element of hazing that was officially banned. Officially, hazing was off limits, but one or two of the instructors introduced endurance exercises that ostensibly were meant to simulate challenges that might occur in the course of police work. More accurately, these exercises were payback for hazing these particular instructors had been forced to endure, once upon a time. Sadism, passed down from a few members of one graduating class to the next. Not the majority of instructors, but a few, influential rogue individuals reveled in corralling recruits for a walk, or sprint, down memory lane. Sprinting while blindfolded was one such exercise. Being handcuffed, blindfolded and put in a room filled with tear gas, in which the key was hidden, was another. Such exercises were off limits, but were given sometimes to cadets who were perceived to have discipline problems.

Dora was one such cadet. She had a penchant for sarcasm, bordering, she had been told, on insubordination.

She did not like being ordered around for the sake of being ordered around. She did not like being abused. She had lived through enough abuse, extremely violent abuse, as a child. She had watched her mother be a helpless victim of abuse and, as a small child, had tried to do something about it. Unsuccessfully.

And the guilt she felt over her inability to save her mother had haunted her all her life. To this day, she was unable to rid herself of a deep, even cellular belief that she had been somehow responsible for her mother's pain —and for her own—that they both had endured at her father's hands. He had beaten her and screamed at her until he was too exhausted to lift his hand.

Hell week brought all that back.

Coughing and crying, she found the key in the gas-filled room, but out of that exercise, that forbidden hazing, came an unbidden, involuntary intention and obsession for revenge. She did not consciously want revenge, but the need for it welled up inside her, until it found release.

On the third day of hell week, she found herself in a room with Sergeant Kontaxis and two other instructors, who quickly surrounded, then attacked her.

She did not want to strike an instructor and be thrown out of the program, so she waited; she wanted to be sure of their intentions and make her best decision as to what was expected of her. On some level, she must have known that she would not allow herself to be violently abused, and if the academy required that of her—the chips would have to fall where they may.

Kontaxis leaped at her, and suddenly, the years fell away, and it was twenty years earlier and she could hear her mother whimpering in the corner of the living room, cowering on one knee, both hands shielding her face, while her father slapped her mother with brutal, heavy hands and little Deborah—she was Deborah then—hurled herself at his legs.

"Fuck! Fuck!" Kontaxis was screaming. "What're you—yahhhhhhh!"

She was suddenly aware that Kontaxis was on the floor, his hands over his left eye. One of the other instructors was unconscious, the side of his face quickly swelling and turning purple, while the remaining instructor was bending over Kontaxis while looking at her and yelling, "Whoa! Whoa! Whoa!"

An hour later, she was home and sipping a beer, waiting to be told what would be done with her, given such violent insubordination. She had tried to explain what had happened, but the instructors involved denied her version of events, which, she claimed, had been part of her hell week, but no one else's as far as she knew.

She had talked back a few times—she hadn't meant to. Her backtalk had come out of her, and so she had been told to stay home the following day; the higher-ups at the academy had to decide what to do with her.

· · ·

Vanessa's phone rang. "Laila?"

"Did the cops call you to ask about a jacket?"

"Well, not exactly. I did learn that they saw a jacket on someone in a video of a drugstore robbery—but no, they didn't call me. At least, not yet."

"They asked if Julius has a jacket with a Columbia logo on it—you know, from the outerwear company?"

"Oh, shit. Jesse has—had—a jacket like that. Gotta go, Laila."

She hung up and ran upstairs to her bedroom, which had been their bedroom, and went through the shirts and jackets on the hangers on his side of the closet. No Columbia jacket. She went to the coat closet, just inside the front door. No jacket. She went into the laundry room and looked around.

No jacket.

• • •

The following morning, at a few minutes after ten, the call came. Dora was strongly advised to quit. To resign. Technically, she could stay if she wanted to, but would spend at least her first two years on traffic duty—which was not all that uncommon, but it would probably be eight years before she made detective, if she ever did, which was unlikely. Unofficially, she was told that her nice red Subaru turbo would probably garner more than its share of parking tickets and moving violations, and would be towed at least a few times and perhaps accidentally dropped off the tow hooks once or twice.

She resigned, then went home and drank three beers and two scotches before calling Missy, but her call rang seven times and went to voicemail. She didn't have the heart to leave a message. She knew where the key was.

She was choking back tears by the time she arrived at Missy's building, parked, retrieved the spare key, and let herself in.

Comfort let out two barks that were part panicked shrieks, then stopped when he saw it was Dora. She entered the apartment and lay down on the living room carpet with her cheek to the floor. Comfort lay down next to her with his head also to the floor, mimicking her posture. He understood. She covered the back of his head with her hand and allowed herself to feel the tightness in her chest, which spread to her throat, and left her body as tears from her eyes.

"I can't believe it," she said to Comfort. "They tell you over and over to just not quit, and...and I quit."

Several hours later, she was telling Missy the same thing.

"This wasn't your fault," her friend insisted.

"How come nobody else quit?"

Missy wrinkled her forehead. "Because they're asshole lemmings. They'd follow the instructor off a cliff."

"Maybe I need a little more of that."

Missy shook her head. "You wouldn't be you if you were like that. You're an independent. An original. You're anything but a follower."

Dora managed a bit of a smile. "Well, I agree with that."

"Please don't give yourself a hard time about this." Missy looked into her eyes, and Dora could feel how genuine her sentiments were.

"I have some career decisions to make."

"Not today," Missy urged. "Don't make them today." She bent over Dora and kissed her gently on the lips. Dora held the kiss, and neither added to it nor took from it. She just let it be the short, sweet kiss it was.

"Okay, then," Dora said.

Her cell phone rang. She took it from her pocket and looked at the caller I.D., then pushed the accept button. "What's up, Vanessa?"

"I found it."

"What?"

"The jacket—with the Columbia logo. He had buried it at the bottom of my closet—not his closet. Mine."

"Huh. So, he did rob the drugstore—or, as I'm sure the cops will say, he could have robbed the drugstore, but it's not a definite since there are probably plenty of similar jackets out there. I suggest, Vanessa, that you call Detective Ganderson in the morning and let him know."

"I'll do that." Vanessa sighed and ended the call.

Dora looked at Missy. "Gotta tell you something."

"Okay," Missy said.

"You've got one seriously cool dog."

Missy laughed. "That I do. Listen"—her expression turned serious—"why not stay with me tonight—in my room?"

Dora didn't answer, just looked at her. Missy held up a hand.

"Hear me out."

"I'm listening."

"I have absolute and utter respect for you and Franny, and I have no..." She was suddenly at a loss for words.

Dora smiled, sat up and folded her arms. "No ... what?"

"Designs on taking her place."

"Good, 'cause no one could."

"I know that. I'm me. But here's the question. What would she say about what happened at the academy, and you being here?"

Dora thought about this. "I ask myself a lot about what Franny would say about this or that and, frankly, I don't know. She went through the academy and was a very good police officer. She used to surprise me. I couldn't predict her when she was alive."

"She did want whatever was in your best interest. Whatever protected you, comforted you, loved you—"

"All true."

"So, stay here."

Dora looked down. "I'm not sure I can do that."

"Sleep in the bed," Missy insisted. "I'll take the couch."

"I can't do that to you."

"You're not. I'm doing it, and I'm doing it because I want to."

"Um, well...."

• • •

The next morning, Missy brought a tray with two cups of coffee and two blueberry muffins into the bedroom, set it on the bed, and poured for each of them.

"So, I have a question I'm wondering if you could ask the Goose or the Gander," said Missy.

"Okay."

"What exactly was stolen from the drugstore?"

Dora shrugged. "I'm guessing pain meds—oxy, Percocet—that sort of thing."

"Don't guess. Find out."

"Okay, I'll try. Why, though?"

"A few things came together for me last night."

Dora gave a rueful smile. "You mean while I was falling apart?"

"You weren't falling apart. You were doing what you had to do. You are who you are."

"I am who I am." Dora waited. "Want to tell me what those things are?"

"Not yet. Well, I'll tell you one of them. It was something you told me, a while back. That Vanessa said she didn't know her husband anymore. He was spending a lot of time at the library. I'm actually pretty sure I remember him being there, and I remember something he asked me while I was working in Reference. But let's wait, since I'm nowhere near sure about this. Can you look into it—what was stolen, I mean?"

"Sure, if they'll tell me, and I'm not sure they will. I was only a cadet. Now I'm not even that. I'm not even with the damn academy! I'm *persona non grata*."

Missy hesitated. "I wonder what the Goose and the Gander will think of that."

Two and a half cups of coffee later, Dora summoned the energy, courage, and motivation to call the police station and ask for either of the detective pair.

Moments later, Mallard picked up.

"Is this the cadet who gave Scott Kontaxis what's been coming to him for nine years?"

"I'm not a cadet," Dora answered.

"Hah!" Mallard roared. "But you should be!"

"You mean that?"

"Damned right. All well and good to churn out those who can pass the class, but leaders are a whole other thing—and you, girl, are a natural leader, if ever I saw one!"

"Well, that means a lot to me. Would you mind stopping by Chief Stalwell's office and telling him that?"

"Sorry, but this isn't something the chief can reverse. They run their own fiefdom over there. You showed up their guys—a girl, no less. They won't take you back. They'll label you as dirty—a cheat, but at least take my word that I think you'd be a great cop. Hell, you'd probably be great at anything you really wanted to do."

Dora sighed. "Well, thanks."

"So, what's up?"

"First of all—turns out Jesse did have a Columbia jacket."

"I know. I spoke with Vanessa Burrell over an hour ago."

"Great. Also, I was wondering if you had a list of what was stolen from the drugstore."

"Why?"

"Listen, if you can't tell me, it's fine. We have a theory."

"We?"

"Just…can you look into it?"

"I'll see what I can do."

• • •

She went for a long walk on the beach with Missy, and found the salty ocean breeze and chilly water on her feet invigorating. They walked along the water's edge, carrying their shoes, careful to step away from the jellyfish. The stinging creatures littered the shallows every year beginning the second week of August.

"I'd like you to give this some thought."

"What?"

"Your future."

Dora bent to pick up a particularly beautiful gray scalloped shell.

"You think I haven't been thinking about my future? Are you kidding?"

"I think you've been freaking out, but not necessarily thinking. At least not thinking clearly."

"How do you know?" Dora's voice had an edge to it.

"Easy. Easy. I *don't* know. Maybe you've been mapping out a coherent, cohesive, utterly sane plan."

Dora stopped walking. Missy stopped too, and looked back. "What?"

"Enough with the sarcasm."

"Who's being sarcastic? I'll help you." Missy grinned and held her arms out to either side, palms forward. "I'm a research professional! We can research your future!"

Dora was about to answer when her phone rang.

"Dora? Mallard. I have that list. I'm going to spell each item—better yet, I'll read them, then text them to you. That okay?"

"Sure."

"Oh, and I was told to be careful with what I shared. I'm told I've been a little too free with information, and I think that was meant to mean you. So, you didn't get this from me."

"I'm sure it was, and no, I didn't."

"But I'll tell you what. They'll never admit it, but they are loving what you did to Kontaxis here at the station—only, don't tell anyone I told you that. And I mean not a soul. He was his own brand of renegade and he had it in for you. I know it's too little too late, but there it is."

Dora laughed. "You're making my day."

"Here's the list. Oxycodone—the only one I've ever heard of, along with aprepitant, trametinib, durvalumab and dabrafenib and osimertinib."

"Yeah, you'd better text those."

"They're coming."

A moment later, Dora sat down next to Missy on a jetty and showed her the names.

• • •

Dora spent the late morning and early afternoon trying not to feel sorry for herself. She knew that nothing good would come of having nothing to do. Idle hands… She drove to City Hall, thinking she might ask for her old sanitation job, but she couldn't bring herself to enter the building and face John, the front desk concierge, or anyone else she knew in the building. She had failed and they would probably know it by now.

Instead, she went over to the Starbucks that was a block from City Hall and had another coffee. She had really wanted to be a police officer. She had been so sure it had been the right career choice, given her love for solving criminal cases and bringing offenders to justice. Even if she could bring herself to enter the building, she didn't think she could go back to tipping garbage. What else could she do? She had never considered the question and had no idea what the answer might be.

Her phone rang. She saw that the caller was the Beach City Library—probably Missy calling from work.

She answered.

"Hey there," Missy said, too cheerfully for Dora to appreciate.

"Hey yourself."

"I don't like the sound of that."

"The sound of what?"

"You sound down."

"I am down. I just lost my career—a career I really wanted—because I didn't have the self-control to get through an aspect of my job training."

"Not the way I see it. I don't think this was the right fit for you. You might think you wanted to be a police officer, but you didn't want to be ordered around and hassled, which would have been part of the deal. I know you, Dora—at least, I have for a little while—and I'm pretty sure you would have been unhappy if you completed the academy and joined the force. You're too much of a free spirit."

Dora didn't answer.

"You there?"

"I'm here. I don't know about free spirit, but I sure am free."

"So, I have some pretty interesting information about the drugs that were stolen. All except the oxy are off-label drugs that fight cancer that's resistant to conventional therapy. They are not likely to be prescribed because many doctors don't know about them."

Dora digested this. "So…you think Jesse was researching these drugs at the library."

"I do."

"I think we need to talk to Vanessa and maybe Rudy and Agatha about this."

...

They met at Mae's Diner for a late lunch. Vanessa's shift at The Bernelli Group had not started yet. The same was true of Missy's library shift. Rudy was not needed to open his bar, and Agatha was on her lunch break from the library. Dora, of course, had all the time in the world.

They were waited on by Carolyn Trask, sister to Catherine the police lieutenant, and now part owner of Mae's. She insisted on continuing to wait tables, a job she had worked for years and claimed to love. Dora, who was giving thought to any job she happened to come across, could not imagine herself waiting tables, being treated badly by unhappy or unruly customers. Customer service of any kind would probably not be her gig.

She had expected Vanessa to want to meet alone, but Vanessa surprised her and insisted that Rudy and Agatha be there too, since they were Jesse's family and the new information concerned them.

"First of all," Dora began, once Carolyn had brought them all coffees, "we're not completely certain that Jesse even committed this robbery."

"There were other robberies," Missy explained. "So, even if he committed this one, we don't know if he committed the others."

"But the jacket?" Vanessa asked.

"We don't know if the jacket's in the other videos," Missy ventured. "And that company sells a lot of jackets."

"There's circumstantial evidence," Dora explained. "There's motive and opportunity, but nothing conclusive. So, let's focus on the information we have right now. What was stolen were all off-label cancer drugs, used most often when conventional therapies are not working."

Vanessa turned to Rudy and Agatha. "What do you know about this? Is this to do with Miz Liz?" She looked at each of them in turn. "Is she sick? It would explain a lot."

Rudy and Agatha looked at one another. "Maybe we should try to get Mom down here," Agatha said softly, "so everybody gets all the information at once."

"I'll call her and go get her, if she's available," Rudy offered, taking out his phone. Everyone watched him as he spoke softly into the phone, ended the call, and turned to them.

"She was resting, but she said if we know something about what happened to Jesse, she wants to hear it. I didn't want to say anything beyond that. I'll be back in fifteen." He disappeared out the door.

Agatha stood up and turned her back on the group. When she turned to them again, she had tears in her eyes. "This is all on me. I tried to do the right thing. I tried to help, but I screwed it all up."

Vanessa went to her and rubbed Agatha's arms. "You tried to help him. No one's going to fault you for that."

Agatha turned to Vanessa, her expression terrified. She shook her head. "No, this is on me. Wait 'til you hear. Wait 'til you hear!"

They sat quietly, ordering another round of coffees, which Agatha insisted on paying for. About twenty-five minutes later, Rudy held the door for Miz Liz, who tottered in, wearing full makeup and an evening dress.

"What're you all looking at? I clean up nice, and I clean up fast —'specially where my Jesse's concerned. Now let's have it!"

Everyone except Liz sat down.

Agatha stood up and faced the group, who looked at her expectantly.

"Several months ago, Jesse and I were with Mama, and she told us she was sick."

"Hey, hey! Don't be telling them that! You didn't get my permission to—my health is nobody's business. Agatha! I did not give you permission…"

"Hush, Mama." The look Agatha gave her mother was beseeching. "You want to know about Jesse? You hush."

Miz Liz went silent, but looked pained and unhappy.

"We love Mama so much." Agatha turned toward her mother. "Mama, we love you so much."

"Don't you think I know that?"

"All of us do," Rudy added.

"But Jesse and me most of all. We're your blood! We would do anything to make you well. Anything."

Miz Liz remained silent, but her eyes grew large and luminous, and her body seemed to shrink in comparison, though she remained standing.

"Mama told us that the treatments weren't working, in part because the cancer had spread, and now it was a few different types of cancers. I was beside myself and I didn't know what to do, but Jesse did. He went to the library and he learned. He battled that cancer with knowledge." Agatha put a hand to her mouth, as her eyes filled with tears. She shook her head. "I'm the librarian, but Jesse's the one who fought the cancer with research—and at my library too!" She gave a bitter laugh. "He never could keep anything from me. Twins are like that. We were close on another level. In a way, Jesse *was* me. We occupied the same spiritual space. So, I knew, and I knew early on—when he was talking to Doyle—that Doyle couldn't help him and had put him in touch with Corb Egar, and so I knew he was going to go to Egar, and I knew why. And…"

She started to cry. "I just couldn't bear to lose Jesse *and* Mama. I couldn't bear it—even with the joy Samuel has brought into our lives. So, I decided to try to stop Jesse—to keep him away from Egar. At first, I tried to talk him out of it, but if you know Jesse, you'd know that I couldn't do that.

He wouldn't let me. He wouldn't listen. He had it in his head that he could find the right medicines—the right combination of medicines."

Agatha looked at her mother, afraid to tell the part that came next. "Egar didn't have what Jesse needed either, so he told Jesse he would have to…" She bit her lip. "Steal the medications—rob a drugstore."

"He what?" Miz Liz put a hand to her throat and backed into a chair that Rudy slid beneath her. "What'd you say?"

"Egar told Jesse that the only way he could get the drugs he wanted to help you—to help Mama, was by robbing a drugstore. So, he decided to do just that."

Miz Liz leaped to her feet. "That's a lie! My Jesse was as honest a man as ever lived!"

Agatha wore a tortured expression, as she looked at her mother and explained with great reluctance. "He did, Mama."

"No! I don't believe it. I refuse!"

"There's more, Mama."

Miz Liz wiped her nose and sat back down. "Well, you might as well tell it," she said, calmer now. Resigned to hear what she had to hear, what her daughter had to say. "I'm already dying."

"I decided to stop him—to stop Jesse. Keep him from getting involved with Egar and keep him from stealing. So, I asked around to see how to find Egar."

"Whoa!" It was Rudy, staring at his wife. "This part's news to me! You went looking for Egar? Without telling me? Are you crazy?"

"Why not just go to his store?" Dora asked.

"Because I didn't know who he was. I just knew Doyle knew someone who could help Jesse get whatever he wanted. I asked around, and…and it took a while, but I wasn't told about Egar. I was never told about Egar… Egar was told about me."

"Ohhhh," Rudy breathed. "Holy…"

"Eventually, he heard I was looking for him and he heard why, and he wasn't happy that I knew he was connected to Jesse."

"What does that mean?" Miz Liz demanded.

"It means that Jesse went to Egar to get help getting these drugs. Jesse didn't know how he would get them, but Egar influenced Jesse to do the burglaries. He showed him what to do. I don't know the details, but he facilitated Jesse doing those burglaries, and now that I was coming to get Jesse to stop, and Egar was involved, Egar was—I don't know, freaked out? Pissed off? Enraged. Anyway, he wasn't having any of it, so he told Jesse that if I got involved, that their deal was off. Not only that, but if I got involved—I guess because of my position on the city council, there would be trouble. And Jesse figured Egar was going to kill me."

"Kill you? What? That's crazy!" Miz Liz's voice was weaker now. She was fading.

"No. Egar's crazy. If he's pissed off or freaking out, he's liable to do anything—I've heard the stories. Or, more accurately, he's liable to have one of his people do just about anything. He's got some murderous guy working for him. The murderer of the murderers. A contract killer. Not only that, but Egar apparently answers to someone. A guy a rung above him. He's not the top dog in the criminal world around here. This other guy is, only no one knows who that guy is."

Dora saw it now. "So, Jesse tried to stop Egar from killing you?"

Agatha nodded. "That's why he went to The Elegant Lagoon that night —to try to stop Egar."

"And Egar killed him."

"Or had him killed."

"How much of this do the police know?"

Agatha looked at Dora, who shrugged. "Some, but there's no way they know all of it. They definitely don't know about Miz Liz's diagnosis."

"Might be," Rudy began, "Corb Egar would've rather killed Jesse than Agatha. Maybe he was afraid of killing Agatha, since she's so well connected—possibly to the police. Jesse might've had a good reason for his crime, but he was still on the wrong side of the law. Egar knew who he was dealing with and besides, he had access to Jesse. Anyway, it all adds up to Egar killing Jesse or having him killed."

"So, my Jesse was killed trying to save my life?" Miz Liz was staring at her daughter, her eyes gone wide and a twitch beginning in her left eyelid, which had begun to droop. Her voice was faint and she sounded confused. She tried to push herself to stand, but couldn't, and she shouted something but no one understood the words; they were gibberish. Even later, in hindsight, no one could repeat what she'd said. Her eyes glazed and then closed and she listed to the left, like a thin tree in a strong wind.

"Catch her, Rude!" Agatha cried, and Rudy did catch her.

Dora remembered something from her training. "She needs a doctor. Either call 911 or take her to the hospital."

Chapter 14

The day was one of those late summer days that carry a hint of fall—days that tell you to enjoy your summer while you can, because colder days are coming.

They went in Rudy's SUV—Rudy and Agatha in the front seat, Vanessa and Dora, who had asked to come along, in the back. Missy had hoped to go too, but she was covering for Agatha at the library. Everyone was silent, alone with their thoughts. The rehab center was a modern facility with three floors—a main building and two wings. The four went to the front desk as a group, all wearing masks, which a sign said were required. They also had to show proof of vaccination. They rode the elevator in silence to the third floor and proceeded along a long hallway.

They passed a large, open room in which a young man Dora thought might be Kelvin Franklin was singing sweetly to twenty-five or thirty compromised people. As Dora slowed to watch, she couldn't help but notice that two of the women, both of whom were in their eighties or thereabouts, had rapt expressions of joy on their faces. They looked as though in that moment, they were once again the girls they used to be.

The four continued down the hall.

In another room, a woman was yelling, "I can't get out of here! Help! Help!" Through the open doors to some of the other rooms, Dora couldn't help but see withered, immobile patients, some of whom were near catatonic, breathing via tubes, while other connectors drained their wounds or stomach contents, carried waste from their bodies, or were connected to monitors that kept track of life functions.

When they arrived at room 317, a nurse was changing Miz Liz's saline IV. Her eyeglasses, which normally magnified her eyes and, perhaps, her personality, were gone. She wore a faded green hospital gown and lay under several blankets.

"How is she?" Agatha asked the nurse, who shrugged.

"As good as can be expected. Are you family?"

"I'm her daughter."

"So, you're on the HIPPA form?"

"Yes, and it's okay to speak in front of these people."

The nurse exhaled. "She's had a major stroke. We're keeping her alive, but her condition is quite serious."

Agatha covered her mouth with her hand. "Will she wake up and regain function?"

"Hard to say. Anything is possible." The nurse left the room.

Miz Liz looked so tiny in the big hospital bed, between machines that were keeping her alive and beneath the blanket. Agatha stood beside her, while Vanessa stood at her feet and ran her hand over the blanket there. Rudy and Dora stayed several steps off to one side. They stood that way for a few minutes, then Agatha took her mother's hand.

"I'm so sorry, Mama. I did this, and I'm just so sorry." She swallowed; tears ran down her face. She looked at Rudy, whose expression didn't change. After a long moment, Agatha said, "I'll be back soon, Mama. You hang in there. I love you."

Vanessa, who was still touching the blanket that lay over Miz Liz's feet, said, "I'll see you soon, Mom," and they all filed out, rode the elevator silently to the main floor, and made their way back to Rudy's SUV.

The ride home began with stunned silence.

After a few minutes, Rudy spoke, his eyes on the road.

"How could you have gone looking for Egar—a violent criminal—and not tell me?"

"I—" Agatha began, looking at her husband.

"I would have helped!" Rudy interrupted.

From the back seat, Dora could see the pain on Agatha's face; Vanessa tensed beside her while looking out the window.

"I couldn't let you get involved," Agatha explained. "I couldn't put this on your shoulders."

"That's not for you to say. I'm your husband."

"I thought I could maybe talk to whoever Jesse was involved with—I didn't know who Egar was. I just wanted to keep bad people away from my little brother. So I told him that, or else…"

"Or else what? What are you threatening anybody with?"

"I'd go to the newspapers."

"To Sarah?"

"Sarah's a good person. She's standing behind C3 and she was willing to help me."

"So, you threatened this Egar person, and he killed Jesse. Jesus!" He slapped the steering wheel with a heavy palm. "Jesus! Jesus! Jesus!" He hit the steering wheel on each word.

"I got him killed, yes."

No one spoke for the rest of the ride.

When they arrived at the bar, Rudy got out of the car, slammed the door, and disappeared inside. Dora, Agatha, and Vanessa hugged one another and briefly stood together.

"Nessa, I'm so sorry!" Agatha sobbed.

"Shhh." Vanessa held her sister-in-law as Dora looked on. "You did what you thought was right. You tried to protect him."

But Agatha only cried harder.

Dora looked at them both, her expression grim. "Agatha, you might still be in danger. I'm going to try to find out who it is that gives Egar orders, and who this contract killer is."

Vanessa and Agatha looked at her like she was crazy. "How?" Agatha asked.

"I'll start by finding Egar."

• • •

The following morning, Dora was up at 5:00 a.m. and out the door by 5:30. The sun was not yet up. A purple and pink glow shone from just beyond the horizon and hinted at the morning to come.

The sign outside the storefront in the little strip mall read, "Egar's Meats—With That Extra Special Ingredient." Dora wondered what that might be.

A blocky young man was behind the counter in a blood-stained apron. He was about the size of a high school lineman, with cheeks that might have been jovial if his eyes had been smiling.

"Help you?" he asked.

"You Mr. Egar?"

The young man's expression changed to either a smile or a sneer. "That'd be my father."

"Where would I find him?"

"You wouldn't. Tell me why you want to see him and I'll see if he wants to see you."

Dora pressed forward at the counter near the register, where there was no glass and steel deli case between them. As she had hoped, Egar Jr. stood directly opposite and leaned forward on his hands to meet her.

"Well, this involves the murder of Jesse Burrell."

The young man curled his lower lip outward, so it covered his upper lip, raised his eyebrows, and shrugged. "Don't know anyone by that name." He shook his head and appeared confused.

Dora's hand flashed forward and took hold of Egar Jr.'s wrist and yanked it toward her, throwing him off balance so that he had to use his other hand to keep him from falling face first onto the butcher block. Dora slid her hand to the end of his middle finger in a joint lock—one of Wally J's finest.

"You sure?"

"Who the fuck…?"

She pulled harder and twisted, feeling his tendons and ligaments reach the limits of their flexibility.

"Did you take much science in school?" she asked, but didn't wait for an answer. "Of course, you didn't, did you, Junior? You don't mind if I call you junior, do you?"

He was trying to twist away, to reach her hand with his free hand, to pry her fingers from his, but Dora twisted away from him, so all Egar Jr. could do was twist with her and writhe in pain.

"The human finger is an amazing creation," she explained. "Did you know that a finger like this one I'm holding—and not nearly as tightly as I could, I might add—one finger has four bones, three joints, three sets of ligaments, and I guess you'd call it four tendons. Isn't that something?"

"What? C'mon, let me go!"

"Let's see. You've got the proximal interphalangeal joint, the collateral ligament, the metacarpophalangeal joint, the flexor digitorum profundus tendon…"

"Aww, c'mon! Oh, man! Let the fuck go!"

"Hang on, hang on. There's this one tendon and I can never think of it…"

"Fuck. Fuck! Let go!"

"Oh, I know. It's the flexor digitorum superficialis tendon. Thanks for helping me remember."

His eyes were tearing up now, and she was worried he might pass out from the pain, so she looked him dead in the eye, continuing to twist his finger tip as she did, with steadily increasing pressure, until she felt the tendons give way. The boy screamed.

"But the best thing," Dora continued. "The very best thing about the finger and its attributes is that there are ten of them." Without releasing his hand, she slid her grip to his ring finger and took hold of it in a similar manner. "And we've only done one."

"Okay! Okay! Okay! Lemme go! Whatya want? Waddya want!"

"Sorry, Egar Jr., I'm not letting you go until you tell me how to find your father."

"Awright—he'll be at the Nassau Cigar and Gun Club from seven until they close. He's there every night."

"What time do they close?"

"How should—ahhhh! Okay! 11:30!"

She released his hand and gave him a smile that was as mirthless as his own. "Thanks so much, Egar Jr. I hope we can be friends."

He was bent over his hand, shaking it and grimacing in pain.

• • •

That night, Dora waited across the street and a short distance up the block from Egar's club. She was prepared to do this as often and for as long as it took until she found him.

Egar left in the company of two friends that night. The following night, he left with three friends. On the third night, she was rewarded as the five or six cars there all left at the same time, leaving Egar's grey Escalade as the only car in the lot. She waited, but no one came out, and after another twenty minutes, she decided to risk the possibility that Egar was inside with guests, perhaps several, who had come with him in his car.

She went around to the back of the building, found a door to the kitchen, and listened for several minutes, but heard no sounds from inside. The door was unlocked, so she opened it and went in, pausing every few steps to stop and listen. She heard nothing and saw no one in the kitchen, which showed signs of recent use. Pots, pans, plates, cutlery, and glassware were on a drying rack, still wet. A refrigerator held the leftovers of a ziti, marinara, sausage, and broccoli dinner. Empty bottles of red wine—a California Zinfandel—littered the garbage can in the kitchen.

She stopped again and listened, and thought she heard a sound—a tone of some kind. Perhaps from a musical instrument. The tone continued intermittently, and Dora followed the sound into the cavernous dining hall where she found, sitting in the middle of the dining hall, an older version of Egar Jr. having some kind of seizure. Saliva was dribbling from his mouth, and he was shaking all over, his eyes twitching—not the lids but the eyeballs themselves. The sound Dora had heard was a persistent moan coming from Egar—a moan with a purpose, as though he were trying to say something or possibly call for help. She also saw what looked like red blisters and welts on his right hand.

"Fucking hell!" She pulled out her phone, and dialed 911 without leaving her name. She had no idea what criminal activity Egar was involved in, beyond her suspicions, and she didn't want to have to defend herself against any perception on the part of the police that she might have been working with him or had caused his condition; hence, her anonymity. After the call, she turned back to Egar.

But Egar was dead.

• • •

She drove back to her apartment and called Missy, who said she would call once she was off work. A few minutes later, her phone rang. She assumed it would be Missy, but she was wrong.

"Agatha?"

"Mama passed."

"Oh. Oh, I'm so sorry, Agatha!"

"I know. She was—unique. Not someone you ever picture dying."

"She was a cool, cool lady."

"Yes, she was."

"How is Rudy?"

"Not speaking to me."

"At a time like this?"

"At a time like this."

"Are you going to have a funeral?"

"I'll talk to Vanessa and maybe Rudy if he comes around, but it's really up to me, so I'd say probably something private with a memorial, once Jesse's death is settled."

"Vanessa knows?"

"She does."

"And her boys?"

"You'd have to ask her."

"What can I do to help?"

Agatha sighed. "You're already doing it. Being my friend."

"I am that. And I'm so sorry. We'll always remember her."

"She's not someone you forget, you know?"

After the call, Dora went to the kitchen, opened a Rolling Rock, then returned to the couch and put her bare feet up on the ottoman. She let her thoughts drift to Miz Liz. The woman was one of a kind, all right—a firecracker of a woman, even in her seventies.

Her phone rang. Missy.

She explained about Miz Liz and they commiserated, sharing bittersweet memories. She then explained about her run-ins with both Egars.

About Egar Jr., Missy said only "Dora" in a maternally chastising way, and Dora could picture her shaking her head, as one would toward an obstreperous child. But when Dora related the way she had found Corb Egar Sr., Missy said, "Wait a minute," and sounded excited. "Run that by me again."

Dora did and Missy was silent.

"What are you thinking?"

Missy said, "Huh. Holy crap. Huh!"

"What? What?"

"Do we know who was at that club tonight?"

"Not offhand, but maybe we can find out. I know zero about the place."

"We need to find out who was there."

"Okay. I can try the Goose and the Gander, but I called Egar's death in anonymously, so I have to figure out how I'm supposed to know about this."

"You'll figure something out."

"You're right. I will."

"While you're at it, we need to know what they ate. And if we can get some samples of it, so much the better."

"Well…"

"What?"

"I know what they ate—a pasta dinner with red sauce and sausage, along with wine and I don't remember—maybe bread. Oh, and broccoli—not sure if it was roasted or sautéed. Does it matter?"

"I guess you didn't take a doggie bag," said Missy.

"Um, no. But don't tell Comfort."

"Pretty sure what matters is what spices were used."

"Mmm. Maybe the police lab can figure that out."

...

Dora waited a day before she called the two detectives. She wanted to give the police enough time to get their teeth into the investigation into Corb Egar Sr.'s death.

Dora called the direct line Ganderson and Mallard had given her. Ganderson picked up.

"I thought you might want to know that I was with Corb Egar Sr. when he died."

"What? You need to come down to the station. Now."

About a half hour later, she was at the station, seated next to Ganderson's desk. Mallard wasn't present. She explained to Ganderson that she had gone to see Corb Egar Sr. to ask him about his relationship with Jesse Burrell.

Ganderson's gaze hardened with fury. "What qualifications did you have to do something like that? Did you want to compromise our investigation? Do you have any idea of how much trouble you're in?"

Dora stared right back at him. "I'm a friend of the family. I went there to talk—no law against that, is there?"

"Are you kidding? The man is part of a murder investigation, and he died while you were there!"

Dora shrugged. "So? Arrest me." She held out her wrists and continued to hold his gaze. "How's that investigation going, by the way?"

"Your involvement in any and all aspects of this case at this point is inappropriate and could potentially hinder the investigation, so if you care about seeing Burrell's killer brought to justice, you'll back off, while being ready and willing to answer any questions we may have."

"Happy to discuss anything, anytime." She looked away, which kept the disagreement from escalating into legal territory.

Ganderson pointed a finger at her. "We may need to revisit your involvement. Stay away from this case, Ellison. Got that?" She didn't answer, so he repeated with emphasis. "I said—got that?"

Her answer was sullen and intentionally vague. "I heard you."

Ganderson ignored her for several minutes, shuffling papers on his desk and staring into his computer screen. The silence was punctuated by a few taps on his keyboard. Finally, he reluctantly explained that Egar's cause of death had been attributed to respiratory failure, and when Dora described the additional symptoms—the dribbling saliva, the tremors, the twitching eyeball, the welts and blisters on his hand—Ganderson assured Dora that these would be passed along to the medical examiner and noted. His assurances were barely that; they were perfunctory and rote. She was also told that both the contents of Egar's stomach and the leftover food would be fully explored.

She wondered how she might acquire a list of the guests at the hall, when she didn't know if the evening's get-together had been a formal event with a name, a celebration honoring an individual, or a club meeting.

• • •

The following day, Missy supplied the answer. She invited Dora to come to her apartment in the late morning, before she left for the library.

Dora arrived to find two steaming mugs of coffee, one apple walnut muffin, and one blueberry muffin on Missy's kitchen table.

"What would you say if I was able to get a list of everyone who was at that hall where Egar died, along with photos of everyone there?"

Dora was pouring the contents of three packets of sweetener into her coffee, followed by a generous portion of half and half. "I don't know what I'd say, but I'd be impressed." She grinned. "For sure I'd ask how you managed it."

"I used one of the most frequently overlooked sources in the field of competitive intelligence."

"What's that?"

"The organization's website."

Dora raised an eyebrow. "Really? The Nassau Cigar and Gun Club listed who was at their event on Thursday on their website?"

"Yup. Kind of an investigatory version of Occam's Razor. To paraphrase: the simplest source might just be the best. And it is, unless they videotaped the event on Thursday, which, given the egos of these guys, wouldn't surprise me."

Dora slid her chair closer to Missy's, and they looked at the webpage with the photo of the attendees of Thursday's meeting at the Nassau Cigar and Gun Club. The photo showed eight men who appeared to range from their mid-forties to about seventy years of age. Below the photo were the names of those in the picture along with helpful pointers such as "at left" or "third from right."

Missy slid the computer nearer to Dora and smiled. "See anyone you know?"

Dora squinted and read the names, then turned to Missy, recognition dawning on her face. "Lenny Altamont."

"Who else?"

"Wait... Ferret Wallace."

Missy pushed her chair back and stood up. "C'mon, we've gotta go for a little ride, take a few pictures..."

As they headed for Dora's car, Missy spoke her thoughts aloud. "I remember something about his yard, and if I'm right, it explains how Egar Sr. was killed."

Missy waited while Dora popped the passenger lock, then got in. "Yup. And maybe who killed him," Dora answered. "And maybe answers another major question for the police and the Burrell family."

They drove in silence, each with her own thoughts, theories, and questions. They drove past Altamont's house, then parked around the corner, where Dora's car wouldn't be seen.

"So, we're taking pictures?" Dora asked. "I already barged in on two of these guys—the father and the son—and in doing so committed God knows how many crimes."

"Take out your phone," Missy said. "We're going to walk by like we're going for a nice walk, which is in fact what we'll be doing. Maybe we're bird watchers or something, taking lots of pictures." To demonstrate, Missy took out her phone, an iPhone 12, and began walking, apparently focused on her surroundings, idly snapping pictures.

"What if he's home and near a window or outside? He'll recognize us."

"Unlikely. When we drove by, I saw that there were no cars visible on the property."

Dora frowned. "I saw that too, but I also saw his locked garage."

"So? We're a couple of friends who like walking and taking pictures of nature. And if we happen to be walking by—so what? Maybe you make puzzles out of the pictures. I paint. No crime in that. And if he thinks we're some kind of a threat—well, I suspect he's not going to shoot us on sight, while we're walking around the neighborhood."

"True. But what if you're wrong? What if he's at a window and he keeps his rifle nearby?"

Missy stopped walking and turned to Dora. "Since when have you ever been so worried about anything?"

Dora raised her eyebrows and tipped her head to one side. "Not worried. Prepared. I want to always, always be prepared. I don't want to ever be surprised."

Missy began walking again and resumed taking pictures in every direction. "Good luck with that," she said.

They continued walking to the corner, then hurried around the block and back to Dora's car.

"We seem to have made it in one piece," Missy observed.

"You know," Dora said, "for a librarian, you've got a lot of courage."

They got into the car, buckled in, and were on their way.

"Since when are librarians supposed to be afraid? If anything, we operate from knowledge—from gathering information, from research. Like you, we want to be prepared."

"Hah!" Dora laughed. "Tou-freaking-ché!"

They arrived at Missy's apartment and downloaded all the images to her computer and began separating out all of the relevant pictures of Lenny Altamont's property. Missy scrolled slowly through them, stopping and looking at two. She expanded both of them on her screen to reveal closeups of his garden.

"I have no idea what I'm looking at," Dora said, "except that it's some pretty flowers in a sweet old guy's garden."

"That's okay," Missy said. "Give me a couple of minutes. I'm just looking for something." She opened a browser, performed an internet search, and arranged the photos and an image from her search so that they were side by side on her screen.

Missy sat back and looked at the pictures. "Now I can tell you pretty conclusively what killed Egar, and how, and very likely who did it."

Chapter 15

C3 sat on the toilet seat cover, listening. He could hear Sarah bustling about the apartment—cleaning, putting things away, straightening up, vacuuming. He wondered if she was going through his things, looking for drugs. The cleaning and straightening up could well be a cover for searching for his stash. But he had fooled her. He kept his stash on him at all times. He felt in his pocket for the little tin that had once held mints and now held his pills. He felt for the flat, virtually invisible tin every few minutes; its touch brought him comfort.

He had not been able to find a job as of yet, and was living and coping with his father and Christine, who were apparently getting married in a few weeks. He had learned of their wedding by stumbling upon their engraved invitations. He had been neither given nor sent one.

He had driven a taxi for a few days and hated it. The dispatcher was a jackass named Don, who cared only about everyone doing whatever Don said. Don and on and on.

Driving the taxi was good, in that he could get what he needed pretty much whenever he wanted. He could text or call and drive by, and make a pickup.

But he'd had enough of driving the taxi. He was switching to Uber—even more freedom.

He kept himself on a steady five milligram dose pretty much all of the time, which he boosted to ten when he was stressed. He knew that this would not be enough for long—that his tolerance would increase and he would need ten and fifteen for the same effect soon. His habit would soon become unaffordable, and this was a major concern.

He wished Sarah would stop looking for his stash—stop pretending she was cleaning the apartment. He wished she would leave him alone.

· · ·

"Look at this closeup of Altamont's garden. What do you see?"

Dora looked closely, scanning the image, but nothing jumped out at her. "I see some plants. Stalks, and red flowers—pretty pink and white roses maybe, and are those deep red ones roses?"

"They're dahlias," Missy explained.

Dora was impressed. "Girl knows her flowers."

"Librarian does her research. What else do you see?"

"Little white flowers."

"Ah! Tell me about those."

"I don't know what to tell you. They're small, and pretty. Like—what do flower shops put around roses in bouquets?"

Missy nodded. "Baby's breath. But that's not what these are."

"Okay, Sherlock. What are they?"

"Ostensibly, they're called Queen Anne's lace."

"Ostensibly?"

"Mm hmm. 'Cause they're not. They're hemlock."

"Hemlock? Isn't that what killed Socrates?"

Missy lit up. "Girl wins the daily double! Librarian is impressed!"

Dora shrugged. "Back in the day, I read a little. Actually, I still do. Before going to sleep."

Missy gave her a long look. "Guess I haven't been around you at that time of day."

"Yes, you have."

"Well...oh, never mind. Look at the stalks of this plant at Altamont's. What do you see?"

"Purple thingies."

"Thingies—that actually is, in fact, the technical term. Those purple thingies or splotches are what differentiate Queen Anne's lace from hemlock. And guess what the symptoms of hemlock poisoning are?"

"Let me guess. Drooling and seizures."

"Girl's on fire! Tremors, welts on your hands where you handle the plant—pretty much everything you saw with Egar."

Dora sat back, blinking as she concentrated. She sipped her coffee and broke off a piece of her muffin, popped it into her mouth. "So, Altamont poisoned Corb Egar Sr.?"

Missy had some of her own coffee. "Looks that way, though we have no proof. Altamont or someone who worked for him."

"We oughta give the Goose and the Gander a call."

Missy looked surprised.

"Don't you think so?" Dora asked.

"Absolutely. I'm just surprised to hear you say it."

• • •

Mallard answered Missy's call and suggested that they have a discussion at the police station, so Dora and Missy drove there together, and sat side by side alongside the officers' desks.

Missy explained about the hemlock and Egar being poisoned; she had brought her computer to show them the pictures. The detectives listened quietly, then looked at one another.

"First of all," Ganderson began, "I'm glad you came to us before going off and doing something crazy—or crazier, I should say." He opened his mouth, about to add something, but Mallard interrupted.

"Going rogue," Mallard added, and Ganderson looked at him as though his comment was unwelcome.

Ganderson rose to his feet, placed both hands on the desk in front of him and leaned forward on them. "This is what you ladies are going to do. Nothing. You're going to do nothing. Understand?"

"Nothing, as in…" Dora shook her head, as if she didn't understand.

"As in nothing related to this case or to police work in general." Ganderson glanced at Mallard to see if he was going to add anything. "We, on the other hand, are going to look into this information and see if it has any merit."

...

Early that evening, Dora took a chance and drove by Shay's MMA with her workout clothes. She was delighted to find Shay teaching an advanced class.

Shay noticed her standing in the doorway, jogged over, and extended an elbow in greeting, which Dora appreciated and reciprocated. She was still a bit freaked out about COVID, which seemed to have new and dangerous variants springing up every month or two. She didn't like vulnerability of any kind. Vulnerability frightened her; loss of control frightened her. She knew she was a control freak, and she was fine with that. Dangers she couldn't control, like pandemics, were well worth the fear they instilled.

She watched the class, noting the techniques Shay was teaching. They were subtly different from those that had been emphasized a year and a half earlier, when Dora had studied at the school. The techniques following the takedown were different, with the focus being on holding your opponent's legs tightly together, to keep the opponent on the ground.

Deadly striking was also taught, though not demonstrated other than in slow motion. Groin, throat, eye, and kidney strikes were emphasized and drilled at slow speeds.

Shay showed the class how to do joint locks beyond the Wally J-type finger locks; she demonstrated wrist locks, heel hooks, neck cranks, *kimuras*—which are shoulder locks—and arm bars. She emphasized that they would all be subject to testing.

After the teaching segment of the class ended, Shay came over to greet Dora. "How's the up-and-coming lady in blue?"

Dora blushed. "Afraid that's not happening."

Instead of asking probing questions, Shay just nodded, absorbing the information. "You look well."

"As do you. I see you've expanded what the advanced students are expected to learn."

"Sure have. I try to keep up with what's out there. Much of what I've added in is from Sambo—the competitive kind and the street version. You can't do a lot of the locks, like *kimuras* for instance, in Sambo competition, but in the street, of course..."

Dora smiled. "That's what it's all about." She indicated her gym bag. "Spar a little?"

Ten minutes later, Dora was changed, had selected headgear, and was back on the mat.

The class had been sparring, but at a signal from Shay, everyone moved to the perimeters and sat down cross-legged along the wall.

Shay and Dora bowed to one another. Dora jabbed, and Shay slid effortlessly out of the way. Dora jab-hooked, and Shay angled away and kicked Dora's left calf with her right instep, hard.

"Whoa!" Dora breathed and refocused, circling to her left, jabbing, then sliding in for a takedown. She managed to grab behind one of Shay's knees, turned, and flipped the instructor to the floor. But Shay immediately pulled Dora into the area above and between her legs—the classic guard position.

Dora postured up, attempting to ground and pound, but Shay held Dora behind the neck, pulling her down and holding her close, so that Dora, despite being bigger and physically stronger, was unable to free her hands for punching.

Suddenly, Shay released Dora's right arm, and when Dora attempted to punch with it, held Dora's arm against her body, lifted her left leg, and wrapped it around Dora's side, then flung her right leg up and around Dora's head, isolating Dora's right arm. Then she simply extended her legs, using their power to force Dora's arm back, bending it at the elbow in a direction the elbow was not designed to go.

"Think you've got me?" Dora asked, her voice tight from the pain.

"Yah," Shay managed to reply. "I do."

"We'll see." Dora stood up, lifting Shay into the air, then fell forward, so that Shay's head would have impacted the mat—or the concrete, had they been elsewhere—if Shay hadn't let go of Dora's arm and used her own arm to break her fall.

The two relaxed, laughing and pointing mock-scolding fingers at one another. "I'd have broken your arm," Shay said.

Dora shrugged. "Cool stuff."

Shay was out of breath and leaned a hand on Dora's shoulder. "The sport's always changing—or rather, new information is always becoming available. Russian—specifically, Dagestani—influence is big now."

Dora bowed and sat down to catch her breath. "I know."

Shay was red-faced and breathing heavily. She sat down beside Dora and they embraced loosely. "It's those black beards. They're everywhere you look."

Dora kept her hand on Shay's shoulder. The woman had been part of her newfound, rebuilt confidence, and the positive channeling of her energy that had reshaped her life these past two years. "Moral of the story," Dora said. "Don't fight guys with big black beards."

Shay took a few deep breaths. "So, what are you gonna do?" She was asking about Dora's plans for her future.

Dora's jovial mood vanished. "Damned if I know."

• • •

Dora had left her phone in the turbo's glove compartment. After showering and exiting the gym, she laid the gym bag on the passenger seat and saw that she had missed a call from the Beach City Police Department. The call was from the main number, but she called back the number she had for the detective team.

"Beach City Police—Mallard here."

"Dora Ellison, returning your call."

"Can you and your friend get down here right away?"

"If you mean Missy, I've gotta call her. I'm not with her now."

"Yes—her. Soon as you can."

She called Missy, but her call went straight to voicemail. "Miss—just heard from the Goose and the Gander—the Goose, to be specific. They want us to come down to the station ASAP."

Several seconds later, she received a texted reply. *Meet you there.*

Twenty minutes later, they were seated where they had been several hours before, beside the detectives' desks.

"Here's the thing," Ganderson said, leaning forward in his chair, all business. "We have long been aware of local drug traffickers and violent criminals because…"

"Because we arrest their friends and we squeeze them and they talk to us," Mallard continued.

Ganderson took a deep breath. "We have long been aware that Corb Egar is a man who is pretty high up in the criminal food chain." The senior detective picked up a pencil and began tapping its eraser against his desk. "And we knew he answers to someone — someone who is connected to the big boys — the cartels and murder-for-hire groups. But someone local. A local boss at the highest level."

"We knew there was such a person," Mallard continued, and this time Ganderson nodded.

"And we knew he was powerful," said Ganderson, "and rules with an iron fist…and a smile. He was reputed to be a nice guy, at least outwardly."

"Until someone turns up dead," Mallard finished.

"Something else we knew," Ganderson said. "He employs an enforcer who's at least as secretive as he is."

Mallard agreed. "Moreso, in fact. We know nothing about him, except that he exists, is responsible for upwards of two dozen deaths, and is expert with a whole host of murder techniques … and he blends in with the local population."

Everyone looked at Ganderson, who appeared to make a decision. "We think you stumbled upon both these guys."

"The local boss and his enforcer?" Missy asked.

Dora smiled and touched Missy's forearm. "Altamont and Ferret Wallace."

Mallard nodded. "Also known as Charles Wallace."

Ganderson remained focused on what he was saying; he ran his hand back through his hair, combing it with his fingers. "We do know that he's a sniper. A marksman. And an expert with several different kinds of knives."

"And, apparently, poison," Mallard added. "But he's known, to the degree he's known at all, as a military sniper—Serbian, I believe."

"Yes, that's right," Ganderson nodded. "While we don't know anything about his current identity, we do know his given name."

"It isn't Charles Wallace?" Dora asked.

Ganderson shook his head. "The name he went by in the Serbian militia where he was apparently something of a legend." Ganderson looked at Dora, then at Missy. "Bogdan Pavlovic."

"There's something I'm not understanding," Missy interjected. "Why did Altamont and Wallace, or Pavlovic, want Egar dead? Wasn't Egar of value to him?"

"He was, but Egar was compromised."

Mallard nodded. "By Agatha Raines."

"Ooh. You know about that?" Dora asked.

"Hard not to, when she was running all over the place asking how to get ahold of Corb Egar. That drew a lot of attention." Mallard looked at Ganderson, who continued for him.

"Not smart. It drew Egar's attention and it drew Altamont's."

The intercom on Mallard's desk rang. He answered, "Beach City Police—Mallard." He glanced at Dora and Missy. "Sure, Chief. Will do." He hung up. "Chief wants to see you."

"Us?" Dora asked. Mallard nodded.

Chapter 16

Chief Terrence Stalwell was seated behind a neat, shiny desk. Behind him were awards he had won and photos of him with a host of renowned Long Island athletes and entertainment celebrities.

He stood up as Dora and Missy came in. He did not shake their hands. Stalwell was known as a CDC, by-the-book guy when it came to COVID protocols. "Nice to see you, Dora. Missy Winters, right? I've seen you at the library."

"Pleased to meet you, Chief Stalwell," Missy said. "We also met briefly at the dinner last year."

"I remember," the chief said, with a warm smile.

"Hey, Chief." Dora grinned.

"Have a seat." The chief sat, followed by his guests. He smiled proudly at Dora, then turned to Missy. "You know, Dora is not only a hero—heroine, that is—in this town, she is also one to me, personally. Lady has some serious courage, and an undefinable leadership quality." He turned his attention to Dora. "You keep on following your gut and you'll do great things."

Missy smiled, the crinkles at the edges of her eyes showing her joy. "She's a cool lady."

"Thank you, Chief," Dora said quietly.

Chief Stalwell's eyes widened and his smiled broadened. Then, just as suddenly, his smile vanished.

"Now, you ladies have done a lot—gathered information and looked into things. I know Dora was planning to be a member of the force—a plan for which, for better or worse, I feel responsible. But it wasn't to be. But!" The word cut the air like a knife, and both Dora and Missy twitched in their seats. "But"—he pointed a finger—"you have to know when it's enough. Citizens can only go so far." He was speaking slowly, emphasizing every word. "When citizens go too far, they put themselves, and often others, in danger." He looked each of them in the eye for several seconds. "And it's enough now." He shook his finger at them. "No more! No more."

"Chief..." Dora took a breath.

"I'm not finished."

"Yes, sir."

"I want to make absolutely clear that we all know the level of danger we are facing. We have professionals—profilers, SWAT teams, detectives, lab technicians, cybercrime experts, narcotics officers... That's who will deal with this dangerous, dangerous man you have helped us discover. So —" He slapped the table and stood up. "You're a heroine all over again, a year and a half later. You've uncovered another dangerous criminal. But here's what you must understand." He looked at each of them again, to make sure they were riveted to every word. "You must understand that Altamont is going to send someone, maybe Bogdan Pavlovic after"—he held up a finger—"not you or you, but after Agatha Raines. Trust me. So, any action you take may hurt Agatha or Rudy or their son."

Dora nodded, wondering whether she was permitted to speak. "Samuel."

Stalwell nodded. "So, here's what I suggest for you two. Go on a vacation. I don't care where. Go to the Caribbean."

"I have a job," Missy ventured.

"I don't care," Stalwell went on. "Go to the mall. Go look at the late summer foliage upstate. It doesn't matter. It can be a metaphorical vacation, but take one...from this case. Please, please—leave this to the professionals, which you two emphatically are not! These guys, these criminals are the professionals of the professionals. This fixer—he's high up, at the top locally, and he's connected to both the national and international syndicates as well as the best freelancers." Stalwell pointed toward the ceiling, then thrust his face forward for emphasis. "And his gunman, this sniper and cut man is a killer's killer—a real Luca Brasi type. And they both need to be handled by professionals. So, listen to me. Lie low."

Dora and Missy remained silent.

Stalwell shook his head. "I mean it, and I need to hear you say it."

Dora stood and Missy followed suit. "Chief," Dora said, "I can promise you, we have no plans to get involved any more than we have been already. We are not going looking for these people."

Chief Stalwell looked at both of them somberly, then nodded.

As they exited the police station and were about to head for their cars, Missy turned to Dora. "How about we start with a food vacation—lunch at the new Greek place?"

Dora gave a smile that was part wince. "I think I'm going to head home. I'm kind of tired."

"Call you later?" Missy said, peering at Dora, trying to discern her mood.

"Of course."

• • •

When Dora arrived home, she went straight to her bed and buried her face in Franny's clothes. "Miss you so much, baby."

She felt useless and alone after the chief's diplomatic but emphatic warning. She was a big believer in refusing to give up, in never quitting—and here she had quit. She had been on her way to achieving her dream job. She loved police work. She loved solving crimes. In a way, she had always known that. She loved puzzles that manifested in real life, and she loved delivering justice where it was needed. Where *she* was needed.

And she had let all that go because she couldn't tolerate the pressure; she had caved to her own emotion and had failed to "put the I over the E"—the intelligence over the emotion. The meeting with Chief Stalwell had forcefully driven that home to her. Now she just wanted to be alone to try not to think about her future. She felt humiliated and did not feel worthy of seeing anyone.

Her phone rang several times, but she didn't answer. She didn't even check to see who had called. She surrounded herself with all she had left of Franny and she slept, awoke in tears, then eventually fell asleep again.

When she woke up again, she realized it was the following afternoon and she was ravenous. She didn't want to speak to anyone—particularly Missy, whom she was certain she had let down nearly as much as she had let herself down.

Missy had planted the thought of Greek food in her mind, so she called the new Greek restaurant and ordered a Greek salad and a gyro. When she drove over to pick up her order, she thought she spotted a faded green Mercury Grand Marquis behind her at several points. The car was a few cars behind her, and each time she looked, the car was there.

And then it wasn't.

She left the restaurant with her bag of food, parked in the lot behind her building, went in, and ate about half her meal. She really wasn't as hungry as she'd thought. It occurred to her that Missy had probably called, so checked her phone and saw that she had called seven times.

Seven times!

Not calling her back would've been selfish, so she dialed.

"Hey!"

"What's up?" Dora asked quietly.

"What's wrong?"

"Nothing."

"It's not nothing. Something's obviously wrong."

"I don't really want to talk about it."

"Is it our meeting with Stalwell?"

"You're one smart cookie."

"And I don't give up, so out with it."

"You are so spot on."

"And?"

"You just said it yourself. You don't give up. Well, guess what I did?"

"I'm not following—"

"Don't disappoint me now. Come on!"

Missy said nothing for a few moments. *She's going to make me say it,* Dora thought. "I gave up, Miss."

Missy didn't answer right away, then said, "The academy."

"The academy. It's what I wanted. It's what I was meant to do. And I was doing it. Stalwell—the chief himself had invited me to be a police officer, and I took him up on it, but I quit because I couldn't cut it."

"That isn't true."

"'Course it's true! It's exactly true!"

"No, honey, it's not. You left the academy for a reason. Yes, you wanted to be a police officer. Yes, you loved being involved in bringing the mayor and his people to justice last year. But you've always stood up against abuse, against unfairness, and people being treated badly. I know you, honey. You've done some wild things, standing up for people who need someone in their corner."

"I guess that's true."

"You guess. It *is* true. Only eventually, *you* were that person. Unfortunately, when you were at the academy, you ran into a situation where you were the one being treated unfairly."

"But that's part of the deal," Dora insisted. "To cut it as a police officer, you've got to be able to take a certain amount of shit."

She heard Missy exhale. "Not what *you* took. That wasn't part of the program. Hazing is not part of the program. While it might be done, I'm sure it's not sanctioned. I guarantee it isn't. And you, my sweet girl, you were a lone voice in standing up to it. Hey, maybe that helped the next person."

"If it did," Dora replied, "I have no way of knowing it."

"So?"

"So, why don't you come by? I have something I want to show you."

Dora sighed. "Okay. Give me twenty or thirty minutes."

"Good!"

She took her time getting dressed. Then got undressed again, showered, dressed, and headed for her car.

And saw the green Grand Marquis again.

Rather than go to Missy's, she drove around for a while, to see what this tail would do.

She had been feeling more and more depressed, and while Missy's talk helped because she had a friend who so obviously cared for her, she was still depressed. She still believed, though perhaps less so, that she had quit and left her dream job—her job of destiny—behind.

But a strange thing happened.

The car following her helped.

The car sent a jolt of invigoration through her—a jolt of purpose.

She began driving around the block, stopping and then starting, parking but then driving away again—just to see what the Grand Marquis would do.

A smile crept onto her face. She was enjoying this.

She had promised Chief Stalwell not to go looking for Lenny Altamont or his henchmen. But it seemed that Altamont or his men might have found her.

Dora parked several blocks from Missy's, began walking toward her apartment, then stopped and took out her phone, holding it up and bringing up the camera, then reversing the image as if to take a selfie. She took several pictures, hoping to see if the person who had been driving the Grand Marquis was now following her on foot and, if so, to shed some light on who that person was. Then she called Missy.

"Miss."

"Hey! You sound better!"

"You can tell from one syllable?"

"I'm a librarian. We have storehouses of wisdom. Meta data, in fact."

Dora laughed in spite of herself. "I have a request."

"Request away."

"Meet me at the Starbucks on the north side of town?"

"Sure. Any reason?"

"There is, but I'll fill you in later."

• • •

Once at Starbucks, Dora ordered a Venti Americano coffee, added three Splendas and some half-and-half, and sat down to wait, keeping an eye on the front door and windows, though she suspected that whoever Altamont had sent after her was smart enough to avoid being seen. Of course, she was pretty sure she had already "made" him—which gave her pause.

Missy came through the door, saw Dora immediately, walked over and gave her a long, rather embarrassing hug.

"How're you doing?" Missy peered at her with concern.

Dora shook her head, trying to dispel Missy's worry. "I'm good. So, listen. Don't look around, but a guy has been following me for a while—first in a car and now, maybe on foot—though I'm not sure."

Missy didn't turn her head, but her eyes looked from one side to the other.

"What do you want to do?"

"I want to find out who he is and why he's tailing me—and maybe throw a monkey wrench his way."

Missy swallowed. "Let me get a coffee, then I'd like to do something else, before we address this guy you're talking about."

Missy got in line behind three other customers. Once at the front of the line, she ordered herself a tall blonde roast coffee, to which she added two Splendas and a splash of half-and-half. She returned to the little round table, where Dora was seated.

"So, before we do anything else, when we were speaking earlier, I thought of something that might be helpful. I'm going to teach you to meditate."

Dora was dubious. "Here? Now?"

"Yup. No time like the present."

"But there are so many distractions."

"Exactly. Meditation teaches you to tune out the distractions." She settled into her seat, wriggling just a bit. "So, sit up nice and straight."

"Should I close my eyes?"

"Nope. Keep them open. Now fix your gaze on a point across the room. Something stationary."

"Got it."

"Great. Now just follow your breath. Notice it coming in…and going out. In fact, you might think the words 'in' and 'out' along with your breath, but you don't have to."

They sat for a moment in silence.

"Is that it?" Dora wanted to know.

"It is—but keep it going. We'll keep it up for twenty minutes."

"Oh, man." Dora raised both eyebrows and drew her head back slightly. "How do I not think about this guy who's following me?"

"Now, you're going to have thoughts that want to intrude." Missy was speaking softly, calmly. "Let them. Don't try to stop them. Just…gently return your focus to your breath and that spot across the room."

A minute passed. Then another. And another.

"Something else you can do is notice your senses, but passively. Notice what you see—what's in your field of vision. Notice any sounds. Notice the smell of coffee or…whatever."

Another two minutes passed. Then two more.

"Notice the feel of your behind on the chair, of your feet on the ground. All of these things make up the moment. You can hold them—these mini experiences—in your mind, or you can let them go and continue returning to your breath."

Five minutes passed. Then another five. And another.

Finally, Missy looked at her watch.

"Twenty minutes—great job! How do you feel?"

Dora thought about it. "Good. Relaxed. Better able to focus, I think."

"Now you've got that in your toolbox and you can use it anytime you like."

"Wow. Thank you."

Missy beamed.

Dora's eyes drifted to the window. Outside, someone passed by in the street, six or seven feet beyond the window. She had seen this person, but somehow not exactly this same person, before. He had been charming and friendly when she had last seen him; now he was radiating power and menace. His features had changed, and he seemed to have grown in stature.

Alarms were sounding in the lizard part of her brain, as her limbic system, which was in charge of her fight, flight, or freeze response, went into high alert.

Missy noticed Dora's change of expression. "What is it?"

"Someone passed by, and I'm pretty sure he was the guy who was following me. He was a ways past the window, in the street, and at the last second, just as he went by, his eyes swept this room and he looked me right in the eye." She shuddered. "Gave me chills."

"Who was he?"

"If he's who I think he is, we met him at Altamont's house. I think he works or worked for Lenny's Auto Repair. He's also a friend of Rudy's—part of that crowd. A regular at Rudy's Bar. He's Ferret Wallace."

"Huh."

"I think he's Altamont's sniper. Hang on." Dora took out her phone and opened the most recent picture, reverse-pinching it with her fingers to enlarge it. "Look. There he is. I took that on the sidewalk a block from here, as I was walking from my car."

Missy looked at the picture. Nodded. "I think I remember him, but I'm not sure. He looks different."

"Like that guy in that movie we watched over Fourth of July weekend — that killer."

"Keyser Söze," they said together.

"Except," Dora said, "he never really was Ferret Wallace. He's Bogdan Pavlovic."

• • •

Sarah Turner sat in the painted white chair staring out of her living room window at one of her neighbors, who was walking an enormous black and white Bernedoodle. Sven and Liga had brought "Toodles" home five months before, and in that short time he had gone from the size of a shoebox to the size of Sarah's dining room table.

She had been waiting for fourteen hours, but C3 had not returned home. He had said he was going out to pick up a few groceries—chicken thighs, corn meal to use as breading, and some frozen broccoli. They had planned to prepare and eat dinner together. That had been just after five o'clock. Now it was 7:00 a.m., and he had not returned from the store...which had closed ten hours ago.

Sarah didn't wonder where C3 was. While she didn't know the exact address or the names of the people he was with, she knew what he was doing. He was copping and using. Probably OxyContin. She prayed he was not using fentanyl, because that drug was more likely to kill him than any other, since it hit harder and faster than heroin and required far less of the drug to produce a high—which meant a faster road to an overdose.

She called her friend, Joanie. Her hand shook as she tried to push the button on her phone.

"Joanie? Sarah."

"Are you okay?"

She only called Joanie when C3 was using or missing.

"He's been gone since dinnertime last night, when he said he was going to the store."

"Just remember, Sarah. You didn't cause this and you can't cure it."

"No. I know. And I damned sure can't control it. But it's still fucking painful. He was doing so well. He had clients who would talk to no one but him—who depended on him."

"Sarah, listen to me. Are you listening?"

"Yes."

"Sarah. Tough love. You don't have to take his B.S."

"But I love him."

"All the more reason. If you take his shit, he's going to keep doing it and drag you down with him. But if you set and keep the boundary—"

"He might kill himself anyway!"

"That's right." She heard the gentle iron in Joanie's tone. She had been there. She knew. And yet…

"There's nothing you can do about it, if that's what he wants to do," Joanie continued. "What does his father say?"

"Charlie? Pretty much what you're saying, but with a bunch of four-letter words thrown in."

"Yeah, well. He knows. He's been there too."

Sarah sighed. "He installed the kid's operating system." The sky was overcast—drab sheets of gray, with blackened edges and hints of light. She wished she knew what to do.

"Joanie."

"I'm here."

"I'm pregnant."

"Oh, God."

Sarah gripped her knees with both hands and began to cry quietly.

Chapter 17

"What are we going to do?" Missy asked, trying to keep the hysteria from her voice. She was sliding into a panic attack. Dora covered Missy's hand with her own.

"We're going to be okay. You're going to be okay. I've got this."

"You've got this? He's a killer! A professional's fucking professional!"

Dora was taken aback. "Miss! Language!"

Missy could only swallow and groan. "Ohhh man. Ohhh man."

"Shh." Dora took Missy's hand, stood up, and began to lead her out of Starbucks, then stopped. "You forgot your coffee."

"Fuck my coffee!"

Dora shook her head. "Language! I'm turning out to be a terrible influence!" She laughed. She felt so much better now. "First, we're going to drive, and while we drive, we're going to figure this out."

"Okay," Missy said, sounding shaky.

"You gonna be okay?"

"I'm with you, right?"

"Good answer. Okay then." They arrived at the turbo, got in, and Dora began to drive, glancing frequently at her rear-view mirror. Eventually, she smiled. "There he is. Right on schedule. Mr. Green Grand Marquis."

"Huuhhh," was all Missy could manage to moan.

"Hey, Siri," Dora said next. "Call Agatha Raines."

"Calling Another Lanes Bowling Alley," Siri said.

"Aw, hell. Never mind." Dora opened the contacts in her phone, found Agatha's number, and pressed it.

"Dora?"

"Listen, Agatha. Someone's been tailing us and I'm concerned you may be in danger. Is Rudy there?"

"No, and he's still not speaking to me."

"Oh, for God's sake! All right. Stay there and don't answer the door, no matter what and no matter who it is. If they say they're the cops, ask for a badge."

"'Kay."

She dialed Rudy.

"Yo."

"Rudy. Where are you? Why aren't you home? Agatha says you're not speaking to her."

"First of all," Rudy said, sounding utterly exhausted, "Agatha got her brother killed—plain and simple. I wouldn't put it that way to her because I love her — or I did, but she went off looking for Egar without thinking, and he took care of business by going after Jesse. I'm sure he was afraid of Agatha, because she's part of the system. And, you know what? She is probably responsible for her mother's death, and she put the rest of us at risk. I'm at Vanessa's. I'm leaving Agatha—gonna get my own place."

Dora made a *nthu nthu* sound with her tongue. "You think Agatha intended to do any of that?"

"If she didn't, she showed a serious lack of judgment."

"Maybe so—but these were mistakes, Rudy. You're overreacting and you need to calm down. Agatha needs you. She needs support. She didn't do anything on purpose. She was trying to protect her brother, so she tried to talk to people she thought posed a threat to him. That took serious courage. Yeah, it turned out the guy was a vengeful criminal who did in fact pose a threat to him. Was the result her fault, or an unintended consequence? Anyway, let me cut to the chase. That guy Egar, who got Jesse killed?"

"He's dead—ain't he?"

"His boss and his boss's hired killer are after Agatha, right now. And if Samuel's with her…"

There was a fraction of a second's pause, then, "WHAT? I'm going there, now!"

"Good." Dora ended the call.

"Dora?" Missy's hands were clenched at her sides, and she was staring straight ahead. "I get that I'm with you and I'm probably safe, but how 'bout you fill me in?"

Dora nodded. "So, the police say that this Bogdan Pavlovic is an expert killer, but primarily a sniper. That means several things. First, he probably didn't personally kill Jesse. Second, he will probably be setting up to do whatever he's going to do next because that's what sniper's do, so I need to put myself in his place and think like him."

"But you're not a sniper."

"But I've got some police training and I've got a secret weapon."

"What? One of those long rifles with a fancy scope?"

Dora laughed. "No, silly. I've got you—and you're a librarian. Right? One smart lady. So, just follow me here. I need you to think clearly and tell me what you come up with."

"What I think is I want to go home and pull the covers over my head."

Dora patted her knee. "Soon. This guy is employed by Lenny Altamont, so what's he after?"

"Um—wait." Missy frowned, then brightened. "Probably revenge."

"Mm hmm, along with eliminating anyone who might know too much —which would include Agatha and possibly Rudy, and probably me."

"So…not me?" Missy sounded hopeful and relieved.

Dora's phone rang again.

"Agatha?"

"Dora—Rudy was just here and right after he got here, a guy—nice-looking Latino guy who looked a little familiar, but who looked like he wouldn't hurt a fly rang the bell and very politely told Rudy that he had accidentally run into the back of a car he thought might be mine. Rudy went out there with him and he hasn't come back."

"Call the cops. Take down my number and the direct number I give you for the Goose and the Gander and tell Detective Ganderson or Mallard everything you told me."

"Will do."

Dora hung up. "Bet I know who that guy at Agatha's was—the waiter at Altamont's. So, you were saying?"

"I was saying it sounds like they're not after me, personally."

"Well, let's think about this. Here's the problem. Corb Egar Sr. was certainly a killer, and he was responsible for Jesse's death. But he worked for someone—Lenny Altamont, it seems. He got Egar Sr. out of the picture, because he was compromised … by Agatha. Now his son also worked for Altamont, though maybe indirectly. Corb Egar Jr. has an ax to grind—because of what I did to him. I humiliated him, and maybe because I was right there when his father died. Whether or not he blames me for his father's death is anyone's guess, but he's probably not looking at that with a fine-toothed comb. And, he might be the one who killed Jesse."

She scrolled to a number on her phone, pushed it.

"Vanessa? Dora. Listen to me carefully. I think Rudy may be on his way there, and not of his own accord…with someone linked to the guy who killed Jesse. Don't let them in, whatever you do. Agatha's already called the cops, so they should be there soon."

She ended the call and turned to Missy. "Now then. This Bogdan Pavlovic—he followed me. He saw me. And he knows I saw him. So… what would you do if you were him, and if you were a sniper?"

"I'd try to get to you first."

"Right, but now that I'm not at the academy, I don't have a set schedule, which is one of the things a sniper looks for. He has to set up and wait for his target, and watch what they do until it becomes predictable. And yet with the attempted attack just now on Agatha and possibly Rudy, this guy's got pressure on him to move, now. He can't set up and wait for days. And while I don't have a set schedule—you do."

"Ohhh, man! So, you think he's coming after me because I have a much more predictable routine?" Anxiety crept back into Missy's voice.

"Exactly. So, we need to think like he thinks. Where are you on a regular basis?"

"My place and the library."

Dora paused, picturing both locations. "I think it would be awfully hard for a sniper to get to you at your place, unless he was shooting from a car—there's no place for him to set up. But at the library…" She looked at Missy. "The parking lot might make sense to him. You're working this afternoon?"

Missy nodded. "In about three quarters of an hour. Agatha's home and we usually switch off."

"Let's drive by there and look." Dora headed toward the library, drove past it and around the block, then into the library's parking lot.

"That church," Dora said, pointing out her window at a spire that rose over the pines several houses away. "That's where I'd be. Look around. There's no place else."

Missy looked doubtful. "It does have a clear view of the parking lot, but it's nearly a block away. How can you be sure?"

"First of all, that's maybe five hundred feet—close range for a good sniper and just about point blank for a world-class sniper. What we need to do now is go back to my place for a slight wardrobe adjustment."

...

When the buzzer sounded, Vanessa was ready. She pressed the intercom. "Yes?"

"Hi, Vanessa, it's Rudy."

"Rudy? I'm diapering Buster. It's not a great time right now. Can I call you back?"

"No worries, Nessa. I have my key. I'll just let myself in."

She had expected this. Vanessa carried both boys into her bedroom and turned on the TV. "Boys, I'm putting your favorite show on, so just stay here and watch, and wait for Mama, okay?" She set both boys on the floor and put on one of their favorite on-demand shows. "Drew, now you watch Buster and make sure he stays here, okay?"

Drew looked at his baby brother. "Stay heew Busta!"

"Good boy," Vanessa said, then turned the sound way up—she hoped it would be loud enough.

By the time she heard Rudy's key in the lock, she was in the living room and ready. Rudy opened the door and stepped into the apartment, followed by the young Latino man they had seen working at Lenny Altamont's party. The young man was holding a nine-millimeter handgun. Vanessa was standing four or five paces to the man's right, a shotgun leveled at his chest.

"Drop it," she ordered.

He turned toward her, a charming smile on his face. "Aw, lady. You're not going to shoot me." Then his eyes went cold and he raised his gun.

"Bullshit," Vanessa said, and pulled the trigger. Red blossomed in the man's chest as he flew backward, dropped the gun and fell to the floor.

Rudy ran to his sister-in-law and took her in his arms. Vanessa was shaking, but quickly broke free and ran back to her bedroom to make sure the boys were okay, then dialed the police.

• • •

"We're heading back real quick to my place, then your place," Dora told Missy. "We need to do a couple of things before getting you back for work."

"What things? What if I want the day off?"

"Miss, it's going to be okay. You'll see. We're doing a little wardrobe change, and we're going to take your car."

"Why my car?"

"Bait."

"Ohhh. Great."

They rode back to both their apartments and did what had to be done in silence, then came back to the parking lot thirty-five minutes later. Dora insisted that Missy drive.

"I'm too scared to drive."

"You want us both to live? You need to drive, Miss. But take your time. Drive slowly."

By the time they arrived in the parking lot, Dora had slid down in her seat to avoid being seen.

"How long before you would usually be heading inside?"

"Five minutes—maybe a little longer."

"Okay."

They waited. Dora closed her eyes.

"What are you doing?" Missy wanted to know.

"Meditating." After a few minutes, Dora patted Missy on the arm. "Okay, Miss. Time to go."

Missy leaned over as though picking something up from the floor. "Dora?"

Dora looked up. Missy kissed her, then got out of the car. Dora allowed herself a brief moment to enjoy the kiss and the love that was so obviously behind it, then she waited, and listened.

Fifteen seconds later, she heard a distant crack, sat up, and saw Missy lying on her side on the ground several paces from the car. She dialed her direct line to the detectives and explained what had happened, then got out of the car, went to Missy, and bent over her. "You okay?"

Missy nodded, wincing. "Just feel like I got punched in the chest. How'd you know he wouldn't aim for my head?"

"Center mass is the best target. Snipers are trained for that. But these vests are good. I knew you'd be okay."

"He won't shoot again—at you?"

"He thinks he's hurt me more by killing you. He's breaking down his rifle right now. Gotta go. Back soon."

Dora ran into the library and out a side door, ignoring the frantic, "Shh!" from several librarians. Then she jumped the back fence and rushed toward the back of the church, whose parking lot was enclosed on three sides, with the fourth being the church itself. Only one side of the church had a driveway.

Dora was pretty sure the gunman wouldn't expect her to be onto him so quickly. She also doubted he would have risked trying to park on the street, where he may or may not have found a space, and where he would have had to carry his prized rifle in its broken-down storage state. No. He wouldn't leave his rifle behind, and he would want the privacy of the parking lot.

While she wasn't entirely sure of what he would do next, she knew he would need a few minutes to do it, so she made sure to get there fast.

And there he was—walking across the parking lot in a beige sport jacket, carrying what looked like a gym bag.

She leaped up, reached the top of the fence, and vaulted over, yelling at the top of her lungs, "Bogdan Pavlovic!"

He startled and spun. She ran directly at him as he opened the trunk of his car and came out with a handgun. She had known this would be a possibility—a likelihood, in fact. So, she kept running.

Something hit her behind the knees and took her legs out from under her. She rolled with the momentum of the tackle and came up on the balls of her toes and saw a familiar-looking man—short, dark, and muscular. "Remember me?" she said. "I'm the wannabe cop who was shadowing Vincent Doyle." She hoped the sniper wouldn't risk shooting her while she was dealing with this man. The man grunted and leaped at Dora with surprising agility, unleashing a flurry of punches, essentially a leaping ground-and-pound. His shots were powerful and effective, momentarily knocking her back. A fist grazed her chin and she struggled to stay on her feet—she could not afford to go down and be a target for his boots or worse, the sniper's gun. So, she changed levels, went for the double leg takedown, then, when she couldn't manage that, opted for a single leg, powered through and, for good measure, tripped the man's legs from under him, making sure to keep his body between her and the sniper.

Once he was on his back, she knew she had him. She mounted, and rained three, quick, accurate punches at his jaw—knocking him out without leaving time for the gunman to aim, then rolled quickly away and jumped to her feet, just as Pavlovic, who had closed the trunk and opened his driver's side door, raised his pistol. She sprinted in a zig-zag pattern at him. He squeezed off four shots, one of which hit her like a hammer in the lower right quadrant of her torso.

Her mind apparently stopped recording the events that followed, but later she would be told that she had leaped at him, grabbed him by the throat, and squeezed, instantly breaking his trachea. Seconds later, the police arrived, declared the entire area a crime scene, and saved Pavlovic's life with a tracheotomy made from a ballpoint pen.

Epilogue

While an ambulance took Dora to the hospital with Missy riding along, the police taped the perimeter of the crime scene, took their photographs, and recorded what they needed to record.

Dora was released from the hospital nineteen hours later, with what amounted to a hole in her gut; the bullet had somehow passed between her liver and stomach, hitting neither, and continued out her back, without touching her spinal cord. She was, everyone agreed, a very lucky woman.

Later that day, Missy drove Dora to the police station where, using a lightweight travel wheelchair, they met Ganderson and Mallard in the hallway outside the interrogation room.

"How 'bout a coffee," Dora said.

"How 'bout a moment's peace," Mallard responded.

Dora looked at him. "Do you always show up at crime scenes dressed for a wedding?"

Mallard straightened his tie. "Why, thank you."

"Are we under arrest?" Missy wanted to know.

"You should be," Ganderson grumbled. He held a half-full bottle of water in his hand. He took a packet of Alka Seltzer from his inside coat pocket, tore its top off with his teeth, and broke the tablets into pieces small enough to fit through the top of the bottle.

Dora looked steadily at the detective. "These murderers hunted us down and tried to kill us, and you're giving us a hard time?"

Ganderson stared back at her, his chin tucked, his eyebrows low. "You took the law into your own hands. Nobody does that."

"I wouldn't have had to if you'd—what is it you guys do—oh, yeah, if you'd *detected* the assholes first and arrested them."

The detective pushed his face closer to her, his expression a mask of fury. "You're in my house, young lady. My house!"

"Well, maybe you need to clean…your house."

"All right, McGregor and Nunes—let's take it down a notch." Mallard stepped between them and motioned for Missy to follow him with Dora's wheelchair. "Let's remember that Altamont and Pavlovic are going to jail." He led them into the interrogation room, then pointed at his partner. "You, get them coffee. Now." He indicated seats for the two women.

"I'm impressed," Dora said. "You actually know some real MMA names!"

"Watch it all the time. All the pay-per-views. And I'm a fan of yours, believe it or not."

"Thank you. Oh, hell. Did someone get over to Vanessa Burrell's apartment?"

"Way ahead of you," Mallard replied. "Nice-looking kid named Teófilo went there after being unable to gain entrance to Agatha Raines's apartment. He grabbed Rudy Raines, and used him to gain entrance to Mrs. Burrell's apartment."

"Jesus. What happened?"

"Vanessa Burrell was waiting for him with a 12 gauge. He's not quite so nice looking now."

Ganderson returned with the coffees, which he placed in front of each of them on the table.

Dora peered at her coffee, then at Ganderson. "Got Splenda? Half-and-half?"

Ganderson rolled his eyes, left the room and returned with the items. "You'll be happy to know that Altamont was arrested at the airport, trying to fly to Puerto Rico."

Mallard grinned. "So there's a spare plane ticket?"

Ganderson ignored him. "And Cathy Trask just arrested the Egar kid for killing Jesse Burrell."

Mallard was astonished. "Based on—?"

Ganderson sat down, now looking supremely satisfied. "Based on a spanner wrench found in someone's rhododendrons two blocks from the murder scene. On it were Burrell and Egar's DNA. Blood and prints." Mallard went over to his partner, and the detectives exchanged high-fives.

"So, we're not being arrested?" Missy asked.

"No, we're not being arrested," Dora said, with a hard look at Ganderson.

• • •

Several hours later, they were back at Missy's apartment and Dora was lying on her side on the living room carpet, her wound-side up, with the side of her face pressed against the floor. Comfort was next to her, mimicking her position. He kept getting up and trying to lick her bandages, and the two, human and canine, ended up pressing their faces together.

"Ooh, that's my good boy, Comfort. Oooh, who's my Comfort?"

Missy was on the couch with a beer and a scotch, her second. "I've been meaning to tell you something."

"What's that?"

"Your leaving the academy wasn't your fault."

"Aw, hell. I know that."

"Really, Dor. It wasn't. It had nothing to do with your not being able to cut it."

"Oh, really."

"Really."

"Then what was it?"

"It…just wasn't meant to be."

"So, tell me. What should I be doing? I've been trying to figure that out for weeks. You're going to tell me you figured it out?"

Missy smiled. "I did."

Dora sat up. Comfort sat up beside her. "Hey, he wants to know, too. So? What should I be doing?"

"It's not what you should be doing. It's what *we* should be doing." She paused, for effect. "We should start a private detective agency."

Dora sat motionless for nearly a minute, absorbing this. Then she slowly smiled. "You know what? We should."

"Isn't it a great idea?" Missy breathed.

"But don't we need a license or something?"

"Yes, we do. And we'll do what needs to be done."

"You know about this?"

Missy smiled again. "I'm a librarian. I know about everything."

Dora closed her eyes, then opened them and looked at Missy. "So, I have something to tell you."

"Really?"

"Mm hmm. I had a dream a few nights ago about Franny, and it was really, really vivid."

Missy was silent, listening.

"She was with me, and it was like she really was there. It was so real! She was telling me about death, and she was really positive, really encouraging."

"What did she say?"

Dora considered the question. "She didn't describe it, really. She didn't talk at all. But she did communicate that it's not an intellectual, cognitive experience. It's more of a visceral, feeling type of experience. Death is not about thought; it's about existing in a different way."

"Okay," Missy said carefully. "And what did you think about that?"

Now it was Dora's turn to smile. "I feel really good about it. Could be the pain meds, but I think she was telling me she's okay." Dora sat up, wincing, and managed to cross her legs. "Know what else I think she was telling me?" She looked down at her hands, which were clasped in front of her.

Missy started to smile as she began to understand. "What?"

"Maybe I'm ready for something new."

・・・

The following Saturday was Charlie Bernelli and Christine Pearsall's wedding. Dora and Missy attended as a couple—their first outing, so to speak, together. They didn't tell anyone that they were now a couple, though they did hold hands, and when the happy Bernelli-Pearsall couple shared their first married kiss, Dora and Missy shared a quick kiss as well.

The reception was wonderful. Now that Dora no longer needed the wheelchair, Dora and Missy danced happily, if gingerly, together. Dora saw that Rudy and Agatha were in attendance, and together. She wondered about that but understood that whatever happened between them was none of her business. She was happy they had worked it out, especially for Samuel's sake. She also noticed Sarah Turner and C3 sitting quietly at a table on the outer perimeter of the room. Sarah's hand was on the back of C3's chair. C3 was drinking a beer and pretending to look at ease.

Some time later, Charlie Jr. sought Dora out.

"Congratulations," Dora said, giving Charlie a kiss on the cheek. "How does being married feel?"

Charlie laughed. "Like I've had a lot of champagne."

"Good to see C3 and Sarah here."

Charlie grew serious. "Yeah, well. There hasn't been much improvement there."

"I guess when the pain gets great enough…"

Charlie shook his head. "We'll see." They watched the couples dancing and enjoying themselves for a few moments, then Charlie looked at Dora with a knowing smile. "I see you're having a nice time."

"I am."

"Not going to say anything more?"

Dora laughed. "I'm agreeing with you. I'm having a nice time."

Charlie bent his head close to hers. "Since you won't be working for the police department, I have a client who wants to talk to you about work."

"About work? Doing what?"

"Modeling."

Dora was stunned. "You're kidding!"

"I'm not. They saw your ad for the tourism campaign last year, and they loved the idea of a series of ads featuring a strong woman."

Dora laughed. "What's the product?"

"It's not a product. It's a local store called Real Women."

"Wow! I'll do it!"

The rest of the evening was a happy, love-filled haze.

THE END

• • •

Not far away, a deeply troubling sequence of events was unfolding at the Beach City Medical Center, as people had begun growing unaccountably, deathly, grotesquely, painfully ill, and eventually dying. First one. Then two. Then a handful. Now a dozen.

And the doctors were baffled as to the cause, diagnosis, or treatment.

Please visit your favorite book store to read:
Book 3 in David E. Feldman's *Dora Ellison Series*—*A Sickening Storm.*

Dear Reader: Thanks so much for reading **A Gathering Storm.**

I hope you will join my mailing list to learn more about my next books at:
https://www.davidefeldman.com/books.shtml

If you enjoyed this book, I would be grateful if you would post a review online.

See you again soon!

-DF

Made in United States
Orlando, FL
15 May 2025